Fathers House
C. Edward Baldwin

Ink-Stone Publishing
ISBN 13: 978-0692280980

I0525552

Fathers House

www.cedwardbaldwin.com

Cover Design by Clarissa Yeo
Yocla Designs
www.yocladesigns.com

Ink & Stone
PUBLISHING
The Carolinas * Georgia * Virginia

C. Edward Baldwin

For my parents, Matheral & Webster Anderson, who even in the afterlife continue to be my inspiration and a driving force behind what I do.

To my wife, Natasha, your love and encouragement get me rising and moving every morning. I love you.

To my dad, Curtis Sr., your worth as my father and mentor is immeasurable! I love you.

To my stepmother, Tyrann, your zest for life and willingness to try new things is truly motivational.

To my siblings (Lisa, Ron, Jason, Felicia, La-Sharla, and Navonya) your faith in me is beyond words inspiring. Thank you!

And lastly, but in no ways least, to my Aunt Moody, I haven't told you this. But I think of you every day. I love you. As a child growing up in Lumberton, you were a huge heroine to me!

©Praise for Fathers House

"A resounding story of fatherhood packaged as a tense thriller." - Kirkus Reviews

"I will start from the bottom line: this is one helluva page turner!" - Gali, onlinebookclub.org

"The story is full of suspense and intrigue. The twists and turns, subplots, and the characters make it an interesting and compelling read." - Mamtan Madhavan, Readers' Favorite

"C. Edward Baldwin does it with panache! Fathers House is well-constructed and devilishly delicious reading." - Simon Barrett, Blogger Network News

"Dots connected in ways I hadn't anticipated. Twists and turns meandered into one big whole. A story so complicated it feels like a Sherlock Holmes book, except bloodier!" - iheartreading.net.

"Mayo Fathers is a suitable villain and Ben Lovison is a worthy hero. The writing and editing are excellent." - Patricia Eddy, Author Allliance

"Given how powerful the Father's Disciples are--they have infiltrated the DA's office and most of city hall; the odds are certainly against Lovison." - Publishers Weekly

"Fathers House is a bloody and suspenseful debut thriller by C. Edward Baldwin that deals with the brutal undercurrents of crime in modern society." - Chanticleer Book Reviews

C. EDWARD BALDWIN

FATHERS HOUSE

Ink-Stone Publishing

C. Edward Baldwin

Chapter 1

It was ironic, maybe even a little funny that every decision the agent had ever made in his entire life led to the two choices now before him. He sat at the table in the kitchen nook of his small apartment. The blinds were pulled tight, shutting out a gorgeous, bright morning. The sweaty palms of both his hands lay flat atop the surface of the table. Above his left hand lay his service revolver. Above his right hand lay his cell phone. He closed his eyes.

The irony was that either choice could be viewed as either bravery or cowardice. On the surface, putting a bullet to his head would take guts. The mere thought of metal blasting into his skull made his heart shiver. The pain would be intensely brutal, if only for a second. It was the thought of that second that gave him pause. Of course, after his body was discovered and people later found out what he'd done, they'd all say that he had taken the cowardly way out. No one would give him credit for withstanding that one brutal second. The funny thing was, if he chose the latter option it could eventually lead to him having to face the legal system. That could result in a lengthy prison sentence, but not the death he was so strongly contemplating now, which would anger the very people who would cry foul if he committed suicide. There was no pleasing some folk. Of course, that option would also mean continuing on as he had the past seventeen years, letting Father continue to control every aspect of his life. It would mean making the call to Father and giving the old man the information he'd requested.

It was cowardly not standing up to Father, not facing the music in the here and now. But it was surely an act of bravery to know that not putting a bullet into his own head today would ensure that one day he would have to publically acknowledge his past misdeeds. Sooner or later the agent would face the music. One day soon he would have to confess to God, and everyone else, all he'd done. That day would require great courage, all he'd be able to muster up. His heart trembled at the thought.

He squeezed his eyes closed tighter, and then his life flashed before him. He saw his mother in all her maternal splendor. Then, his father who was once there, then was gone, and then was there again. He saw his brothers, all of whom had been much older than he. It had always been as if he didn't really have any brothers at all. Then again, there was Ben Lovison.

Ben had been a friend, a best friend, a blood brother. Their relationship had been thicker than any blood connection. It had been years since the agent had last seen him. It was even longer since the agent's love and admiration for his blood brother had suddenly turned to envious thoughts and hatred. The agent quickly pushed that memory away, only to have it replaced with another painful one…Fathers House. Then he wondered if it was better to live in a house with invisible, yet obstructive walls, or if it was better to be trapped in a house where you could see the walls of your limitations. If one successfully, albeit unknowingly, navigated through a house with invisible walls, one would still have the sense of being free. But in a house with thick visible walls and locked doors, one would surely know that he was not free. Was blissful ignorance akin to freedom? Today the answer seemed so obvious. Trapped was trapped. And one day Ben Lovison would see the obvious. One day he was going to hit a wall and then realize just how trapped he'd been. At that time, maybe the agent would get his blood brother back. Shared pain always brought people together. Maybe then the two of them could figure out a way to get beyond the walls. That was, of course, if finding out the agent's most atrocious act didn't provoke Lovison to kill him first. Anyway, he had finally reached a decision.

He sighed, opened his eyes, and then after wiping his clammy right hand across the front of his shirt, he picked up the cell phone.

* * *

Maalik Jackson's breath was lodged in the middle of his throat like cornered wind trapped inside a balloon. He stood motionless at the top of the basement steps, staring into the blackness at the just slammed basement door. He listened intently, trying to determine if Uncle Mayo was still on the other side of the door. He could hear nothing. He could see nothing. No sound, total darkness, and no Uncle Mayo. Despite his fear, he wasn't totally surprised with his current predicament. He'd expected the old man to do something. After all, Uncle Mayo had warned him about the drugs. But Maalik hadn't expected this, whatever this was. What type of punishment did the old man have in mind?

Slowly his breathing returned. He swallowed hard, turned around shakily, and then proceeded down a couple of stairs into the darkness. There, he paused again and looked back up at the basement door. He could barely make out the outline of it, as it disappeared into the darkness. Only moments before Uncle Mayo had pushed him into the basement, the door quickly snapping shut behind him as if its hinges were taut rubber bands. He sucked in a long, nervous, deep breath. Once again, he turned his head back toward the basement floor. He goose necked forward, trying to peer beyond the darkened stairwell. After another breathless moment of indecision and uncertainty, he decided it was probably best to just keep moving. Haltingly, he continued downward.

Drugs are dangerous, was a refrain that he'd heard a

thousand times before, at school, on TV, and here at Fathers House, a place where, ironically, most of its young inhabitants had more than a passing familiarity with most illicit drugs. Maalik had been under no illusions when he had chosen his new career path; he'd seen firsthand the ill side effects of drugs. But users and dealers generally accepted the high risk-high reward nature of the drug trade. For Maalik, it had been no different, even if it had meant jeopardizing his stay at Fathers House.

He had lived under the Fathers House roof for the past six months and had been a regular participant in the House's afterschool program eighteen months before that. There were seven other boys that also lived at the House, and another eighteen in its afterschool program. As far as Maalik could tell, at least four of the House residents dabbled in the drug trade. And unless the old man was totally clueless to the obvious, (which Maalik seriously doubted) those four had apparently been given a pass that wasn't being afforded to Maalik. "I don't want you doing drugs," the old man had said to Maalik on more than one occasion. "You know what drugs did to your mama." It had been a needless reminder. Of course Maalik knew what drugs had done to his mama. He'd been there. He'd suffered through it. But his mama had been a user, not a seller. Eleven-year-old Maalik understood the difference. In the drug game, you were either a taker or a giver. Users were givers. His mama had given all she had, including her body, and ultimately her life, to the drug game. But Maalik had no intentions of using drugs. He was going to be a taker. He was going to make that money. He needed to make that money.

However, he had to admit to himself that he hated disappointing Uncle Mayo. The old man had been good to him. Maalik truly believed that Uncle Mayo only wanted what he thought was best for Maalik. Maybe that was why he had been tougher on Maalik than those other boys. But

Maalik had been born with his eyes wide open to the real world. In the real world, money was might, and might make right. In the real world, a safe penny-ninny job wasn't going to cut it.

It wasn't as if Maalik hadn't considered all his options. He had. But in his mind there were few, if any. He couldn't sing. He couldn't rap. So child stardom was definitely a pipe dream. And as for society's favorite— staying in school and getting a quality education, well that only represented an even chance to potentially earn more than the minimum wage. And even if he wanted one of those so called respectable jobs, he'd most likely need to go to college to land one. Going to college would cost money and not to mention, years away. He needed money now, lots of it. Drugs equaled now money. With it, he could pay back Uncle Mayo for all he'd done for him. And more importantly, he could get his grandfather's farm back.

He reached the halfway point and paused again, dreading what he might find at the bottom of the steps. He had expected Uncle Mayo to do something drastic after the police had released him into the old man's custody. As far as he knew, none of the other boys had ever been snatched up by the po-po. That he had was probably justification enough for the old man to exact some form of punishment. It had crossed Maalik's mind that the old man may have considered giving him an old-fashioned whipping, or simply kick him out of Fathers House altogether, hurling Maalik into a careless childcare system. But now it didn't appear as if either of those things was going to happen. The old man hadn't even looked very upset when he'd picked Maalik up from the police station. Not a word was shared between the two of them the whole ride home. And when they got back inside Fathers House, the old man's words were few before he grabbed Maalik by the collar, pulled him to the basement door, opened it, and then threw Maalik inside as if he was tossing a lamb to the wolves. Now that

Maalik remembered it, the old man had been calm the entire time, perhaps too calm.

In the six months that he'd lived at Fathers House, Maalik had never before been inside the basement. In fact, he hadn't known there was a basement. Now he was descending into the bowels of Fathers House. What did the old man have in store for him down here? He froze in place as a blanket of dread draped over him. He remembered that Fathers House was connected to Uncle Mayo's funeral business. It wasn't exactly a frightening thought as Uncle Mayo had never shown any ill will toward him, certainly not of the magnitude of causing his death or dismemberment. Still, right now, being in the vicinity of a funeral home where handling dead bodies was commonplace and its owner was more than a little upset with him was unsettling. After a moment he pushed the crazy thought aside and got his legs moving again, gingerly creeping downward as if trying to avoid possible landmines.

After a couple of steps, a smell assaulted his nose. The strong stench was almost recognizable, though he couldn't quite place it. The first thing that came to mind was his grandfather's hog farm. Those big, nasty hogs could be smelled from miles away. The hogs would spend the day rolling about in slop and their own crap, oblivious to their foulness, or simply uncaring. He had often wondered if a part of them, knowing their fate, had created such stinky chaos as a way of slinging one last odious shot at his grandfather.

He descended a few more steps. Then it hit him. He knew exactly what it was that he smelled. The thought made him as nauseous as the smell itself. Had a toilet overflowed down here? Was he expected to clean up the mess? As he continued timidly down the remaining steps to the basement floor, he began to feel somewhat better. Cleaning up crap was gross. But gross he could deal with.

He reached the last step and braced himself. He needed to stay at Fathers House and if this was what it was going to take, then so be it. But he wasn't going to promise not to sell drugs. He still needed the money. Besides, it wasn't something he planned to do forever. He just needed enough money to get his grandfather's farm back. That farm was his birthright. The farm hadn't made his grandfather rich. But it had made him free. He'd answered to no one but himself. It was the kind of life that Maalik had come to respect. He, too, would one day work his grandfather's farm—his farm. He would work his own hours, live his own way. But first, he needed money to make that happen.

As if on cue, an intercom crackled from somewhere in front and above him, issuing a deep voice that sounded birthed from a barrel. "Do not let your heart be troubled. Trust in Father. Trust in me. In Fathers House there are many rooms; if it were not so, I would tell you. A place is prepared for you. Come, trust in Father."

Maalik remained still. The voice stopped and the room returned to an almost eerie quiet, except for a muffled creak coming from somewhere in the walls. It sort of sounded like a mouse was caught in a trap. A desire to flee surfaced, and Maalik turned his head around, looking back up the stairs he'd just come down. He could barely see the steps in the darkened stairway. But it didn't matter, since he quickly dismissed the thought anyway. He'd brought this on himself, and he would see it through to the end. Besides, running back up the stairs to pull on a door that was surely locked would be a childish waste of energy.

Out of nowhere a bit of anger bubbled within him as his thoughts turned briefly to Cain. The older boy was just as much to blame for his current predicament as Maalik himself was. If only Cain would have allowed Maalik to work for him, instead of giving him that holier than thou bullshit about the dangers of selling drugs. Cain sold drugs. Cain made money. Why wasn't it okay for Maalik?

And it would have been, except Maalik got caught. If only Cain would have shown him the ropes, taken him under his wings, taught him the tricks of the trade. But Cain hadn't. But that was just pissing in the wind now, he thought, his anger flaming out as quickly as it had risen. He'd been busted, fair and square. "Luckily," Uncle Mayo had told him, "I know the officers that nabbed you. If it would have been anyone else, you could have been removed from this house and thrown into the system or worse…jail. Is that what you want?"

Of course it wasn't. He needed to be here at Fathers House. He needed the roof over his head, and if coming down here in the basement, facing whatever there was to face would ensure he could stay, well then, that was what he was willing to do. Uncle Mayo had added, "There will always be consequences for your actions. In the basement you will face those consequences. Accept them and you'll be allowed to stay here."

He stepped onto the basement floor.

His heart started racing. He sucked in another deep breath, this time rushing it out. He tried to calm himself, to steel his nerves. How bad could it be down here? Surely he wasn't the first to be sent to the basement. He was suddenly struck with the realization that the other drug-dealing boys of Fathers House had also been sent down here. He was not a trendsetter. No one had been given a free pass. And out of that realization was born another: the others had survived. He hadn't heard of any broken bones or seen any burn marks on their bodies. He hadn't heard of any kind of torture happening at Fathers House. That sort of thing would have surely gotten around. No, he was being indoctrinated into something. He felt it. This was an initiation of some sort. Of that, he was becoming increasingly certain. He was going to have to clean up crap or pass some other vile test. It would be nasty work, meant to be scary, but ultimately it would be harmless.

The deep voice returned, "Move forward two steps."
Hesitantly, Maalik did as commanded.

He found himself in some sort of hallway. Ahead of
him, a row of dimmed recessed lights lined either side of
the ceiling from where he was standing and ending at the
other end of the hallway. He had the sense of being in a
narrow tunnel. At the end of it, a flat screen monitor
suddenly materialized on the far wall. Onscreen, a
digitalized computer head appeared. The head's eyes glared
at him. A few terror inducing minutes passed by before the
digital head spoke. It was deep voice. "Turn to your left," it
commanded.

Maalik turned to his left. The row of lights on the left
side suddenly brightened. The sudden burst of light caused
his dark-adjusted eyes to blink rapidly and water. After
several seconds, his eyes re-adjusted to what was fast
becoming welcomed brightness. He wiped away tears and
looked. What he had assumed was a wooden wall was in
fact the exterior glass wall of a room. He noticed to his
right was a door slightly ajar. Inside the room, a spotlight
flashed on, highlighting to his horror, Nas Robinson.

Nas Robinson was a flashy high roller, and though you
couldn't tell by his current condition, an impeccable
dresser. Inside the room, he was stark naked and dangling
from thick braided ropes which ran through the pulley of a
long metal crane which reached up to the ceiling. His body
was tilted forward slightly in a hanging fetal position. His
arms were banded to his chest while his legs were folded
beneath him. A bucket was placed under his head and
another bucket was placed beneath his buttocks. His
midsection was encased in some type of metal contraption,
that judging by the pained look on the young man's face,
caused him an extreme amount of displeasure. His
classmate Khali had introduced Maalik to Nas just last
week. Nas was going to be his ticket to drug riches. Nas
was awash in money. He drove a custom built SUV and

never wore the same pair of sneakers twice.

"Do you know this man?" The digitized voice was eerily calm, but was nonetheless threatening.

Maalik blinked several times in Nas' direction as if trying to place him. Seeing Nas hanging like that made Maalik realize that he wasn't there to just clean up crap. His very life could very well be in danger. Suddenly he wanted to be a normal eleven-year-old kid. He wanted to be somewhere else now, anywhere else, somewhere where a young kid should be, at a friend's house playing videogames, or even at school recess playing what he used to consider a boring game, kickball. After a moment, a desire for self-preservation made him consider lying about any connection he had with Nas. But his lips wouldn't follow suit. He stammered, "Ye...yes sir. I do."

"How do you know him?"

"Kh..." he started to say Khali's name, but suddenly regained control of his lips. Khali had tried to help him get a gig, there was no need getting him mixed up in this. So he said, "I don...I don't know. Kids at school. Dey..dey... dey said he's a drug dealer."

For the first time, Maalik noticed that Nas was not alone. There was another man, a rather large man, in the room with him. Though Nas, who was perhaps about ten years older than Maalik, wasn't exactly a big fella himself; the huge man behind the glass would have no doubt dwarfed most anyone. He was wearing a black, metal studded mask that looked similar to an executioner's mask worn by one of Maalik's videogame characters. The gigantic executioner obviously did not like Maalik's response to the last question, and he took it out on Nas. He turned a chrome handle that was connected by a long rod to the metal contraption. Nas grunted and then vomited in and around the bucket that was placed in front of him. At the other end of his body, Maalik saw the source of the horrid smell he'd first encountered coming down the stairs. Most of it hit the bucket, though drippings of it also dotted the floor around it. As Nas' bodily fluids trickled to stops at both ends, a ghastly moan escaped his lips.

"Did you sell drugs for this man?" the digital head asked.

"No," Maalik answered quickly with the thankful truth.

But the digital head's follow up question came just as quick. "Did you try?"

Maalik hesitated, again briefly considering lying, but then with reasoning that belied his eleven years of life, he realized that if he and Nas were both there at the same time then digital head most likely already knew the answer to that question. "I wanted to," Maalik answered in a quavering voice. "I tried to. But I was busted before I was able to make a sale. I just wanted to make some money. I just wanted to pay Uncle Mayo back for helping me, being so nice to me." He was talking fast and heard the shrillness in his voice. He knew he sounded like a scared little kid. But he didn't care. That's what he was— a scared kid. He hoped digital head would see that. Understand that. Maybe Digital head was Uncle Mayo, he thought hopefully. Maybe Uncle Mayo would let him go back to just being a kid.

Digital head said, "This man has no authority to sell drugs in Duraleigh. This is Father's territory. Understand?"

"Ye…yes sir," Maalik replied. Tears streamed down his face. "I'm sorry, Father."

For a few minutes, Nas's whimpering was all that was heard. Then, the digitized voice spoke again, "This fool has taken food out of my mouth and the mouths of my children. It's food I intend to get back one way or the other."

Inside the room, the huge man walked over to a table that was lined against the back wall. He picked up a book from it and flipped through a couple of pages. He arrived at a spot and tapped it with his thick finger. "Nas Robinson," he said as he stared intently at the book. "For the crime of encroachment into Father's territory, your name is listed in the Book."

Maalik shook uncontrollably as he watched the masked man hold the black, bible-thick book in his enormous hands. After reading Nas's charges, he placed the book back onto the table and then walked back over to the metal crank.

The fused sound of metal turning, bones crushing, and Nas's agonized shrieks soon filled the air, intensifying with each passing minute before abruptly ending, leaving only the sounds of Father's food being returned to him, drip by drip.

Maalik dropped to his knees and vomited. His childhood was now lost forever and he knew it.

Chapter 2

At four a.m. Monday morning, Ben Lovison's eyes popped open. Beads of sweat peppered his forehead. His breaths came in short, quick pants. He lay in bed for a few moments, listening. Finally, he heard her. She was lying next to him. The light sounds of her breathing dimpled the quietness of the bedroom. Thank God, it had only been a dream! It was not time. He stared off into the semi-darkness of the bedroom, allowing his eyes a chance to focus. As they did, the overhead light fixture materialized. It was a three-light, gold-hued ceiling fan, almost as ostentatious as a chandelier. He always thought that it was a bit too gaudy for the bedroom. But April had insisted on having it. He was now staring at it because he'd conceded to her wishes. Seeing the fixture too clearly now, he turned away from it and closed his eyes again.

After another calming moment, he reopened his eyes, turned to his side, and looked at his wife. They'd been married two years, two of the happiest years of his life. She was so beautiful. Strands of her silky jet-black hair fell aimlessly about her face. She was sleeping peacefully, almost soundlessly. She was definitely not a snorer, he thought, unlike himself. His occasional nocturnal nose wailing was getting him dangerously close to being exiled from the bedroom. Curing that nighttime blasting was in the top five on his honey-do list. Still staring at his wife, he concentrated his gaze on her midsection. Her babies-mound was slowly, rhythmically, moving up and down. Perhaps nothing produced anxiety more than the realization that one was about to become a father, he thought. The babies weren't due for another eight weeks. Dr. Shepherd said everything was progressing on schedule. Still, Ben worried. He leaned over and gently pecked his wife on the lips. She did not stir.

Not able to return to sleep, and not wishing to disturb April, he moved from the restless quiet of the bedroom to the stillness of the kitchen. Ben stood comfortably over six feet tall. A broad shouldered man of thirty-three years of age, his face was lightly stubbled with a whisper of boyishness.

He made coffee, poured himself a cup, and then sat down at the kitchen table where the night before he'd left his county-issued laptop and a couple of file folders. He punched in his password and sipped his coffee as he waited for the laptop to finish its startup. After a few moments, the desktop was visible. He tapped the icon for the district attorney's office web system and signed in. A seemingly endless, orderly row of case numbers with names hyphened next to them appeared. He scrolled down the list until he reached case number 234455-Peyton Lars. He clicked on it.

The Duraleigh County District Attorney's office had gone green eight years ago. All its case files were digitally converted. Witness statements, police reports, plea agreements, discovery items, everything was virtually recreated, sending bible-thick files the way of the dinosaur. The only hard files Duraleigh prosecutors carried around nowadays were just folders with yet to be converted file additions such as plea forms to be signed or witness statements taken outside the office. It was twenty-first century prosecution at its finest.

It had been Ben's first year in the DA's office, and with all that first year prosecutors were expected to do, adapting to a new system had been the least of his concerns. Besides, the system had been no newer than any other aspect of the job. Like the other newbies, he'd spent the majority of his time in the courtroom, handling a multitude of misdemeanor cases. The misdemeanors were mostly simple drug possession cases, DWI cases, simple assault and battery cases, and some minor domestic

violence cases. Most had been easy to prosecute, but then
most of the frustration felt by young prosecutors was
seldom related to the level of difficulty of any particular
case, but rather in the sheer number of the cases. Ben had
found out in short order that crime never stops wasn't just
an adage, it was a fact of life, as was the prosecution of that
never ending crime. Prosecuting crime could be long,
arduous, and oftentimes, thankless work. It could also be
overwhelming and chaotic. Still, he loved it.

   Organization was the key to having a shot at keeping
on top of things. The DA's web system was a great benefit
in that regard. It helped keep the DA's office neat and
orderly. All files were within a fingertip's reach with all
necessary forms easily accessible. Ben couldn't have
imagined what life had been like before the paperless era.
During his first year, there had been so much to keep up
with, and the office had provided very little assistance.
After a month long training period, that seemingly went by
faster than the speed of light; he had been cut loose and
literally thrown to the wolves. He'd later figured out that
had all been by design. Counselors who couldn't handle the
hectic, fast pace of the DA's office were weeded out early.

   After scrolling through the Lars case summary, he
turned his attention to the file folder that contained the plea
agreement. He removed it from the folder and looked it
over. Everything appeared in order. The deal had been
offered and accepted on Friday: two years prison time
followed by three years' probation. It was basically a slap
on the wrist for the amount of drugs the kid had been
caught with. But it would get him off the streets for at least
a little while, and with any luck, the short prison stint might
be just enough to convince the kid to try to do something
more productive with his life.

   I keep giving these boys the chance my father probably
never had, he thought wistfully. Although he'd never met
the man, or knew anything about him, Ben wanted to

believe that his dad was locked up somewhere, a victim of the Man and the System, rather than the very real possibility that he was dead, or worse, alive somewhere and not giving a shit about him. Anyway, he thought, pushing that craziness aside, he'd better make sure Peyton Lars hadn't been the recipient of a prior plea agreement. He was scheduled to meet the teen and his attorney at noon today during the Storrs' trial lunch break. The meeting was to take place in the chambers of the Honorable Judge Felix Mannielo where they would formally attach signatures to the plea deal. Mannielo was a fair judge, but he wasn't exactly a big fan of second chances, and he sure as hell wouldn't be that fond of a third one.

He tapped a couple of keys, bringing up Peyton Lars' case history. A single case file appeared. It was from 2002, his first year as a prosecutor. He clicked on it. "Hmm," he mumbled as he scanned through it. He had been the handling prosecutor. But he couldn't recall a thing about the case. A fact that really didn't surprise him; that first year on the job had been a blur. Besides, except for the true regulars of whom there were a few, his brain shuffled most cases out of his mind as soon as the cases reached a resolution. As he continued reading through the file, he saw that the Lars kid's other crime had basically been small potatoes, relatively speaking. As a ten-year old, Lars had shoplifted some candy and a toy from a convenience store. For sure, any sane parent would prefer their children be crime-free. But for some parents that threshold had necessarily been raised to a line just short of strong-armed robbery.

Lars had received two months' probation. It had been a juvie crime, and therefore, it would not affect Lars' current plea arrangement. But as Ben started to close out the file, he paused. Something struck him as odd. He went through it once more and eventually pulled up the initial police incident report. He immediately saw it—1024

Holston Street. The address was that of Fathers House
where Ben had stayed for five years after the murder of his
mother. The home catered to disadvantaged, or otherwise
wayward, boys.

That was strange, he thought as he continued reading
through the file. Why hadn't he noticed it at the time?
Slowly he scanned the file, looking to find an
acknowledgement that he, the prosecuting attorney had a
link to the house, but he didn't find one. There was no
mention of the address or any potential conflict of interest.
How could he have overlooked such a thing? Of course, he
hadn't known Peyton Lars before that time, and he was of
no relation to the boy. And the fact that the two of them had
shared the address—1024 Holston Street, albeit separated
by eight years was of no real relevance.

Fathers House was run by Mayo Fathers, who was
somewhat of a father figure to many of the boys. But being
a father figure wasn't the same as being a father. The boys
weren't actually brothers. So there hadn't exactly been an
ethical lapse. An acknowledgement that he and the boy had
had a shared link, even a skeletal one, would have been the
professional thing to do, but Ben hadn't broken any laws in
not having done so. He'd had other cases involving boys
from Fathers House and to his knowledge; he'd
acknowledged his link to Fathers House in those cases or
had recused himself. He would mention the previous Lars
link to Etlzer later that morning. But since the previous
case had been a juvie crime, there would be no need to
bring it up with Mannielo. Juvenile records were generally
kept sealed.

He closed out Lars' old file and reopened the current
one. He rechecked the boy's current address and saw that
Lars was no longer living at Fathers House. It was possible;
he admitted to himself, that he was having reservations
about the current plea deal because he didn't think for one
minute that young Peyton Lars hadn't been in any other

trouble over the past eight years. However, he quickly realized that in the final analysis, no one but Peyton Lars and perhaps the kid's inner circle knew whether or not Peyton Lars had really been a solid crime-free kid for the last eight years or so. But that was of no consequence now because Lars had managed to stay out of the system. And as far as the current plea deal was concerned, that was all that really mattered.

He closed out of the Lars file and returned to the home screen. He then keyed in the Cindy Storrs murder file. The case file materialized on the screen as he drained the last of his first cup of coffee. He went over to the counter and poured himself another cup.

No one could say with any amount of certainty what makes a particular crime a high profiled one. Everyday somewhere in the country, a child is abducted, killed, or has wandered off. A girlfriend or wife has been killed by her boyfriend, lover, or husband. Some people simply vanish, never to be heard from again. The latest crime statistics claim that a murder is committed every 30.9 minutes. But of all the horrendous crimes that occur basically every second of every day, only a small pittance of them will garner the public's collective imagination. One such infamous crime, at least amongst the citizenry of Duraleigh, was the brutal beating death of Cindy Storrs at the hands of her husband, Deacon Storrs.

A part of the fascination with Cindy Storrs' death could no doubt be attributed to the circumstances surrounding her murder as provided by her husband. Deacon Storrs claimed that he'd found his wife's bloody body that morning in their marital bed. She'd been beaten to death with a hammer that was found at the scene. Deacon Storrs insisted he'd had nothing to do with her murder. According to Deacon, he'd left the apartment the night before, after an argument he'd had with his wife. The argument had been a loud one and had been heard by at least three of the couple's neighbors. Deacon told police that he'd walked to a nearby bar, gotten drunk, and then returned to the couple's apartment around 11:30 or so. He believed the door had been locked when he got there. He sort of remembered fumbling around for his key. Once inside the apartment, he relocked the door and then stumbled over to the couch where he passed out, not even bothering to check the bedroom where he now believed his wife had laid, already dead.

Deacon Storrs was a very believable individual. He was thirty-one years old, medium height, medium build, a very unassuming figure. He looked his questioners directly in the eyes. He showed considerable remorse for the last argument he'd had with his wife. The argument, he'd said, had been a rarity. Although he'd had past disagreements with his wife, they'd never before reached the shouting phrase. His neighbors also attested that the Storrses had been a very quiet and friendly couple. Detectives could not find a single person to speak ill of the man. He was friendly, neighborly, went to work every day and was always on time, a very dependable employee. In fact, if not for his very implausible story, Deacon Storrs may have very well been left alone to mourn the loss of his twenty-nine year old, attractive wife in peace. But a ghost did not kill Cindy Storrs. A human did. And there'd been only one human locked inside that apartment with her. Deacon Storrs.

Ben was second chair on the case. The lead prosecutor was a twenty-year veteran of the DA's office, Jeff Stone. Stone was old-moneyed. His New England family had made its fortune in shipping. Stone had wanted no part in the family business. Though he stopped the line of renouncement at the monthly dividend check he received as part of his share of the family's vast holdings.

Stone rested the state's case early Friday morning and anticipated a quick end to what appeared to be an open and shut domestic murder case.

"When this gets to the jury," Stone had said confidently, "they should get back in record time."

However, Ben wasn't so sure. He'd remembered how Deacon Storrs had so cavalierly rejected the plea offer as if he'd had an ace up his sleeve. Still, Stone had insisted that Ben keep the plea form at the ready during the prosecutorial phase of the trial, as if Deacon Storrs would suddenly come to his senses after having heard the facts of the case repeated in the light of day in front of a jury. So Ben had dutifully brought the form, nestled in a thin manila folder, to trial with him every day. But he didn't believe for one minute that the form was in any danger of getting an attack of signatures anytime soon.

"I have no earthly idea," Stone had said in response to Ben's query of why Deacon Storrs would reject an involuntary manslaughter charge when the evidence clearly pointed to murder in the first degree. Stone, who had more than twice as much prosecutorial experience as Ben, had added, "I have long ceased trying to figure out the criminal mind. Maybe Storrs thinks killing his wife during a drunken rage doesn't count, or maybe his defense will be that while he was passed out dead drunk on the couch, a spook teleported through the locked door and bludgeoned his wife. I really have no earthly idea. But it's not my job to know. My job is to defend the rights of the people of this state. To speak for the victim who can no longer speak for herself. Deacon Storrs murdered his wife in cold blood. I believe we've proven that beyond a reasonable doubt. And the sooner the defense wraps up their bullshit, the sooner the jury can get the case, and the sooner we'll be able to go about the business of putting other deviants behind bars."

"Maybe," Ben said to himself in the empty kitchen. He took another sip of his coffee. Though he didn't have a heap of murder trial experience, he knew enough not to underestimate the ability of twelve people in a jury box to see things entirely different than the prosecution. Especially if the defense continued bringing forth character witnesses as credible as their lead witness had been on Friday.

The Reverend Ethel Storrs was an associate pastor of the First Faith Baptist Church. She was gray-haired and kind-faced with an old-fashioned grandmotherly demeanor. It was easy to imagine her preparing fruit bags on Christmas day for all of her grandchildren, even the grown-up ones. Her entire manner, from her graceful walk to the witness stand, to the careful and deliberate way in which she spoke, screamed honesty and forthrightness. She wore an understated flower-print dress and her hair had been set back in a bun. She was a used car dealer's dream. If she said she'd only driven her now-for-sale car once a week and twice on Sunday, it would sell faster than a salesman's fake grin could disappear. As they watched her being sworn in, Ben sensed a sliver of Stone's over-the-top optimism evaporating. However, after the defense counselor, Keithan Jones, got deeper into his questioning of Rev. Storrs, Stone had perked up again. It appeared the reverend's total devotion to the truth and honesty could cut both ways, even if one way could prove potentially harmful to her son Deacon.

"Are you saying that you believed Cindy Storrs?" Keithan Jones had asked her. He posed the question delicately. Ben could only assume that Jones had covered this ground with the witness in his pretrial preparations. What he likely hadn't anticipated was the courtroom's reaction to the good reverend's statement that Deacon's wife, Cindy Storrs, had seen an omen predicting her own death at the hands of a stranger, and Cindy had consulted a psychic regarding it.

"I believe in signs from God," Reverend Storrs answered.

"Would a sign from God necessarily be a white pigeon on the roof of a house?"

Reverend Storrs smiled. "Surely God is capable of using whatever methods suits his needs or desires to communicate with us." Her voice was strong and steady. Still, there was a measurable groan in the courtroom. Judge Henry McMichaels banged his gravel.

Jones altered his line of questioning. "Would you have recommended that your daughter-in-law go see a psychic about the white pigeon she'd seen on the roof of her apartment complex?"

"No," Reverend Storrs said matter-of-factly. Jones smiled. But she quickly added, "I would have recommended that she seek the Father, as I would have recommended to anyone else who'd ask my advice. I would have encouraged her to pray and study his word." She glanced around the room as if speaking to everyone in it.

"Did you recommend she go to the authorities?" Jones asked.

"And tell them what exactly?" Reverend Storrs asked defiantly. "That she had a premonition that some stranger would break into her house and bludgeon her to death? They wouldn't have believed her, just like the prosecution doesn't believe me now. But, it's true. Cindy saw her murderer and it wasn't my son. But God's will, will be done. The truth will come out, one way or the other."

Ben noticed a couple of jurors nodding their heads as if in agreement. Evidently, Jones noticed it too and he took it as an opportunity to steer the reverend away from the supernatural, and toward stories of the defendant's upbringing. Her testimony ended the court day. Afterwards, Stone felt rejuvenated. He told Ben just before they left court that he was planning to revisit omens and psychics during Monday's cross. It would be fair game, Ben supposed. If the reverend was seen as willing to use any means necessary to free her son, including espousing the virtues of omens and psychics, then there was a good chance her testimony could be refuted as just blatant hogwash. Blame it on nature. Blame it on the rain. Blame it on psychics and omens. But please oh please don't blame sweet, innocent Deacon.

To Ben, a belief in omens and psychics was a complete waste of time. He could not imagine why anyone would spend their hard-earned money on psychics, soothsayers, or any other such nonsense. Crap in life happened, pointblank, end of story. Sometimes it happened for no reason at all. You were in the wrong place at the wrong time, or even the right place at the wrong time, and something bad or good just happened to you. And you would have to deal with it. In other cases, crap happened to you because of you. For instance, if you didn't pay your light bill, your lights were turned off. Or if you didn't work, you didn't eat. Of course, those types of crap you could reasonably control. The others, you just had to deal with and hope that your share of potential crap would be as limited as possible. To him, these were simple truisms that needed no crystal ball. His single-parent mom, may she rest in peace, had taught him these simple facts of life. And Mayo Fathers had reinforced them. Why most people spent a lifetime in a wilderness of misunderstanding on such matters was a big mystery to him. Life wasn't that complicated. There was no man behind the curtain pulling strings, sending omens and white pigeons to hint about his intentions. It was only you and how you dealt with things. If the defense was preparing to blame Cindy Storrs' death on the ethers, open and shut may in fact be a distinct possibility.

He drained the last of his coffee and then closed out of the Storrs file. He looked at the digital clock on the stove. It was five minutes after five. He decided he had enough time for a jog before getting ready for court. Seven minutes later, he stood on his front porch, his breath forming intermittent fog-like wisps in the chilly January morning. He first looked to the east where the rising sun's rays began to push across the sky, and then he looked west, before slowly taking off in that direction, a nice and steady run into the retreating darkness.

His mind floated to thoughts of April. She'd still been asleep when he'd changed into his sweats, which was a good thing he told himself; especially since lately she'd had trouble sleeping. Everything on her body seemed to ache, her back, her legs, and just about every muscle. Her sense of smell had become acute. Most scents bothered her, including his aftershave. He'd had to switch to an unscented brand. She was nauseous most of the time. The doctor had assured him that all of this was normal during pregnancy. But it pained him to see his wife in so much discomfort. She had a routine doctor's appointment later that morning, and he wished he could be there with her. But she'd insisted he go on to court. That she'd be okay. He figured that she only wanted him to go to court because she knew that he'd insist that they leave for the appointment a little early. His routine was to leave for any appointment well before he was due to arrive. His mantra had always been be early, even way early, but never late. Which was completely opposite of that of his wife. Whose mantra was undeniably—no mantras, period, end of discussion

The two of them often jokingly wondered how they even fell in love in the first place, he of the rather be-an-hour-early-instead-of-a-minute-late-breed and she preferring late grand entrances over timely arrivals. But the chemistry between them had been instant, and the marriage, depending upon the onlooker's perspective, had either been whirlwind or shotgun. A baby was conceived on the night of their first date, and the marriage had followed suit two months later.

From the moment he'd first laid eyes on her, he was sprung. And when he'd found out she'd felt the same way, well that was nothing short of a miracle. They both had decided not to wait on the inevitable, electing to start their lives together immediately. The baby had miscarried shortly before the nuptials, but neither felt as though a mistake had been made. Their love was real and their feelings for each other were as strong as ever. And now, two years after having first laid eyes on her, they were going to have that baby after all, two of them in fact.

Lights dotted on just about every other house in the neighborhood as the neighborhood slowly stirred to life. He ran past three cars idling in their driveways, their engines warming up, their mufflers billowing grayish-white exhaust fumes into the coldness. So far it had been a typical noncommittal North Carolina winter. On Friday morning, it had been a pleasant and spring-like sixty degrees during his jog. Now just three days later, it felt downright arctic. He ran up and down the two streets parallel to his own and then returned home. There was no need catching pneumonia while trying to stay in shape.

After reentering the house, Ben went directly into the upstairs main bathroom for a shower. It was now 6:00. Fifteen minutes later, the steamy shower was completed and Ben emerged from it, dropping one wet foot after the other on a purple throw rug. Before April, the bathroom floor itself dried his feet. He smiled. Civilization had arrived in his life and it was a good thing. Considering all he'd been through in his life, losing his mother to a senseless crime, never knowing his father, and growing up in what was essentially a group home, he'd managed to accomplish a lot. He'd graduated college and law school. He was a rising star in the district attorney's office. To boot, he had a beautiful wife with two beautiful baby boys on the way. To be sure, Mayo Fathers had been an essential reason behind his success. Ben didn't know what would have happened to him if Mayo hadn't taken him in. And he didn't want to know. He'd overcome his past and that was all that mattered. His future was very bright.

He finished toweling off and then wrapped the now damp towel around his toned midsection. He reached under the sink and grabbed his electric razor. He picked up a folded newspaper from the wicker stand that was against the wall behind him. It stood next to a matching white wicker wastebasket. After lining the sink with the newspaper to catch falling stubble, he began the tedious task of shaving.

Despite the newspaper lining and his best efforts to avoid having them do so, fine black hairs still speckled around the edges of the white porcelain sink. After only completing one side of his face, he frowned down at the antlike hairy specks, and then heard the first of his wife's shrieks blazing into the bathroom.

Chapter 3

James Etlzer was a numbers guy. It was an obsession that had started in grade school with his first passion—baseball. The numbers didn't lie. If you wanted to know if a hitter was having a great season, you'd look at his numbers—his batting average, the number of home runs he'd hit, the number of runs batted in. Was a pitcher worth his salt? Well what did the numbers say? What was his earned run average? How many strikeouts did he have? How many walks? How many hits given up? The numbers didn't lie. Consult them and there were no mysteries.

In his current capacity as Duraleigh County district attorney, he believed not only in the prophetic capabilities of numbers, but also in their perception-setting abilities. The numbers always told the tale. Was Duraleigh the safest county in North Carolina? Why, just look at its ten percent decrease in the number of overall crimes from last year. While you're at it, take a gander at its twenty percent decrease in violent crimes over the last five years. In fact, look at all of the mind boggling statistics during DA James Etlzer's entire eleven year reign. His office's conviction rate was truly staggering. Why Mr. and Mrs. John Q. Anybody, don't you feel absolutely safe in Duraleigh? Of course you do, because the numbers didn't lie.

Etlzer sat at his desk in his office, partaking in one of his favorite pastimes—thumbing through the county's latest crime statistics. The stats were truly impressive, and the county had shown improvement in every major category for each year of his tenure. No small feat considering his predecessor, Bruce Waters, had himself touted obscene numbers. The thought of Waters brought a touch of sadness, as well as a feeling of concern. He put the statistics guide back into the upper left desk drawer and then looked expectantly at his desk phone.

As if he'd willed it, the phone rang. "Etlzer," he barked into the receiver.

"Have you heard?" asked the voice on the other end.

"Yes," Etlzer replied. "His wife called me last night. She's worried. She doesn't think he's going to make it. It was a massive heart attack. He had over ninety percent blockage." He paused, then, "It's amazing. I just saw Waters last week. He looked incredible, appeared in great shape. He was very excited about running for governor. I guess you never know."

"No, you don't," the voice answered blankly. "We have to move quickly."

"I don't follow."

"The governorship. You are going to run in Waters' place."

Etlzer leaned back in his chair. "Governor. That's a big leap from DA. AG is one thing, but governor…" his voice trailed off.

"It's makes perfect sense. Waters was popular because of how he'd cleaned up Duraleigh. That was the catalyst behind his successful attorney general's bid. You're his protégé. If the people can't have Waters, you're the next best thing. The campaign infrastructure is already in place. Money, donors, volunteers, everything is at the ready."

"What if Waters survives?"

"It doesn't matter. He's already lost the election. Heart attack equals weak candidate. He's done as a politician."

Etlzer rubbed his chin. "There are some other concerns."

"Such as?"

"Waters heard talk of a federal investigation into Father's Disciples."

"I'll tell you as I'd told Waters. Any federal investigation into Father's Disciples will be hindered. My people don't talk. And those who do don't do so for long. In any event, if the feds want Father's Disciples, I'm prepared to give it to them."

"I don't understand."

"You don't need to understand, counselor," the voice said calmly. "Just prepare yourself to become the next governor of North Carolina, and afterwards, well, dream big counselor, dream big."

"Alright, alright. But there is one other thing. The Leeson boy. The Duraleigh Standard is starting a narrative on the return of gang violence. Now it's possible that the police and mayor will take the immediate negatives on that. But there could be some blowback on my end as well. I mean ending gangs was one of the main issues I ran on."

"I admit we were a little messy,' the voice said with a trace of irritation. "But a fix is already underway. I'm sending someone over. He'll cop to it. He'll say that it was just a beef between friends."

"Can we sell that? I understand the Leeson boy is busted up pretty bad."

"It'll sell. Assign one of your regulars to it, someone who doesn't ask many questions, like Lovison. It'll go away."

"It's that simple?" Etlzer asked doubtfully.

"It's that simple, Governor," the voice replied.

"Governor," Etlzer repeated softly. It had a nice ring to it.

Calvin Leeson was having an O.O.B.E. He'd learned the term from his high school physics teacher, Mr. Egbert Moreland. It meant out of body experience. Moreland was a short, eager-faced man, with thinning hair that he combed over in a wasted attempt to camouflage his bald head. In describing his own O.O.B.E experiences to his students,

Moreland said, "Oh little friends, I travel all over. Sometimes I even visit some of you. I hover over your beds while you're sleeping."

At the time, Calvin had doubted that his teacher was being serious, or if such a thing was even possible. But here Calvin was, hovering over his own hospital bed, looking down at his badly bruised face. He studied his face for several minutes. His jaws were balled out as if he had a mouth stuffed full of chewing tobacco. His puffy eyes looked like little ant mounds. His complexion was now strangely purplish. In his current O.O.B.E state, Calvin struggled to remember what had happened to him.

Police car. He vaguely recalled a police car. Or was it policemen in a car? He wasn't sure. Cain Simmons. Yeah, Cain had been there. Cain and policemen in a car. How did it all fit? He struggled to remember. After a few minutes, he gave up. It hurt too much trying to remember. Mr. Moreland hadn't mentioned having headaches in his O.O.B.E state. If Calvin was out of his body, was he a spirit? Could a spirit have a headache?

He floated upward a little more, backing further away from the bed, taking in a panoramic view of the room. It was a tight little room, perhaps no bigger than a generously sized walk-in closet. He took the full measure of his body and then looked away. A flat screen television fitted snugly into the upper left corner wall. A Cosby show episode, its sound muted, played onscreen. At the front of the bed, near his body's head, there were three or four machines, each either beeping, or blinking, or both. An IV bag dangled over his head, its tube extending into his right arm. He scanned the rest of the room, and then stopped suddenly as his eyes happened upon the body folded in the recliner at the other corner of the room.

"Momma," he cried out. He floated over to the recliner and hovered over his mother. Sarah Leeson looked extremely uncomfortable. She was fetal-curled into the crevice of the chair, her toes lightly scraping the edge of the leg rest.

Policemen. Cain. His mother. There was a connection. Remember, damn it, he commanded himself. Seconds later, an image surfaced—policemen. Slowly, the memory became clearer. A dark blue sedan pulled up alongside him as he walked home. A head had leaned out the window of the passenger side. Calvin hadn't known him. He'd never seen him before. It had been a young dude, in his late teens or early twenties. He was brown-complected with one long bushy eyebrow. "You're Sarah Leeson's boy," he'd said to Calvin. He didn't ask; he accused.

"I don't know you, partner," Calvin responded hastily and continued walking.

"He's cool, C." The voice came from the backseat. Calvin stopped and stooped down, peering into the car. It was Cain. "That's my nigga, Morant," Cain said. "He works for Father too. Get in. He just wants to holler at a brother."

Calvin hesitated. He wasn't sure. But Morant quickly jumped out of the front seat of the car, yanked opened the back door, and roughly shoved Calvin down into the backseat. After Morant got back in, the car dislodged asphalt, sped down the road, and eventually ended up on the south side of town behind W.H. Knuckles Elementary School.

Morant quickly hustled Calvin out of the car. It was no secret who was running things. Both Cain and the driver, a short man with a muscular George of the Jungle upper body attached to stunted but equally muscled legs, exited the car as well. Neither said a word.

"You're working for the FBI," Morant said. Again, it was an accusation, but this time, Morant flavored it with a punch to Calvin's gut, dropping him to his knees and leaving him gasping for breath.

Morant stood over Calvin. "You biting the hand that

feeds you boy," Morant said menacingly, spicing it up with another blow, this time to Calvin's jaw, knocking him over on his side. He stomped Calvin's head into the ground and grinded it into the dirt.

Blinded by pain and confusion, Calvin trembled on the ground, struggling against the weight of the Nike on his head. He'd met the FBI agent only three times and had yet to give any information that hadn't already been known. Calvin was only a bit player in Father's Disciples, a mere street hustler. He'd given the agent nothing because he'd had nothing to give. He didn't even know how the agent had gotten his name in the first place. But apparently, Father had somehow found out about the meetings and now Calvin was getting the shit beat out of him because of it.

Morant lifted his foot from the side of Calvin's head and readied it for another stomp, before pausing knee-high at the crunching sounds of another car slowly moving across the gravel. Morant looked toward the car and let his foot fall harmlessly down, next to Calvin's head.

Through slightly closed and dirt-filled eyes, Calvin saw the white sedan with the blue siren on top. A sense of relief swept through him. It was the police. He watched the patrol car's driver side door open. Shiny black dress shoes exited the vehicle and walked over to the back of the blue sedan from which Calvin had been unceremoniously pulled. "What's going on here?" the officer asked. The question was directed at Morant.

Morant squared up and slightly nudged Calvin's head with his foot. "Nothing officer. This is Father's business."

"Hmm," the officer said. He lowered his voice as if sharing a secret. "You guys should be more careful. People called in. Said some young boy had been kidnapped. Ya'll are going to have to get the hell out of here."

Morant said, "We got to finish this up."

The passenger side door of the police car opened. Another shiny black shoe hit the gravel.

"It's okay, Peters," the first officer shouted towards the patrol car. "I got this."

The shiny black shoe stayed planted for a long moment, before hesitantly rising up again and returning to the patrol car. The passenger side door of the patrol car slammed shut.

The first officer faced Morant once more. The volume increased slightly and the range lowered. "Hurry this crap up. People saw. I've got to call the ambulance."

Morant glared at him for a full second. "Calm your nerves, man. We got this. He then turned to Cain and George of the Jungle. "Let's get to it." The blows came in abundance, courtesy of fists, feet, and elbows. Calvin curled up in a fetal position in a futile effort to protect himself. His hopes for protection, so strong just a minute ago, evaporated into a mist of comprehension. Father was too powerful. He even had the police under his thumb.

Now, Calvin drifted in and out of consciousness. During his fleeting moments of wakefulness, an understanding of his situation had sunk in. He faced death. He could see it across the way where his father stood in its midst, open-armed and beckoning Calvin to come join him. He surely missed his father. It had been almost three years since the elder Leeson's death. The wound it had caused still hadn't sufficiently healed. Their potential reunion would be sweet.

Calvin smiled. Death could be a good thing. But then, Calvin turned his head away and looked in the corner at his mother. She was still asleep in the recliner. She needed him alive. He remembered Morant's initial greeting, "You're Sarah Leeson's boy." Maybe they had something on her too. He had to warn her.

"Momma," he cried out. She didn't answer. He called out again and again; and again and again, there was no answer. Suddenly he felt himself being pulled up from the hospital bed. He looked down at the bed that was changing form. It now sported grass and weeds as if it was becoming part of the earth. He tried reaching for it, but could only grab the top edge of the inclined mattress. It turned to a fine dust in his hands. "Momma," he cried out again.

"Calvin." The voice came from above him. He turned to face it. It was his father with outstretched arms.

Calvin waved him off. "I got to go back. I've got to warn Momma."

His father waited patiently as Calvin continued ascending toward him.

"I got to go back," Calvin said.

Finally, Calvin reached his father who gently pulled his son into his embrace. "It's over son," he said gently. "It's over."

***

Everything was a blur, seen through a sleep-fueled haze, and leftover tears induced from a just interrupted dream, a dream that had unfortunately been based on an unfolding reality. Calvin was dying.

Sarah Leeson stood, wedged between the recliner she'd been sleeping on and the wall on which her back was now pressed. In front of her, her only child lay on a bed, doctors and nurses scurrying about him. There were beeps, pings, and wails from various machines mingling with the frantic verbiage of medical personnel fighting what she knew to be a losing battle.

She'd seen this scenario play out before.

Nearly three years ago her husband suffered a heart attack. The heart attack was the merciful ending to Pete Leeson's courageous, albeit unsuccessful battle against cancer. He'd fought the disease for eighteen months, running up a mountain of false hopes and medical bills before the heart attack had mercifully brought what cancer had threatened all along. It was life's irony, she'd thought

then as she'd watched the doctors and nurses frantically try
to save a man who was dying anyway.

Now here she was again, losing another man from her
life, a young man who'd had so much promise and who had
desperately tried to fill his father's shoes. It had been a
desperation that had undoubtedly contributed to her son
being here. No, she said to herself, pushing the thought
away. She would not blame Pete's death on this. Still, she
needed to lash out at someone or something.

The maddening activity soon trickled to a stop. A
restless and uneasy calm fell over the room, washing over
her as the cacophony of death battling medical noises
morphed into a single elongated ping. She shifted from
behind the recliner and slid down the wall onto her
backside, pressing her thighs up against her bosom. "Why,
God, why?" her anguished scream slashed through the
hospital room.

Chapter 4

Ben had known Dr. Gordon Shepherd literally his whole life, the good doctor having delivered Ben thirty-three years ago. Shepherd was a throwback, an old fashioned family doctor still apt to making house calls, and who still took pictures of every baby he delivered. He knew his patients intimately, taking great pride in remembering a lot of their birthdays, anniversaries, and graduation dates.

When Ben had called Shepherd early that Monday morning, Shepherd was already at the hospital making his rounds. At seventy-two years of age, the doctor had no intentions of retiring anytime soon, and Ben had no doubts that Shepherd accomplished more in a half-day than most doctors half his age accomplished in an entire week. When Ben had found out he and April were expecting a baby, he'd instantly thought of Dr. Shepherd. April had been skeptical at first, but it had taken just one consultation with the doctor for her to change her mind. His mind was as sharp as a tack, and as he told her, "I have over forty-one years' experience delivering babies. I think I am quite capable helping get these two into the world."

"Two?" Ben had asked, not quite trusting his ears.

"Two," Shepherd repeated. "You two are having twins."

Now it seemed the twins had been just as anxious to get here, as their parents had been to see them. A bit too anxious, Ben thought now as he stood outside the neonatal intensive care unit, watching as his newly arrived boys were each placed into an incubator. "This is all standard procedure," Shepherd had assured him earlier as the boys were being weighed, measured, and prepared for transport to the NICU. "At thirty weeks, we have to make sure the babies are getting the right amount of minerals and fluids. We also have to monitor their body temperatures. And make sure they're not losing too much fluid."

"Are they going to be alright?" Ben asked nervously.

"I'll be honest with you," Shepherd told him. "This is not an ideal situation. Nothing takes the place of a mother's womb. Right now the odds are about 40-60 that we could lose one or both of them. But we've been here before. We have experience in these situations. In addition to that, premature care has advanced a lot in the last few years."

It had been an honest assessment. Ben expected no less from Dr. Shepherd. The doctor was an eternal optimist, but he was also a realist. If the situation was hopeless, Shepherd would have had no problem saying so. It wouldn't have been the first time he'd had to give Ben sobering news.

When Ben was thirteen years old, he'd returned home from school to find his mother lying near death on the sidewalk in front of their home. A puddle of blood from a single gunshot had widened in her chest. Despite seeing his mother in such a horrific state, he'd remained calm enough to go inside their home, dial 911, and afterwards, the number of Dr. Shepherd; a name his mom had scotch-taped to the door of the refrigerator.

Shepherd made it to the emergency room fifteen minutes before the ambulance. As the paramedics rolled Lizzie Lovison into surgery, Shepherd pulled Ben into a waiting area and found a spot on a bench near the back of the room. "They will do everything they can for her," he assured Ben. All around them the emergency room teemed with activity.

A little boy, perhaps five years of age, had accidently stepped on a rusted nail at his school and now complained loudly about having to get a tetanus shot. Meanwhile, a young mother, her head wrapped in a red scarf, rushed in, carrying a child in her arms and a little brown plastic bottle. She yelled at the attendants that the child had accidently swallowed prescription pills. One nurse grabbed the baby from the woman's arms, taking it through double doors in one direction while another nurse led the woman down the hall in the opposite direction, all the while trying to calm the hysterical woman. Next, an elderly man came in complaining of chest pains. It was one thing after the other, some major, some minor, and all seemingly happening at one time. It was an ordinary Wednesday afternoon and it wasn't even quite suppertime. Ben, with blood-speckled shirt and pants, sat stock-still next to Dr. Shepherd who had his arm around him, lightly patting his shoulder.

Thirty minutes later Shepherd said, "I'll go back and see what I can find out." A little while after that, he returned and motioned for Ben to follow him to a private room down the hall. Once they were inside the room, Shepherd closed the door, looked Ben squarely in the eyes, and said simply, "She's gone."

Ben stood at the glass window of the neonatal unit, quietly staring at the two newest Lovisons.

"...tably," He turned his head around in the direction of the baritone voice. It was Dr. Shepherd, still wearing his scrubs.

"Sorry, doc," Ben said. "I didn't hear you."

"I said April's resting comfortably," Shepherd repeated.

"Good. May I see her?"

"By all means," Shepherd replied. "I need you as upbeat as you possibly can be. Assure her that everything will be alright."

"Will it?"

"The odds are as I told you before. But you're her husband. Your love and support will give her better odds. She's still weak, and I need her fighting to get stronger. So you need to pray for whatever strength and courage you need before you go in to see her. Okay?"

Focusing on the tubes attached to their babies, and becoming increasingly aware of the two of them lying in what looked like little metal coffins, Ben mouthed silently, "Okay."

The walls in the hospital chapel were decorated in a hodgepodge of religious imagery. There were images of crosses, crescents, Buddhas, stars, moons, suns, Bibles, and all sorts of religious depictions in a harmonious display of spiritual tolerance. It had been a compromise on the part of Lincoln Memorial's senior administration staff after there had been uproar against the decision to remove all religious imagery from the hospital, including all Bibles, crosses, Korans, and anything remotely related to any religion of any kind.

Ben knelt on a mat at the front of the chapel in a place where an altar used to be. Now there was simply a table with candles and a bowl containing written prayers from anyone who'd felt compelled to write one. He hadn't felt so compelled and for that matter, he wasn't exactly sure what he wanted to say. For the longest time he just stared at the candles. His tenuous belief in God was only there at all because his mom had believed. However, in Ben's mind, considering the way she'd died, there wasn't exactly a compelling reason to believe in a higher power. And if he added in the fact that the so called higher power had allowed his father to abandon him and his mother, then God Almighty wasn't exactly batting a thousand. At the very least, he hadn't always shined so favorably on one, Benjamin Clyde Lovison.

Still, he loved his wife and their new family, and he wanted them all healthy and home, so he closed his eyes and prayed. He prayed for the wellbeing of his two little babies. He prayed for his wife April to get better, both mentally and physically. He prayed that he'd be a better man and a better father, much better than his own father had been. Finally, he prayed for the strength to face April with confidence, optimism, and knowledge that everything would be okay. After meditating silently for a few moments, he opened his eyes, thanked God for his time, and stood up. When he turned around, he stared right into tear-filled eyes.

She appeared to be in her mid-thirties. Her face was pleasant, but tired-looking. She looked as if she'd spent a night or two at the hospital. Her hair barely held form, strands of it popped out of place like weeds. She wore a knee length white skirt that sported the haphazard creases of having been slept in, as did her blue blouse. She fingered a small cross attached to a necklace which hung around her neck. Ben smiled. She managed to return a half-one as she eased past him to the spot he'd just vacated. He was almost out the chapel when he heard the crash behind him. He turned around. It was a chaotic mess. The woman had fallen over the table, knocking it over, sending the candles and the prayer bowl along with its contents hurtling to the floor. Tiny bits of paper flickered to the floor like disinterested snow.

***

Sarah Leeson had just lost her only child. She babbled that to him after he'd helped her up from the floor. She was unsure of what she was going to do now that both the men in her life were gone. What had she done wrong, she sobbed. "Why am I being punished," she asked into the air, winging her arms out flamboyantly as if to punctuate the rhetorical question. Ben had no answers for her, so he simply and quietly escorted her to the cafeteria where he offered to buy her a cup of coffee, which she accepted, and some breakfast, which she declined.

At ten o'clock, the crowd in the cafeteria thinned. A

few tables were randomly occupied with an assortment of visitors and hospital personnel. The conversations were varied and muffled, like those in a library before some bun-haired lady ordered complete and absolute silence. There was no such noise-monitor here, but sometimes circumstances beckoned silence. Ben led her to a table near the back, and then quietly and patiently sat with her.

Eventually he learned that the other man she'd lost had been her husband. He'd been stricken with cancer, though it had been a heart attack that delivered the fatal blow. Her son had been the victim of street violence. Ben vaguely recalled skimming an article about the incident in last week's Duraleigh Standard. He listened without interruption, interjecting only when her pause seemed interminable, and then only to gently nudge her along. He asked her son's age. Seventeen, she said. What a wonderful age that was, he said without thinking. She smiled and apparently understood he'd meant no harm by it. After all, her son's death was still fresh to her as well. She asked his name, and afterwards if Ben was short for Benjamin. "Yes," he answered. "But please call me Ben." She repeated his name, "Ben." It slid comfortably from her lips as if she'd known him longer than twenty minutes.

He thought about sharing his story about his mom. How he'd lost her to senseless violence as well. But the thought made him remember how he'd really felt after his mom had been killed. He'd wanted neither sympathy nor empathy. He'd wanted revenge.

"I'm an assistant district attorney," he blurted out as if that fact alone was a sword to be used against any and all perpetrators.

She jerked ever so slightly and looked genuinely puzzled. Then, she abruptly pushed back from the table and started to get up. "I'm sorry," she said, clearly flustered. "I didn't mean to impose."

Ben reached across the table for her. "Impose? You're

not imposing. Hold on a second. I'm one of the good guys."

She pulled back beyond his reach and made it to her feet, snatching up her handbag in the process. "I'm so sorry. I've got to go. I have so much to do. I'm sorry." She spoke rapidly and avoided looking at him as if she'd just found out his embarrassing secret.

"Sorry about what?" Ben asked following behind her. He had to break into a light jog.

"Please Mr. Lovison," she said in a quavering voice. "Let me go. I have things I need to take care of."

Mr. Lovison? Just a few moments ago, he'd been Ben. Why was she acting so formal all of a sudden? He stood a few feet back from her and watched as she entered the empty elevator. She punched the call button and then turned her gaze to her shoes as the elevator doors closed.

In Ben's experience, some people on the low rungs of education and income held a deep distrust of the law and the people sworn to enforce it. That distrust often manifested itself through unreasonable fear or unfathomable hate. As one moved up the income and education scales, distrust gradually became understanding of the rules of law, and with that understanding, often came a deep respect for those individuals entrusted with defending and enforcing it. Of course, amongst the extreme upper end of the income scale there was sometimes a feeling that the rule of law could sometimes be a nuisance, and that policeman, prosecutors, and judges were mere lowly public servants, apt to overstepping their bounds from time to time.

Sarah Leeson's behavior had been surprising only in the sense that she had appeared to be an educated woman of at least modest means. But then again, there were always exceptions to every rule. As he approached the hospital room where his wife had been moved, Ben dismissed thoughts of Sarah. He paused at the closed door. He heard voices inside the room.

He opened the door to find Mayo Fathers standing over April's bed, smiling widely. April, though she looked a little feeble, smiled too. She had a new mother's glow and she seemed…happy. Tired, but happy.

"There he is," she said in a high whisper when she noticed him standing in the doorway.

Mayo turned around. "Congratulations, Ben. Twins, huh?"

"Yes, thank you."

"Mr. Fathers told me what a decent and honorable young man you were growing up. He said our boys will be fortunate to have you for a father."

"I appreciate the compliment, Mayo."

"Well, it's the truth. I never had any trouble out of this one. He always had a deep respect for authority." He smiled at April. "And you sweet one. Call me Uncle Mayo. We're family."

April smiled weakly, "Sure, Uncle Mayo." She closed her eyes and seemed to nod off.

"I called your office and they told me what happened," Mayo said to Ben.

"You didn't have to rush down here."

"I had someone else here to visit anyway."

"Anything serious?" Ben quizzed.

"Nothing you should be concerned about," Mayo deflected. "How are those babies?"

"Fine," Ben said hurriedly also wanting to deflect. He nodded ever so slightly toward his wife.

Mayo caught the hint and smiled awkwardly.

"What did you want?" Ben asked rather harshly before softening it with, "You said you'd called my office."

"Uh, right," Mayo said, appearing somewhat surprised at the tone of the first question. "I wanted to confirm your participation at next week's conference. But I guess in light of the arrival of the babies, you probably won't make it."

"No, I can make it. It's an opportunity to give back."

"Great," Mayo said. "I also got a confirmation from Caleb."

April opened her eyes and perked up a little at the mention of Caleb's name. "Caleb Dawson, Ben's old friend?"

"One and the same," Mayo said. "The Bureau is giving him a couple of days off and he agreed to do it."

"I can't wait to meet him," April said. "I've heard so much about him."

"I don't talk about him that much," Ben said, obviously embarrassed.

"They were two peas in a pod at one point," Mayo offered. "Then Caleb's father came back and moved the family away. But Caleb has always said the time he'd spent at Fathers House helped make the difference in his life. He and Ben are what the home is all about. Next week I plan to showcase both of them. Fundraising will go through the roof."

"Anything I can do to help, just let me know," Ben said.

"Just show up," Mayo said as he walked toward the door.

After Mayo left, April looked warily at her husband. "Why don't you call him Uncle Mayo?"

"Huh?" Ben asked.

"Uncle Mayo. I have never heard you call him that. But he says family calls him that. But you don't. Why?"

Ben thought about her question for a moment. The answer was simple really. When he'd first started going to Fathers House he'd called Mayo, Mr. Fathers. After moving into Fathers House, he'd tried briefly calling him Uncle Mayo like everyone else had. But it felt uncomfortable to him doing that. Mayo wasn't his uncle. He was of no blood relation, kind deed or no kind deed. So one day, Ben dropped the uncle moniker and started calling him Mayo. But he didn't tell April any of that, instead he said, "I don't know."

It didn't matter. It wasn't a pressing concern for April. She yawned and asked, "How do our babies look?"

Ben kissed his wife on the forehead. "Beautiful. Both of them are simply beautiful."

Chapter 5

Maalik drained the last of his milk and threw the empty carton into the trashcan. He grabbed an apple from the bowl and walked to the former butler pantry/library. The wall separating the two rooms had been knocked down, and the combined room was now the study hall. Some of the books from the old library, a few of which were almost a hundred years old, were squeezed tight into a bookshelf built into the wall. To protect the books, the temperature in the room was kept low even in the winter, which gave the room a hint of the authentic dankness of an old bookstore.

Maalik didn't acknowledge the other boy sitting at the table. Instead, he grabbed his math workbook, a notebook, and a pencil from his book bag and sat down at the opposite end of the table. With his eyes fixedly on his workbook, he felt the other boy's eyes on him.

After a few moments of awkward silence, the other boy got up and moved to the chair across the table from Maalik. "It's been two weeks man. How long are you going to keep this up?"

Maalik didn't look up. "Keep what up?"

"This, the silent treatment."

"Dude, I ain't being silent. I just ain't got nuthin' to say."

"Is that right?" The other boy said. "I know you got busted by the police. I know Uncle Mayo picked you up from the station. I know you were punished somehow. And now you're acting strange. It's like you're in some sort of fog. What did he do to you?"

"Ain't nobody done nuthin' to me, Prodegee. Alright? Nuthin'. I'm cool. Okay? I'm cool."

"I ain't buying that," Prodegee said. "Something

happened. I see who you've been hanging with now too. What if I want to get down?"

Maalik smirked. "Get down. You? Man, please. You're just a kid."

"A kid? I'm the same age as you."

Maalik looked up at Prodegee for the first time. He licked his lips and then wiped his mouth with the back of his hand. "I'm telling you this for your own good. Stay away from me. Stay away from Nathan. And stay away from Joe-Joe. Cain knows what's up and he'll tell you the same thing. Just be a kid."

"Nah, man," Prodegee said. "I want to...."

"What the hell are you doing?" The angry voice rushed into the room from the hallway. Prodegee looked in that direction. "Cain, what's up?"

"Don't what's up me," Cain said. "I told you to stay away from him." He faced Maalik. "What're you doing Maalik?"

"I ain't doing nuthin', man," Maalik said. "You need to check your boy."

Cain glared at Maalik. "Get your stuff Prodegee." And then to Maalik, "Stay away from him."

Maalik went back to his workbook. "Whatever," he mumbled.

Outside the study hall, Cain jacked up Prodegee by his shirt. "Either you down with him or you're down with me."

"But I see ya'll hanging out. You down with him," Prodegee charged accusingly.

Cain ignored that. "I'm serious Prodegee. If you're going to kick this music thing with me, you can't hang with him or with me when I'm hanging with him. And I ain't got to explain it to you. You got a choice. What's it going to be?"

"Alright, man. Damn. I'm with you. Alright."

"Good. Meet me at my house at about six-thirty."

"You're staying at your house tonight?"

"Yeah," Cain said.

"Your old man's not going to be there?"

"He's not my old man. He's my mother's boyfriend. And no, he's not there."

"Well bet; let's go kick some music now."

"I can't right now," Cain said. "I got to go downtown and handle some business."

***

"Judge Stanley Kilroy is an asshole," Frank Vass said. He stood at the defense table in an emptied courtroom, talking in a hushed voice to his assistant, Sue Bobbins, as he angrily stuffed papers into his briefcase. The judge had long since left for his chambers; but Vass still glowered at the empty bench.

"You say that every time he's assigned to one of your cases," Sue reminded him.

"That's because he's an asshole every time he's been assigned to one of my cases."

Sue harrumphed, shook her head, and finished collecting the remaining papers from the table, placing them atop a computer tablet in Vass' briefcase.

"Don't give me that look, Sue. You know I'm telling the truth. That man has it in for defense attorneys."

"Frank, Frank, tough break, eh," the voice crawled into the room from behind him. It belonged to Adam Banks, a snarky little prosecutor from the Attorney General's office. Banks was five feet five inches of pompous bullshit.

"Put a sock in it, Adam," Frank said without bothering to turn around.

"You sound upset," Adam teased.

Frank turned around, facing him. "No, I'm not upset. I'm just surprised that you and the honorable Judge Kilroy have such a total disregard for fairness."

"Really now," Banks said. "You feel that allowing in

knowledge of one's past run-ins with the law is somehow unfair."

"What I feel is that knowledge of what may or may not have been embezzlement committed over twenty years ago by my client when he was a nineteen year old impressionable college student will prejudice a jury hearing his fraud case today. But I see the State will stoop to anything to try to prove its case."

"Don't give me that nonsense," Banks said, the cheeriness now out of his voice. "The fact that Jamison Pittman stole money from his employer twenty years ago is very relevant to the charges of bribery and fraud that he faces today. I think it's very beneficial for the jury to know that the conduct leading Mr. Pittman to misappropriate DOT funds, while accepting bogus bids for the state's road projects, had been nurtured during the whole of his adult life.

Vass responded sharply, "Adam, you know full well that twenty years ago Jamie accepted a plea deal to avoid any embarrassment to him and his family. His father had been battling cancer for god's sake. A trial would have been too much for the family."

"The fact remains, missing money wound up in your client's possession. And he copped to taking it."

"Adam, you know..."

"Gentlemen," Sue said, cutting him off. "The judge has already ruled on the issue." To Frank she said, "You have a client meeting at 4:30."

"Smart lady," Banks said and winked at her. "How about coming to work for the other side?"

"Thanks, but I'm perfectly content working for this side," Sue said.

"Well, if you ever change your mind..." He looked at Frank. "I know you were hoping to get Mannielo on this one. He always seems sympathetic to the defense's plight."

"If by sympathetic, you mean fair. Then yes, I could

have used him on this trial."

"I bet," Banks said, and then turned to leave.

"Asshole," Vass muttered.

Vass and Sue left the courtroom. She headed toward the elevators while he decided to take the stairs.

After reaching the first floor landing, he thought he heard a familiar voice. He opened the stairwell door just in time to see Ben Lovison and a few other people board an elevator. He called out to him, "Ben."

Ben turned around and looked curiously at him for a moment, before the look of delayed recognition crept across his face just as the elevator door closed.

***

Ben walked hurriedly into his office where Cain Simmons and his attorney, Melvin Wallingford, had been waiting for about thirty minutes. He apologized for being late to the meeting that he had only learned about five minutes before when he'd stopped in Etlzer's office.

After shaking hands with both the counselor and his teenaged client, Ben went behind his desk and plopped down his briefcase. Then he opened the file folder he'd just received from Etlzer. He sat down in the leather straight-back chair and pulled out the plea form. He stared at it for a minute before calmly placing it back into the folder, which he then moved to the left top corner of his desk, out of the way. He moved the briefcase to the floor down by his knee. He looked from Wallingford to Cain.

The teen met his eyes for all of ten seconds before awkwardly turning away. There was no sense in prolonging this, Ben thought. "Calvin Leeson died this morning." His interlocked fingers rested atop his desk. He swiveled his head from Wallingford to Cain. "He's dead," he reiterated. "I listened to his mother as she described to me how she'd been in the room, helplessly watching her son die before her very eyes. I studied her face as she talked to me about how her son died slowly, in pain, while she was able to do nothing about it. It wasn't a booboo she could kiss and make better. It was real, and it was permanent. She also told me about his dreams, his hopes, and his life. Now, there is nothing neither she, nor I can do about his hopes and dreams."

Wallingford cleared his throat noticeably, indicating his disapproval at what he obviously considered an unnecessary spiel. But he obviously wasn't prepared to do more than that.

Ben ignored him just the same and continued. "What I can promise is that I can give him justice." He stopped and stared hard at Cain. "Son, there's going to be justice. You know more than what you've shared thus far. It's time to give that up." `

"Wait a minute," Wallingford said. "My client has already admitted to the altercation. He has no more to say."

Ben leaned back in his chair and exhaled an exaggerated flow of air. "Okay, okay." He looked for a moment at the folder he'd placed on the left top corner of his desk and then turned back to Wallingford. "This is what we've got—one kid dead, one kid admitting to beating dead kid. Witnesses confirm that the dead kid got into a car with this same kid, who, I repeat, has admitted to administering the beating that ultimately led to the first kid's death. I'm looking at first degree. I can argue premeditation. Your client here picked up the soon-to-be-deceased and drove him to a location for the specific purpose of killing him. But, if I'm feeling particularly charitable, I may give the jury the option of second degree which still carries the option of life in prison without the possibility of."

Cain jumped up. "Man, you're kidding! I told ya'll what went down, and ya'll try to pull this crap. I didn't commit no first degree murder or second degree!"

"Sit down," Wallingford said firmly.

Cain hesitated before dropping back down in the chair like a scolded six year old.

"Look," Wallingford said coolly. "Witnesses may have seen Calvin Leeson get into the car with my client. Kids jump in and out of cars with their friends all the time. Kids also have disagreements. And, unfortunately, sometimes those disagreements lead to fisticuffs. I believe it can be demonstrated that my client did not have a gun, or a knife, or any weapon of any sort. And the facts are both my client and Calvin Leeson are seventeen-year-old kids. Both are approximately the same height and weight. My client's fists aren't registered as weapons of destruction. Surely, even with the boldest vision of grandeur, my client wouldn't have assumed he could have ended a fellow teen's life with only the use of his fists. So premeditation is your wet dream at best. Same with second degree. Now if the state wishes to waste valuable court time and public money pursuing an unwinnable case, then by all means, have at it. But in the best interest of all parties involved, we will accept a charge of simple assault."

Ben confidently drummed his desk with his fingers. "Leeson's skull was bashed in. His eyes had literally been pushed into their sockets. If your client's fists aren't registered weapons, they most certainly should be. But I believe I can prove to the jury's satisfaction that fists alone weren't used here. The deceased's wounds are consistent with those caused by a blunt object. And it's possible that the deceased could have fainted, fallen, tripped, or had otherwise somehow become temporarily incapacitated. At which time, your client took full advantage, ultimately beating Calvin Leeson to death. Even if I acknowledged the difficulties in proving first degree, second degree would be a slam dunk."

Cain fidgeted in his chair, but didn't utter a word.

Wallingford shifted ever so slightly in his chair, a minor, almost indiscernible concession that the prosecutor had a valid point. "Your case is still sketchy counselor. But humor me. What do you want?"

"I want names. Witnesses have placed at least two other people in the car. I want the names of those individuals. It's clear that one person did not cause the injuries that led to the death of Calvin Leeson."

"And if those names are provided?"

"I'll go after them. Your client signs that plea form." He nodded at the folder. "It's a simple assault charge and carries only a few months of probation, no time."

"And if they aren't?"

"We go to trial with first degree at the top of the ticket."

Chapter 6

Loud music blared from two large speakers and shook the walls of Betsy Simmons's smallish three-bedroom, white wooden-frame house. The speakers were located in the tiny back third bedroom that Betsy had allowed her son, Cain, to turn into a makeshift studio. The room contained all the essential equipment for twenty-first century basic music making: a synthesizer, computer, microphones, and a camcorder. In here, Cain and Prodegee created rap songs and underground mix tapes that they burned into CDs. Sometimes they would also create homemade videos and put them on YouTube. It was all part of Cain's strategy. He wasn't going to wait to be discovered. He was going to make shit happen, and Friday night's show was going to go a long way towards that end.

Framed pictures of Prince, Jay-Z, and several other past and current hip-hop and pop stars, all representing Cain's varied influences, vibrated rhythmically to the thumpety-thump beat of Cain's current YouTube offering—Enuff.

Cain bobbed his head and rapped into a microphone, "This is the right stuff. This is the rough stuff. This is the kinda stuff—you know you can't get enuff." This particular song was one of his mind-candy songs, something for the people to enjoy just for the love of music's sake, no thinking allowed or necessary. He'd written it strictly to showcase one of Prodegee's beats. He planned to start Friday night's show with it. It would definitely get the crowd into a partying mood. The lyrics were easy-to-remember rhymes and that type of rap always seemed to get the crowd up. He had some more substantial shit to hit them with too—some make-them-think shit, but he was going to have to be careful how he played that. After finding out about Calvin's death, and his own butt possibly facing murder-one charges, he didn't want to do anything or say anything that would pour gasoline on a fire that Uncle Mayo clearly wanted doused.

He was thankful that Uncle Mayo had hooked up Friday's show, making it part of some anti-gang festivity bullshit. The irony of Mayo Fathers spearheading such an event was not lost on him. But he chose not to think about that part of it. Right now, he wanted to focus on his upcoming performance. He was only one of several acts on the agenda, but in his mind, it was his gig, his time to shine. He prepared as if he was going to perform at Madison Square Garden.

Out the corner of his eye, he saw Prodegee take off his headphones and turn off the synthesizer. For a moment, he pretended not to notice and continued bobbing his head as if the music still played.

Prodegee was undeterred. "Dude, there ain't no coming back from murder-one time." His voice was stern and paternalistic despite the fact it hadn't an ounce of bass and was accompanied by the dropped-ice-cream look of despair on the kid's face.

Cain closed his eyes and did not respond.

"Dude," Prodegee said louder as if the reason for Cain not answering was a sudden case of deafness. "There ain't no coming back from murder-one time. They're going to lock your butt up and throw away the key."

Prodegee's real name was Jamal Morris. But Cain had christened him Prodegee after he'd seen how the eleven-year-old wunderkind could create beats. It was Beethoven-type shit. The kid really had a gift for sound. In Cain's mind, if there were truly such things as child prodigies, then Jamal Morris was their poster child. He was such a little fella, he didn't quite look eleven. But he was hood-tough and walked with a swagger. Cain had first seen and heard him on the turntables at one of the talent shows that Fathers House always put on. It was musical-love at first sight. Right then and there, Cain had made up his mind that wherever his rap destiny was leading him, he'd get there a lot faster with Prodegee by his side, hooking up his beats.

"We got a show to get ready for man," Cain said nonchalantly. "Turn my shit back on."

The pre-recorded Enuff beat was stored on the synthesizer. Prodegee did not turn it back on. Instead he stared long and hard at Cain. For several moments, the two stood in silence, staring at each other. Cain knew the kid was right. There was no coming back from a murder-one conviction. The sentence would be either life without the possibility of parole or death. But he refused to allow himself to worry about that now. One reason why and perhaps the most important reason—he hadn't committed murder-one. He hadn't so much as laid a hand on Calvin. He had been there and had thrown some phantom punches as his consistent nightmares since that incident could strongly attest to, but he had been a bystander, an innocent and reluctant bystander.

For reasons still not clear to him, he was to cop to an assault charge and keep his mouth quiet about the true assailants. Calvin had gotten himself into some shit that he'd been unable to get himself out of, and had somehow gotten Cain caught up in it as well. Someone had ratted to the cops that they'd seen Calvin get into a car with Cain and some other people—who, the rat conveniently could not identify.

Cain knew what Calvin's shit was, but at this point, he didn't care. Cain had done what he'd been told to do. He'd followed orders. He was taking one for the team. It was f-upped that he had to do so. But that was hood-life. He had no choice. Snitching was not an option.

The second reason why he was not concerned was because of the assistant district attorney—Ben Lovison. Despite the man's pretense otherwise, he had been a hood kid, a resident of Fathers House even. And when push came to shove, Cain was confident that Lovison would remember his origins and take care of his own, if not for him—Cain, then for Father. Father had a way of being persuasive— very persuasive.

The way Cain saw it, Lovison's threat about seeking a murder-one charge was only that—a threat, an illusion, smoke and mirrors. There would be no murder-one charge. Lovison knew that. And Cain knew that.

Call it wishful thinking or a feeling in his gut, but Cain did not believe he'd spend a day in jail or prison. Finally he broke the silence. "I got some very important people backing me. Important people who know other important people. So, it's all good. So what I'm going to do is get ready for my show." His voice was strong, confident, and convincing.

Prodegee smiled. The look of panic that had strongly gripped his face only moments before suddenly vanished. Evidently, he understood that important people could change the dynamics of most situations. If Cain was unworried, then things truly were all good. Prodegee flipped a switch and his original artistic beats once more roared from the speakers. And once again the walls reverberated.

***

A light throbbing pain had methodically pushed its way up the back of acting Special Agent-In-Charge Tom Ram's head. Apparently the tension he'd felt at the base of his neck that morning had accomplished its goal of becoming a full-fledged headache by late afternoon. He pulled open his top right desk drawer and grabbed the aspirin bottle. He looked across the room at the coffeemaker. Popping two pills in his mouth, he stood and walked over to it, and then washed the pills down with the last of the morning coffee.

He was a tall man with a moose-thick neck that sat upon wide muscular shoulders. His facial features were friendly and familiar. People always assumed that they knew him from somewhere, though never quite able to pinpoint where exactly. He always reminded them of an uncle or cousin, or some other erstwhile male relative or friend. Or was he an ex-pro football player? Or was he perhaps a TV weatherman?

No one had ever successfully guessed that he was a twenty-four year veteran of the Bureau, having served capably in a variety of capacities from recruitment, to counterterrorism operations, to heading task forces investigating such varied crimes as child prostitution and gangland violence. He'd never played professional football, but he did in fact play one year of college football at Virginia Tech before sustaining the proverbial knee injury that had effectively ended his playing days.

He had no doubt that but for the knee injury, he could have made a successful run at the pros. However, he also strongly believed things happened for a reason. He'd long envisioned attending law school after his playing days were over. After the injury, he'd been able to keep his athletic scholarship. Once freed from the endless commitments that were the life of a college athlete, he doubled his study efforts and worked almost full-time hours at a local convenience store, enabling him to save a good portion of his impending law school tuition.

It was that stint at the Shop-N-Save that had gotten him interested in crime fighting in the first place. He'd been held up twice in a nine-month period by an organized crime syndicate that operated across several states and had targeted gas stations and convenience stores. The syndicate had specialized in holding up lone workers during third shift hours. A smooth-talking, thorough special agent had interviewed him after the second incident, and Ram became hooked on all things Bureau.

Although he'd kept his desire to pursue his law degree, he never lost his fascination with the FBI. After graduating law school, he immediately applied for employment with the Bureau.

He loved being a part of the Bureau. To think that he most likely would not have considered it as an employment option if he hadn't blown out his knee. It was a rewarding career and it had eventually led him here to Charlotte as an Assistant Special Agent-In-Charge. After three months in his new role, SAC Charles Summers had abruptly resigned his position, and the Director quickly named Ram as acting head honcho.

After flushing down the pills with the ancient, over-warmed, and now bitter tasting coffee, he placed his cup next to the finally empty pot, and returned to his desk. Unsure if the two pills would respond to his headache quickly enough, he considered popping two more. He was a chronic migraine sufferer and sometimes the headaches were exacerbated by troublesome problems, of which the drug cartel—Father's Disciples, was one.

Though he didn't know what to make of his latest headache-enhancing problem, he decided against taking any additional pills right now. He would wait out the pain.

Now seated back at his desk, he recalled the morning's briefing from the agents investigating the cartel. Either Father's Disciples were the luckiest sons-of-bitches on the planet, or the Bureau, more specifically his part of the Bureau, had been cleverly, thoroughly, and effectively compromised. Four potential witnesses dead, two of which were inside prison walls. An undercover agent was missing. There were no apparent connections between any of the events to each other or to Father's Disciples, but these had been very fortuitous occurrences for one very ruthless drug syndicate.

The consensus amongst the agents was that the investigation had been dealt a serious blow. It had already been slow-sledding getting even a soupcon of evidence against the crime syndicate, and just when they'd been able to move forward a half-step: bam! They were roughly shoved back to square one.

He rubbed his temples again. The syndicate was definitely troublesome.

From what the Bureau had been able to piece together from very reluctant witnesses, Father's Disciples had operated clandestinely in Duraleigh, North Carolina for at least the past twenty years, enjoying a ghostlike existence. Outwardly, the city had none of the earmarks of an illicit drug organization operating within its borders. Its violent-crime rate was exceptionally low, and instances of gang-fueled violence were practically nonexistent. Occasionally, the local authorities held drug busts, arresting a few peon hustlers and dealers, but nothing out of the ordinary, and certainly nothing unusual. For a city its size—just under four hundred thousand residents, Duraleigh had topped the Bureau's annual list of America's safest cities for the second year in a row. Its crime rate was an astounding 85.6 per cent lower than the national average, a complete reversal from its high-crime heyday of the mid-eighties when it had consistently ranked amongst the nation's most dangerous cities.

He tapped a key, bringing his computer out of sleep mode. He reentered his password and then tapped the icon for the FBI's Automated Support System, ACS, and when prompted, he entered another password. Once inside the secured website, he went directly to the Father's Disciples' case file.

The investigation was still in its infancy. Information about the cartel was piecemealed from Bureau drug busts, some of which were conducted hundreds of miles away from Duraleigh. The connections were as varied as the ocean was wide. The initial connections were veritable slips of tongues. Several drug suspects in unrelated investigations had mentioned a "Duraleigh Father" when drilled during interrogations, but when pressed, the suspects refused to go into any further detail. In other instances, the connections were just receipts found in the cars, homes, or on the persons of people suspected and/or indicted for trafficking in illegal narcotics. The receipts were from Duraleigh gas stations, stores, and hotels. At first, the receipts had simply piqued a curiosity. Why were so many drug dealers frequenting the sleepy city of Duraleigh, North Carolina? It was a mid-sized city that according to FBI statistics, didn't cotton too much to any crime, much less major drug dealing. It seemed the perfect place to raise a family. So why was it garnering so much interest from drug mavens? Initially, none of the suspects was willing to answer the question. By themselves, the receipts amounted to nothing more than very curious occurrences. But when information from various drug cases was placed into the FBI database and then cross referenced, a very different picture of the city of Duraleigh emerged.

Ram frowned as he brought up a chart the Bureau sketched of the syndicate's organizational structure. The information had been gleaned from two of the now dead witnesses, although none of it had been confirmed. Listed at the top of the chart was the suspected head of the syndicate, Mayo Fathers. Fathers was a respected Duraleigh business man who owned a very profitable funeral home business and had, in what the Bureau had originally thought a head-scratcher, turned his home dubbed Fathers House into an orphanage. But Fathers was not the charitable philanthropist he appeared to be. There were indications that Fathers House was simply a breeding ground for young hoodlums-turned-foot soldiers for Father's Disciples.

The next two names on the chart—Lucas McCain and Jermaine Bledsoe were also high-ranking members in the syndicate. Although the Bureau hadn't been able to gather much additional information on either two, it was assumed that the three of them, Fathers, McCain, and Bledsoe operated as a triumvirate in the syndicate's hierarchy.

At the bottom of the chart was the list of names of potential witnesses against Father's Disciples. Part of the list had been compiled by the two deep cover special agents who were in close proximity to the syndicate. The word deceased had been hyphenated next to four of the names on the list, including the two most recent deaths: Cindy Storrs and Calvin Leeson.

At best, their deaths had been unfortunate coincidences. Calvin Leeson had been approached by an agent, while Cindy Storrs had personally contacted the Bureau. Storrs had agreed to provide incriminatory evidence against Father's Disciples. Leeson hadn't been so forthcoming. But there'd been promise. Other than the special agents directly involved in the investigation, no one knew about Operation Heaven Sent. Not even the local authorities. There had been, so far, unsubstantiated rumors that Father's Disciples had a few Duraleigh officials, including several in law enforcement on its payroll. A couple of convicted drug felons claimed that Father's Disciples operated above the law. In light of the rumors, the Bureau didn't want to potentially tip off the syndicate about the investigation, and had therefore blacked out the local authorities. Local law enforcement would be brought in only when the Bureau could be certain that they were clean.

If the Leeson and Storrs deaths were not accidents, but rather planned executions, then the worst case scenario had already been realized which meant not only that the next name on the list was in grave danger, but also that the Bureau had a serious leak.

The syndicate seemed to know every step of the

investigation. And it seemed willing to kill relative minor players in the game in order to encumber those steps. Though Storrs could have potentially provided very incriminating evidence, Leeson was a bit player at best. His death, if syndicate-ordered, was simply a fingers-up at the Bureau.

He looked away from the computer screen for a moment and lowered his still aching head. He was a deeply religious man. In this line of work where he saw firsthand the destructive capabilities of his fellowmen, a belief in a higher power was comforting. As always, he prayed for the health and wellbeing of his family and the men under his charge. He prayed for wisdom and understanding. And lastly, he prayed for the safety of the investigation's one remaining listed witness. Though Cain Simmons was possibly no more than a foot soldier that could only provide information about Fathers House's link to Father's Disciples, the syndicate had demonstrated that it considered no individual too unimportant to be taken out.

Finished with his prayer, he lifted his head, picked up the phone, and dialed Washington. If there was a leak in the Bureau, it needed to be plugged immediately.

Chapter 7

Late Friday afternoon, Melvin Wallingford finally returned the assistant DA's phone calls. Yes, he'd gotten the messages. No, he hadn't been able to get in contact with Cain either. He'd also tried his home, Fathers House, and had contacted Mayo Fathers personally. No, he didn't have any cell phone numbers for his client. And yes, the kid was being very cavalier about this.

When Ben hung up the phone after speaking with Wallingford, his first thought was—forget it. If the kid didn't care about his own future, then why should Ben care about it? If the boy wanted to face a murder-one charge for a crime he swears he didn't commit, then so be it. But after taking a deep breath and slowly exhaling, his second thought was calm down counselor; the boy hasn't flown the coop. He knew where to find him.

Ordinarily he wouldn't have responded so well at being blown off, especially in a capital case. Ordinarily, he would have gotten an arrest warrant and young Cain would have been snatched up by a uniformed officer and then placed in a cell where he'd stay unless and until he could post bail.

But there wasn't anything ordinary about the Cain Simmons case. The case had been handed to him with a prearranged outcome, which wasn't normal procedure. The assigned prosecutor to a case generally worked the case rooter to tooter, deciding if and when to offer plea deals. Of course, Etlzer had the authority to weigh in, but for the most part, he let his prosecutors dispose of their cases as they saw fit. Initially, Ben had bought Etlzer's rationale for having him assigned to the Simmons case. With the premature birth of his boys and April being in the hospital, a little lightening of his workload was welcomed. An open and shut case here and there would be helpful, and he could cut back some on his hours without officially having to take any time off. Any time off not used now, could be used later. With two newborns currently in NICU for an indeterminate length of time, banked paid time off and open and shut cases were more valuable than money. But in Ben's mind, the death of Calvin Leeson meant that the Simmons case was no longer an open and shut one. But for some reason, Etlzer didn't see it that way. The DA was still insistent on a simple assault plea deal, and had indicated to Ben that he wouldn't back any charge against Simmons greater than that charge, despite the dead kid lying in the balance.

An arrest for an arrest's sake, especially in this case, would be a time waster, Ben admitted to himself. Cain Simmons would be back on the street quicker than Ben could clear his throat. Besides, his murder-one bark was worse than the bite. Despite the chest-beating display he'd put on Monday for Simmons and his attorney, he had a weak murder-one case, and it wouldn't exactly be a slam dunk getting convictions for murder-two or manslaughter. If Cain stuck to his story, and there wasn't a compelling reason for him not to do so especially since Etlzer and the police were satisfied with it, then Ben would never find out the truth about those involved in the beating death of Calvin Leeson. Everyone would continue to believe that what had happened to Calvin had been just a matter of beef between friends. A belief aided in the fact that no guns or knives had been involved. Since Cain was not much bigger than a flea himself, any potential jury would likely disregard the possibility that he'd used a rock or a bat in the course of things. It wouldn't take a jury long to set Cain Simmons free.

But Calvin Leeson was dead. And Ben was convinced that one runt-sized teenager was not solely responsible. Ultimately, this wasn't about Cain Simmons, was it? It was about Calvin Leeson. It was about justice. It was about two murderers out there roaming the streets and for all he knew, planning to strike again. So despite Cain's apathetic attitude toward his own life, toward Calvin's life, and toward the wheels of justice, and despite Etlzer's nonchalant attitude toward the case and over the district attorney's objections, Ben was going to be a thorn in Cain Simmons' side. The boy had a responsibility to himself and to his community. And Ben had a responsibility to Calvin Leeson and to the dead teen's mother. And he was going to make sure that Cain Simmons damn well understood that.

He looked at his wall clock. It was five-fifteen. He'd gotten a tip that Cain Simmons fancied himself a rapper and was scheduled to perform tonight. The show at the Britt Heights Community Center was scheduled to start at eight o'clock. He had some time to tidy up a few more files. "I'll see you in a bit, young Cain," he said to himself as he punched in his password on the computer and then clicked on the Matherly file. For the next hour or so, he put thoughts of Cain Simmons on the backburner.

***

At fifteen minutes to eight, the Britt Community Center was awash in teenagers. The loud music could be heard from outside the center, blasting from speakers in fits and starts. Ben stood just outside the entrance to the gymnasium, dutifully asking a pock-faced gatekeeper for early entrance into the center and without having to pay the ten-dollar cover charge.

"You're not allowed to enter now," the gatekeeper said blankly.

"Do I look like I'm here to party?" Ben asked,

expanding his arms outward and upward. "I just need to speak to one of the acts before he goes on."

The gatekeeper was unimpressed. With his stoic expression unchanged, he took quick measure of Ben. "Look mister, I've seen all kinds. You can't enter now."

Ben stared at him for a moment. "I thought the show started at eight."

"It was supposed to," the teenaged gatekeeper said.

"It's almost eight now. "Why aren't we being allowed in?"

"There's been a delay," the gatekeeper said in a matter-of-fact tone.

"When are you allowing us in?" Ben asked.

"In about fifteen minutes," the gatekeeper replied. "And you're going to have to pay the cover charge. All the money is going to help fight gangs, you know."

"I didn't know we had a gang problem in Duraleigh," Ben said.

"We don't," the gatekeeper said. "And with positive events like this to keep the kids occupied, we won't. Now if you don't have ten dollars, I'm going to have to respectfully ask you to step aside."

It had been a long day and he was too tired to continue arguing the point. Charity is as charity does; he thought as he pulled out his wallet and fished out a crisp ten-spot. Handing the bill to the gatekeeper, he asked, "Has Cain arrived yet?"

The gatekeeper took the money and grabbed Ben's hand, pressing a stamp against it. "A fan too, huh?"

Ben pulled his hand back and frowned at his newly pressed marking which looked like a glob of mud. "I guess you could say that. Is he here?"

"Doubt it. He's the last scheduled act. And knowing Cain, he's going to come late and make an entrance. He's a showman."

"Can he rap?"

"The best," the gatekeeper said. "You ought to check out his videos on YouTube. Man, he's..." He was interrupted by an eruption of loud music from inside the gym and by someone standing in the line behind Ben shouting, "We're going to miss the start of the show!"

"Just go to YouTube and type in the real Y-U-N-G (he enunciated each letter) Cain featuring P-R-O-D-E-G-E-E."

"First chance I get," Ben said.

Inside the gym, the overhead lights were on and music roared from two huge onstage speakers. A convergence of teen-speak followed Ben to a spot in front of the stage that had been roped off. The stage was without the benefit of curtains to hide the behind-the-scenes activity, a crew was still setting up for the first group's performance. Ben pulled out a concert flyer from his inside coat pocket. It was all local groups with Yung Cain, featuring Prodegee listed as the headliner. Jessie's Other Girl was the first scheduled act followed by Deal Raw. Our Time Too would be the last act before Cain was to hit the stage.

The gym itself cleaned up rather nicely. The floor sported a spit-shine quality gloss. Even the walls seemed cleaner, whiter than Ben could remember ever having seen them. The Britt Center had been one of his favorite places to go as a kid. He played in countless basketball games, both pickup and league-play in this very gym, though now you wouldn't know from the smell and look of the place that basketball had ever been played in it. Instead, a concoction of body wash mixed with various perfumes and colognes bandied about. On the bleachers that had been folded back into the sidewalls, were decorative colorful images of young people in various modes of play. On the back wall, opposite the stage and covering nearly the length of the wall was large graffiti-style lettering which read, Make Play Not War.

After the first two performances finished and the show

was between acts, Ben gingerly moved through the crowded gymnasium, walking as if there was a scratch-cake in the oven; ready to sink at the slightest vibration from his footfall. As he made his way to the other side of the gym, hordes of teens in low-hanging baggy jeans and way-above-the-knee skirts parted slightly to allow him through. He suddenly felt conspicuous and aged—an old man in a sea of youth.

He scanned the place, half looking for Cain, half wishing for a fellow adult. He saw neither. He did see two security officers walk near the entrance he'd just come through, but he doubted if either one of them had counted twenty-five birthdays.

As he continued walking, he noticed that some of the boys looked older than the security officers. A few had full beards or thick goatees. And their shoulders, my God, what were kids eating these days. It was as if they'd already spent time in County—three hots, a cot, and hundreds of daily pushups. They were broad-shouldered and thick-muscled. Baggy and sagging jeans, over-sized T-shirts, gold necklaces, and tats ruled the night.

But in comparison to the girls, the boys' dress was actually conservative. He saw more than any male should be allowed to see of anyone's teenaged daughter. The clothes were barely there. Skirts barely covered bottoms. Jeans were little more than an extra layer of skin. Tops were either too low on top—exposing too much boob or two high from the bottom—exposing too much midriff, or both.

Finally and gratefully, he spotted Mayo. He was accompanied by two men; one carrying a notepad, the other had a camera draped around his neck. The three of them had come in through a side entrance. As Ben started to make his way towards them, the lights lowered, a heavy synthesized drum roll boomed out of two large speakers, and the host jumped on staged and loudly spat, "Our Time

Too," into the microphone.

**

An hour later, Yung Cain featuring Prodegee finally took the stage. The crowd had grown restless and anxious. A single shout of, "We want Cain!" quickly dominoed into cascading waves of "We want Cain! We want Cain! We want Cain!" And just when the anticipation had reached its crescendo, the lights went out, casting the gym into complete darkness. Everyone fell silent and looked anxiously toward a stage that was no longer visible. A computerized voice counted down, rushing from the large speakers, "Five...four...three...two...one." A blast of music ripped from somewhere on stage, quickly leading into the obviously familiar beats of Enuff. Bomph-bomph. Bomph-bomph, boom-dum-boomph. A sea of teen heads started bobbing in rhythm with the song's beats. A spotlight beamed on the center of the stage, revealing Prodegee furiously playing an electric keyboard. A rush of applause and delighted screams erupted from the gymnasium floor. By the time Cain's voice exploded from the two large speakers, the gym was in total pandemonium.

For the next thirty minutes, Cain owned the stage and the moment. He worked the room like a born showman. He strutted back and forth across the stage, rapping songs that every kid in the gym seemed to know. He artfully plucked towels from a stack that had been placed near the back of the stage. He wiped his face with each before tossing it into the crowd. The girls shrieked with delight. Wherever the towels landed small skirmishes popped up before quickly dissipating, leaving one girl gleefully hopping in place while tightly holding her newly acquired prized possession.

After his last song, Cain stood in the middle of the stage, basking in the glow of perfection. His face beamed; he was clearly enjoying the moment. The crowd screamed for an encore. So he'd ripped Enuff again. The underground song had amassed a great number of YouTube hits. Many of the kids knew the words by heart, and again, rapped along with him.

Cain looked over at Prodegee. Sweat rushed down the kid's face. His eyes were rolled into the back of his head. The kid had totally lost himself in his beats, really feeling them. He didn't look like himself. He looked otherworldly. To Cain, he was looking at Jimi Hendrix reincarnated. The whole moment was surreal. If he could have, Cain would have stopped time, freezing the moment into eternity. At that exact moment, he could not imagine anything sweeter.

He gazed out at his sea of adoring fans. He thrust his arms high in the air. He felt triumphant, confident that he'd just treated them to a glimpse of greatness. He wondered how many of them had truly understood what they'd just witnessed. Really, how many people who'd seen LL Cool J or Lil Wayne perform early on, say at a house party or a block party, had realized that they had been watching future rap legends? Very few, he imagined. Most of those witnesses-to-greatness probably couldn't even see past their own hoods, much less one of their own ascending to points well beyond them. But the naysayers and disbelievers hadn't stopped either LL or Lil Wayne, and nor would they stop him.

There was a smattering of adults in his sea. Any other time this would have pleased him, as he considered himself influenced as much by the music of his mother—artists like Prince, New Edition, and Run-DMC, as he was by his own favorite hip hop artists. He had visions of being a generational star. But he was weary of these particular adults, and he seriously doubted that any of them were there for his music.

He stared for a moment at Uncle Mayo who looked as uncomfortable as ever in an expensive suit. He was standing at the back of the gym with the reporter who'd written the news article on Calvin's beating. Cain knew why the guy was here and it wasn't for the anti-gang message that Uncle Mayo was pushing. He wondered how Mayo could be so blind. Cain frowned at the reporter's photographer who was lurking nearby and was spending considerable time looking at the girls rather than looking through his camera lens.

Then he saw them. The two of them were standing together at the opposite end from Uncle Mayo, near a fire exit, both looking like they hadn't a care in the world. And he supposed not, it was his butt that was on the line, not theirs. The fact that they were there concerned him. He dropped his arms—the signal for Ronnie to cut the lights which he did promptly, casting the room back into complete darkness. Thirty seconds later, the lights flicked back on, and Cain and Prodegee had disappeared from the stage.

***

After the metal air vent cover dropped semi-noisily onto the tile floor, a spray of golden light easing in through the bottom of the room's closed door ricocheted off it like tiny pin-shots of fool's gold. Prodegee came through the air vent first, followed closely by Cain. As soon as both gathered themselves onto their feet, Ben flicked on the light.

Seeing their astonished, sweaty faces, he explained, "I practically grew up in this gym. I know all the nooks and crannies."

"Cool," Cain said sarcastically. "So ya know that Cain and Prodegee aren't magical." He reached for the duffel bag that was next to a metal desk. He opened it and pulled out two towels, one of which he handed to Prodegee. He wiped his face while Prodegee did the same.

"Still," Ben said. "It was a great show. Someone said you were a showman. And you are. I must admit. I got to give you your props."

Prodegee finished wiping his face and begin to relax a little; apparently relived that Cain seemed to know the unexpected stranger. "Thanks man," he said to Ben. "You really liked the show, huh?"

"Yeah, I really did," Ben said.

"But I bet you weren't waiting to ambush us in order to congratulate us on our set," Cain said.

"Well, I wasn't exactly waiting in ambush. But you're right. I wasn't here waiting just to congratulate you. I need to talk to you."

"I told you before; I've said all I've got to say."

"You think you can just blow this off. You think it's just going to go away."

Cain glanced at Prodegee, and then turned to face Ben. "You can make it go away."

"It doesn't work that way. You got to give me something."

"I told you man. I ain't got nuthin' to give. I don't know nuthin'."

Ben stood back, casually looking around the room. There were two metal desks with matching metal chairs squeezed against a side wall. The room was a little bigger than an average-sized dorm room. It hadn't changed at all since he'd last been in it, over fifteen years ago. Britt Center used it as a little study cubby for the kids, especially the ones that hadn't been able to study well with others.

Prodegee grabbed a seat in one of the metal chairs and looked from Ben to Cain.

Finally Ben said, "Calvin is dead. His future is over. You're still here. You have a future. Are you going to allow them to take that future away as well?"

Cain sighed and dropped his head. No one spoke for several minutes. Muffled voices and music coming from the gymnasium seeped into the room. The concert after party had started. Finally, Cain said in a near whisper, "I can't snitch."

Ben grimaced. He had just about enough. He was sick and tired of these so called gangster rules, hood rules, where no one talks. No one snitches. Kids dying, lives ruined, that's acceptable, the cost of doing business. As long as no one talked, everything was okay. "I don't want to hear that," he said sternly. "You call it snitching. I call it doing the right thing. You owe Calvin the right thing. You owe your hood the right thing. You owe your future the right thing. Pay your debt. You owe."

After several moments, Cain looked at Prodegee. "Yo man, get out of here."

"I need to stay," Prodegee protested.

"Nah, you don't. I don't want you involved in this. It's going to be alright. I'll see you back at the house."

With an air of reservation, Prodegee stood up. "Are you staying at Fathers House tonight?"

Cain forced a smile. "Fo show, dude. We got to revel in our greatness."

"Alright, bet," Prodegee said. The two touch fists and then Prodegee left the room, leaving his damp towel on the metal desk, and closing the door behind him. Cain locked it and turned to face Ben. "You know I'm dead, right?"

"No, I don't know that. We can protect you."

"You didn't protect Calvin."

"We didn't know Calvin needed protecting."

"The FBI did."

Ben held his hands up. "Whoa! The FBI? What do they have to do with Calvin?"

Cain cocked his head and stared at Ben for a long moment before answering. "The FBI is the reason Calvin's dead."

Ben pondered the accusation for a minute. He pulled the other metal chair away from the desk, making a high-squeak sound like a nail being scraped across a chalkboard. He sat down. "Maybe you should start from the beginning." He pointed at the chair Prodegee had sat in.

Cain waved it off. "Nah, I'll stand." He glanced nervously about the room. "Have you ever heard of Father's Disciples?"

"No."

Cain released a nervous chuckle. "I guess you never got into trouble while you were at Fathers House."

"What does that have to do with anything?"

"Any kid that gets into any type of serious trouble while staying at the House will get sent to the basement. And if you ever got sent to the basement, then you would know about Father's Disciples."

"You're saying Mayo Fathers is running some type of illegal operation at Fathers House."

"No, I ain't saying that. And I ain't saying anything about Fathers House."

"Okay, fair enough. Then, what is Father's Disciples?"

"I'd rather not say."

"Alright. What does the FBI and Father's Disciples have to do with Calvin's assault?"

"Father's Disciples got word that Calvin was talking to the FBI. How they got that word, I don't know. But Calvin shouldn't have been talking."

"How did you get involved?"

"I was told that some guys were going to come and pick me up and then we were going to go pick up Calvin. I was just a means for Calvin to get into the car."

"Who told you?"

"I can't get into that."

"Then who were the guys that picked you up?"

"I told you. I don't know them. I hadn't seen them before and I haven't seen them since. But, what I do know is that they were cops."

"How do you know that?

"Because some uniformed cats showed up and they knew them."

"That's it?"

"Yeah, you must've forgotten what it's like living in the hood. I can spot a cop."

The kid was right. Even back when Ben had lived in the neighborhood, a favorite pastime was diming out the undercover policemen, the unmarked cars, and the out-of-place bums on the street corner. To be sure, there had been some successful busts stemming from narc-work, but most of those had been aided greatly by informants, aka snitches. It was what made undercover work increasingly difficult and dangerous for law enforcement. A discovered undercover agent would pay dearly with his life. "Alright, so they were cops."

"Yeah, they were," Cain said matter-of-factly.

"And…"

"Someone called 911 when Calvin got snatched up. A witness saw me in the car and told the police. So I was told to take the heat for it. They said that I would only get an assault charge; no time, as long as I kept quiet about the other two."

"But Calvin died."

Cain blew out a long breath and said silently, "Yeah, he did."

Ben leaned back in the metal chair, held up one hand, and ticked off fingers one at a time. "Okay, so what we got is the FBI, some supposedly notorious bad asses named Father's Disciples, dirty cops, and one dead teenager. Does that about sum it up?"

"Yeah, it does," Cain said.

"Is there anything else you'd like to add?"

"You don't get it. Do you? I've already said enough to get me killed."

"I don't see how you've said anything. I still don't have the names of the killers."

"You have more than you did before I started talking. It's on you what you do with it."

"Yeah well," Ben said. "We'll see."

"What about the murder one charge?"

"Like I said, we'll see."

Cain took off the damp shirt, and retrieved a dry one from his duffel bag. He wiped his chest and face with the towel, and then pulled on the new shirt, before stuffing the old one plus the two towels into the duffel bag. He looked at Ben and then shook his head slowly as if to say "My life is over. I hope you're happy." He left the room without saying another word.

Ben stayed in the room for another twenty minutes before deciding to leave. He wanted to make sure no one saw him leave so soon after Cain, lest they'd ascertain that the two of them had been together. Knowledge of the meeting would sprout a cascading amount of snitch innuendo. He turned off the light and opened the door slightly, peering out. The hallway was empty. He looked back in the room and spotted the vent cover lying on the floor. Leaving the door cracked, he went over to it and firmly snapped it back into place over the vent.

If he'd taken an extra moment to look into the air vent before snapping the cover back over it, he would have stared straight into the eyes of the second person who'd been privy to Cain's forbidden snitching. Instead, he left the room, blissfully ignorant to the fact that the walls truly had ears.

Chapter 8

On Saturday morning, Ben awoke with a jolt, breathing heavily. He had the weirdest dream, a nightmare really. He'd dreamed about the twins. One of them had somehow taken the umbilical cord and wrapped it several times around its brother's neck, strangling him, all while inside April's womb, and all very much visible on the ultrasound. Yet, no one—the doctors, nurses, April, or himself was able to stop it. All of them simultaneously yelled at the screen. "Stop that! Let your brother go! Stop that now!"

He lay on his back for a few moments, looking hazily up at the gaudy ceiling fan. A bit of morning sun eased through the blinds' partially opened slats and reflected nicely off the golden crystal, making it appear as if three golden mystic images dangled from the ceiling. Eventually, his breathing slowed and his eyes fully adjusted to his awakening. Still, he could feel his heart drumming along at a fairly good clip. He looked to his left where April would have been had she been at home and not at Lincoln Memorial. The dream seemed so real. But thank God, it wasn't.

He looked at the clock on the nightstand. It was six o'clock. Today promised to be a very eventful and tiring day. He was scheduled to pick up April from the hospital by eleven, and he hadn't made a single dent in his housecleaning. She would be totally astonished if not clearly disgusted at the amount of mess a single man could generate in five days. He had infiltrated every room in the house with an unconscious blitz of untidiness, and now he didn't quite know which room he should clean first.

Droplets of dried urine outlined the base of the master

bath's toilet, compliments of a couple of mornings' worth of missed aims. Scanning the shower, he noticed how the white porcelain finish was now a dusty-gray. If he truly wanted today to be the last time April set foot in their home, then let her happen upon this monstrosity. Even he was disgusted by it. It suddenly became a no brainer; he would clean the bathroom first. He reached under the sink and grabbed the Comet, Soft Scrub, some sponges and an old rag.

The bathroom took about forty minutes. When he finished, his thoughts turned quickly to the kitchen. He frowned, remembering that it was a total wipeout. Fast food wrappers and two pizza boxes littered the kitchen table. The sink was filled to the brim with dirty dishes, which was amazing because he'd been too tired to cook anything substantial. He'd basically spent the week, living off instant grits, scrambled eggs, and takeout. But he couldn't muster the effort to clean pans, plates, bowls, and eating utensils, so he just kept reaching into the cupboards and drawers for clean ones.

As he stepped inside the kitchen, a strange odor—sharp and semi-putrid greeted him. He immediately spotted the possible culprit—a half-eaten container of shrimp fried rice, left on the counter since Tuesday. It wasn't that strong of a smell, yet. But April's feminine powers could detect the faintest of such odors and the source of their issuance from a half of block away. Pulling a trash bag from the pantry, he methodically went about the business of getting the place in order. The kitchen took nearly an hour and a half because he was slowed by his disdain for doing dishes. He was able to put the bulk of them in the dishwasher, but he still had a sink load to do by hand, including pots and pans. Now finally and mercifully, the kitchen was presentable.

By nine o'clock, he'd made great headway and the house was almost once again ready for female occupancy.

He stood in the master bedroom, having made the bed and putting away the last of the clothes he'd flung on the floor over the past few days. Not too coincidently, the old Seven Dwarfs' tune, Whistle While You Work wafted through his mind. He loved the Snow White story as a child, and he supposed that through the years, the tune had probably helped many souls get through many unpleasant tasks. But he hadn't whistled at all during the past three hours and the time still flew by; for as he cleaned, scrubbed, and put away, Cain Simmons had consumed his thoughts.

He'd kept asking himself one main question. Had Cain been truthful? Rogue cops. Father's Disciples. FBI. The boy had told one fantastic tale. One, Ben wasn't afraid to admit, had left him skeptical at best. A major crime syndicate in Duraleigh, policemen acting as enforcers— killing one of the city's youth, these were very serious accusations. For which, the boy hadn't provided one shred of proof.

But he'd been scared. There was no denying that. Ben had seen it in Cain's eyes. He'd seen it in the way the youngster had trembled ever so slightly as he was talking, constantly shifting his eyes about the room as if he was being watched by unseen, but treacherous forces.

It could have been an act. But Ben didn't think so. Cain had appeared genuinely frightened. Besides, the indisputable fact remained—Calvin Leeson was dead. And Ben did not believe for one minute that Sarah Leeson's only child had died at the hands of Cain alone, if at all. But at whose hands had he died? Father's Disciples? Duraleigh's finest? It was still too fantastic a story to believe. But fantastic did not mean untrue.

But if it was true, then a couple of other things had to be true as well. Namely, Calvin Leeson had to have been involved in some illicit behavior. Otherwise how would the FBI have known about him, and why would they have deemed him of some importance? Important enough that this supposedly dangerous outfit—Father's Disciples, had found it necessary to have the kid eliminated. He considered that scenario as he plugged in the vacuum cleaner, clicked it on, and heard it noisily come to life.

Duraleigh had a sordid past. That was common knowledge. What was also common knowledge was that the city had been cleaned up. All thugs, goons, gangsters, aka the Father's Disciples of the world had been shown the door. Gone were the drive-by shootings, violent shootouts, and the out-in-the-open prostitution and illicit drug sale transactions that used to plague the city's streets. It was the stuff of legend how the city's leaders had finally had enough and had literally taken the fight directly to the hoodlums. Getting rid of them, totally rid of them had been long, arduous, and ugly work. People had been lost on both sides, good and bad, but eventually it had been done. Now, nationally, Duraleigh was the model for what a city could do if it set its mind to it. It was highly unlikely that a "Father's Disciples" was operating within Duraleigh's city limits.

But what had disturbed Ben more about Cain's fantastic tale was the part about Fathers House. "Any kid that gets into any type of serious trouble while staying at the House will get sent to the basement. And if you ever got sent to the basement, then you would know about Father's Disciples." Ben had lived at Fathers House for five years, from the age of thirteen, after the murder of his mom, until he graduated high school. He'd participated in its afterschool program for a couple of years before that. He had fond memories of Fathers House. It had been there when he'd needed it. Sure, there'd been some bad kids there. Mayo Fathers specialized in helping all kids, especially the bad ones. Ben refused to believe that the basement talk was true. But why would a kid make something like the basement up, especially knowing Ben could simply ask Mayo Fathers about its existence? And if it was true, then why wasn't Ben introduced to it? Growing up, he hadn't been a hoodlum, but he hadn't been a saint either.

As he methodically pushed the vacuum cleaner back and forth across the living room carpet, he debated about whether or not to ask Mayo Fathers about it. He didn't believe for one minute that Mayo Fathers could be involved in anything that would harm the very boys he'd taken in. It would contradict Mayo's life's work. For a man who'd inherited a big house and successful family business, and who'd, for reasons known only to him, had used both to help underprivileged kids, it didn't make logical sense to then turn around and harm those very kids. But Ben's training as a lawyer and his own natural instincts forced him to look at an issue from all angles.

Cain's story could be true. And if so, what kind of danger would Ben subject the teen to if he went asking Mayo Fathers tough questions about the basement. And without a shred of proof to warrant law enforcement involvement, life could become very difficult for Cain and there'd be no way to protect him in that scenario. If Cain was ousted as a snitch, then it was very possible he wouldn't see the light of another day.

He unplugged the vacuum cleaner and pulled up the cord. He would do a quick sweep of the upstairs master suite and hallway. As he dragged the vacuum cleaner upstairs, he thought about Mayo's conference next week and suddenly realized that there was one person he could ask about Fathers House and an outfit called Father's Disciples.

After hitting the second floor landing, he heard the doorbell. He uttered a profanity under his breath. He left the vacuum cleaner in the hallway and went back downstairs. He was not expecting anyone and didn't care much for the interruption. He almost had all his chores completed, but almost did not equal complete. He wanted everything perfect for April's return home. The last thing he needed or wanted was interruptions—unplanned, schedule-altering interruptions. Looking through the peephole, he thought, oh God, not now. Standing on his front porch, carrying insistent and worried expressions, were his in-laws: Stephen and Patricia Ellison.

Perhaps it was an overstatement to say Ben didn't get along with his in-laws. After all, he didn't really know them. He'd only seen them twice in the two years since he'd met and married April. The first time had been after April's hastily planned meet-the-folks drive to her childhood home in Charleston. It was right after the two of them had decided to get married. She had thought it'd be a good idea if her folks met him at least one time before he actually showed up on their doorsteps as her husband.

"They're old fashioned," she'd said. "They believe a courtship should see months of moons before even the hand holding stage. They will think we're getting married only because I'm pregnant."

Ben said, "People don't do that sort of thing much anymore. For some women it's a conscious decision to start bearing children before matrimony."

"I know that and you know that, but why force my parents to worry needlessly. Besides, I want them to meet you without prejudice. I know they'll love you as much as I do."

"I love you too," Ben said. Pausing a heartbeat, he asked, "What do you imagine they'll say when the baby's here in seven months?"

"I don't know," she answered and then appeared to not give it another thought. They continued the drive to Charleston in contented silence. Occasionally, Ben would steal a glance at his bride-to-be who'd fallen asleep a couple of hours into the drive.

Stephen Ellison seemed more interested in Ben's family

history, or rather his relative lack of knowledge about it. Mr. Ellison—who could trace his family's history all the way back to a slave-holding black man, could not fathom how Ben's family tree essentially started and ended with Ben. For Mr. Ellison, despite African-Americans' numerous historical examples of it, the idea of someone not having even one minute piece of knowledge about their paternal ancestry was unconscionable.

"So, your mother died without bothering to tell you about your father," Stephen Ellison had said after Ben's response to his insistent probing into his future son-in-law's family history. It seemed not a question, but an accusation.

"That's correct," Ben had answered stoically, which would be his last meaningful response that evening and the remainder of the meet-the-folks weekend.

The doorbell rang again.

With a sense of dread that he sincerely wished was not there—for he truly wanted to get along with his in-laws, Ben opened the door and quickly stepped back. Without speaking, Stephen Ellison walked anxiously into the house. Almost instantly, Patricia Ellison—with a whiff of a gardenias fragrance floating alongside her, rushed in behind him and darted in the direction of the downstairs bathroom. "Hello Ben," she called out. "I've been holding it for two hours." She disappeared around the corner.

"Phobias about public johns," Stephen Ellison said apologetically, his eyes trailing behind her. "You could line that thing with Jesus' shroud and she still would not sit on it." He cleared his throat, abruptly signaling the end of his commentary on his wife's restroom preferences. "So, how are they? April? My grandsons?"

"They're all fine," Ben said. He didn't bother asking how they'd known.

Stephen Ellison walked toward the living room. He was a short man and extremely light-complected. He had a thick meaty head, the sides and back of which carried the remains of what used to be a gorgeous jet-black curly mane. He was wearing a white, long-sleeved turtleneck and brown corduroys. He moved with the assured air of a man who was very much used to the benefits of having lots of money. Ben closed the front door and joined his father-in-law in the living room. "I'm due to pick up April in about an hour," he said. "Hopefully the boys will be home in another week or so."

Stephen Ellison sat down on the white suede-leather couch. "Good. Good. Mrs. Ellison and I would have gotten here sooner had we known." He tilted his head at Ben. "Thank God, April felt well enough to call us on yesterday."

"I'm sorry about that," Ben lied. Truth was that with everything that was going on, the emergency caesarean, the premature births, the last thing he wanted for himself and the situation had been additional irritation. And for all the love that the Ellisons no doubt had for their daughter and would have for their grandchildren, they still caused Ben significant irritation.

Stephen Ellison went on. "It's not right for Ellisons to be brought into this world alone."

Ben bit his lip, clamping down the irritation. Though his sons were indeed part Ellison, he understood exactly what Stephen Ellison's veiled statement implied. But now was not the time to correct Papa Ellison on his grandsons' paternal bloodlines. When his wife and sons were safely home and their newly shaped family structure was firmly in place that would be the time to remind the Ellisons and anyone else needing reminding, that his boys were indeed Lovisons. And that even though there were probably only three blood-connected Lovisons left in the free world, it did not matter. He blew out a quick breath and said, "Listen Mr. Ellison. I have to finish up some things here before I go to pick up April. Please make yourselves at home. There are all sorts of drinks in the refrigerator. You can—"

"—don't worry about us," Stephen Ellison interrupted him. "You do what you have to do and when you're ready, we'll ride with you to the hospital. It'll give us a chance to see our grandsons."

"Sure," Ben gritted his teeth. He left, hard-footing it upstairs. When he reached the second floor landing, he angrily snatched up the vacuum cleaner. Seconds later, it roared back to life.

***

At 10:30 that same Saturday morning, all the inhabitants of Fathers House had finished their chores, showered, dressed, and had exited the house. They were headed to Calvin Leeson's eleven o'clock funeral service; everyone that was, except Cain, who because of his involvement in the boy's death, had been excused by Uncle Mayo from attending the funeral.

The funeral was at Hope Christian Church-of-God-In-Christ, which was about a fifteen-minute drive from Fathers House. After the boys left, Fathers House was devoid of its usual assortment of voices and myriad activities. It was unusually, eerily, and completely, earplug-quiet.

Earlier when everyone was getting ready, Cain had feigned sleep, partly because he hadn't wanted to talk with anyone, but mostly because he'd felt like a traitor and hadn't wanted to look into the eyes of those he'd betrayed. Now that the house was empty, he sat up on the top bunk of his sometimes room, letting his feet dangle off the sides of the bed.

He was in the rare position of having a bed here as well as one at his mother's house, which was about a ten-minute walk from Fathers House. His mother was a recovering addict. Back when she'd been deep in the throes of crack cocaine, Uncle Mayo had rescued him and brought him to Fathers House to live. It was an early success story after his mother eventually twelve-stepped her way back from the depths of drug despair and managed to hold onto her inherited house in the process. She'd sent for Cain immediately, claiming she'd needed him home with her.

However, his mother had cleaned up too nicely and had attracted a few suitors in the process. One in particular, Marcus Stevens, quickly nosed his way to the front of the pack. Marcus had a chiseled frame courtesy of three hots, a cot, and plenty of free time. He'd spent three years upstate on various drug charges. He was a recovering addict as well. Right from the start, Marcus and Cain had posted up on opposite sides of the ring. Cain didn't trust the ex-con's newly acquired soberness. But mostly, Cain just didn't like Marcus. He was a rude, brash, know-it-all. But for whatever reason, Marcus made Cain's mother happy and so, Cain tolerated him. But whenever he came around, Cain would get ghost. An understanding Uncle May kept an open bed at Fathers House for him which Cain would use occasionally, as he had last night.

He slid down from the bed and stretched, casually looking up at the ceiling fan. He wasn't sure exactly what he was going to do about last night. In a moment of weakness, he'd felt sorry for Calvin and even sorrier for himself. So, he'd snitched, telling House and Disciple business to someone who wasn't privy to that information. Yeah, he could rationalize it to himself, by repeating that Lovison wasn't really an outsider, that he was family, that he'd been raised at Fathers House. But he knew that rationalization wouldn't hold water. For one thing, according to Lovison, he had never been sent to the basement, and therefore, should have never been exposed to information concerning Father's Disciples. And secondly, Lovison was so far removed from Fathers House and this neighborhood that he was no closer to either than any complete stranger would be. Yeah, Cain had fucked up and he knew it.

Whatever punishment Calvin had gotten, up to and including his death, had been deserved. You didn't snitch. Not ever. Cain should have remembered that last night. He should have trusted Father to handle things. But he hadn't. Now, there would be consequences. His only saving grace was that no one knew about his indiscretions except Lovison, and if it came down between Cain's word and Lovison's, Cain would just have to deny his ass off and claim that Lovison was somehow making all that bullshit up, that he'd probably gotten pieces of information from the FBI and was only trying to incriminate Cain to make him talk.

For a while that idea seemed the reasonable route to take. But he soon realized that Father had a way of finding out things. No, Cain was going to have to confess his sins and hope and pray for the best, taking whatever punishment Father would deem appropriate. Besides, Cain had held back some information. He didn't tell Morant's or Jones' real names. Sure, he had been partially truthful. The two of them were members of Duraleigh's finest, but what police department didn't have its fair share of rogue cops? In his mind, he hadn't said anything that wasn't true of just about every police department in America, if not the world.

Still, he felt uneasiness. Father knew. He always knew. It was a reality that Cain understood far too well, and so it was of no real surprise to him when his bedroom door slowly opened, revealing a man he knew he would have to face sooner or later concerning this situation.

The man walked casually into the room. Cain didn't attempt to offer any explanations. At this point, he understood it would be of no use. His punishment had already been determined. His only hope was that it wasn't the ultimate.

Unfortunately, it was.

Chapter 9

The school psychologist's name was Margaret Younger. She was an energetic, overly cheery, twenty-five year old with blue eyes and short, bouncy blond hair. Her, "I was so sorry to hear about the death at Fathers House," was delivered in the same cheerful overtones as her, "It's a pleasure to meet you, Attorney Lovison."

She led Ben into her office. "Please have a seat Mr. Lovison." She indicated the chair in front of her desk. She took her seat behind her desk and immediately focused on the opened file atop it. "Jamal is such a remarkable young man," she said, reading through the file. "What terrible tragedies he's faced in such a short life. Both of his parents were killed in an automobile accident two years ago. He has no family to speak of. He bounced around in Virginia's childcare system for over a year until someone heard about the marvelous work being done for underprivileged children at Fathers House.

"He started here at Colbert Elementary last year. His teachers tell me he's a great kid, smart, well mannered. He'd adjusted quite well, and now this." Her voice trailed off as she slowly shook her head.

"Does he have any friends? I mean here at school."

She looked up. "He has some lunchroom buddies, Joey Sampson, Justin Wilson, and Xavier Williams. I don't know if he hangs with them outside of the school. But from what I've been able to observe, they seem as close as kids that age can be." She hesitated, looking at him squarely. She spoke deliberately and for the first time that morning, without cheeriness. "I know you have to do your job. But losing both of your parents and then discovering a dead body hanging from the ceiling of a room you sleep in would be too traumatic for most adults. Jamal is only eleven years old, and I'm concerned about his mental health. If there was any way you could delay this questioning, I would appreciate it."

"I understand your concern and I will try to be as gentle as possible. But a young man is dead. And I need to get to the bottom of that."

"What is there to get to the bottom of? From my understanding, the young man committed suicide."

"Appears so. Look" Ben said, shifting uncomfortably in his chair. "This should take no more than five or ten minutes."

She sighed and looked longingly back at the wall clock above her head. "Okay. I'll call him in."

About ten minutes later, Jamal walked into the office. Margaret started to introduce Ben to him, but Jamal told her that they'd already met. She asked if he felt up to answering questions about Saturday's event and he said, "Sure, why not." She excused herself from her office, stopping briefly in the doorway to say in a firm voice, "I'll be back in ten minutes." She punctuated the statement with another hard glare at the wall clock.

After she'd left the room, Jamal, to Ben's surprise, closed the office door. Afterwards he turned and faced Ben. "Cain didn't commit suicide."

Ben's first thought was that the kid was in denial, like the first time a child was told that there was no Santa Claus. There was an abject refusal to believe it, which sometimes ended with the child placing fingers in both ears and yelling to the heavens as if that ritual would somehow make what they knew in their heart to be true, not be. But instinctively, he knew that wasn't what the kid meant. There was something different about Jamal. He seemed, somehow, older than eleven. "But," Ben said, speaking carefully, "you found him."

"I know," Jamal said. "And there were no signs of forced entry into the house. I saw Miss Helm unlock the door when we all came back from Calvin's burial. I watched the policemen as they checked all the doors and windows. And I know the coroner's report stated that the ligature marks were consistent with hanging."

Ben's eyes widened. "Coroner's report. Ligature marks."

In reaction to the man's surprised look, Jamal added, "I read a lot and the preliminary autopsy report is public record."

Ben was impressed and a little freaked out at the same time. It was like he was talking to Doogie Hauser. "Okay, knowing that, why would you say Cain hadn't committed suicide?"

"He wouldn't do it. Cain was street to his heart. He was one of the best rappers I've ever heard. He loved his music and he loved his hood. Cain would have gone to prison; he would have even died in a hail of gunfire. But what he would have never done was take his own self out. And he definitely would not have done it by hanging himself. There's no honor in the streets for that."

"Did Cain have any other friends? Kids he hung out with?"

"Nah, not really. He was into his music."

"How about at Fathers House? Was he close to any of the other kids there?"

"No, just me. We were both into music. So, we usually kicked it alone."

Ben paused and looked around the office. Jamal stood near the door. He looked back at Jamal. "How is it living at Fathers House?"

"Just like any other house I guess. We eat. We sleep. We have chores."

"Does anything strange or unusual ever happen at the house?"

"Like a dead body hanging from the ceiling fan?" Jamal said evenly.

Touché, Ben thought to himself. He hesitated and debated whether or not to ask Jamal what he knew about the basement, and about some of the Fathers House kids apparently slinging drugs. He looked up at the wall clock. He had about one minute left. He decided not to ask him, at least not now. If Jamal knew anything about drugs or the basement, he was unlikely to start babbling with Ms. Younger due back at any moment. Besides, hood kids loathed to snitch anyway. Instead, Ben asked, "Jamal, what do you think happened?"

"You can call me Prodegee." He paused, slowly shaking his head. Finally, he said, "I don't know man. I just don't know."

***

On the Tuesday after the funeral, the flow of cards, plants, flowers, and food in remembrance of Calvin Lamont Leeson finally slowed to a trickle at the modest residence at 1906 East Street. In order to create more space in her living room, Sarah Leeson moved a couple of peace lilies to her bedroom and three palm plants to the kitchen where she'd replaced the table centerpiece with one of the seven lovely remembrance flower baskets she'd received. She put the remaining plants on the back deck. A variety of food dishes still lined the counters. A garden-fresh and woodsy aroma, splashed with the scintillating scents of various pastas and meats, continued to flow freely throughout the house.

She stood in the doorway to his room and looked around. She'd only been in the room once since Calvin died. It was as he'd left it. The room was typical teenage boy, except probably for the neatness. On the walls, pictures of pretty young vixens, sporty cars, and musical

stars she'd long given up trying to name, were collaged.
His bed was made. His desk was free of clutter. A row of
about ten pairs of sneakers were lined up soldier-like along
the wall on the right side of the room. She smiled. Calvin
had to have been the neatest teenager in the world. She'd
never had to get on him about cleaning up his room. If
anything, she'd had to tell him to stop bugging her about
housecleaning. He'd been an obsessive clean-freak.

She walked to his closet and opened it. Seven days ago
she'd been in here to select his burial wear. She had
initially selected his black suit, the one she'd insisted he
buy because, "You need at least one dark suit in your
wardrobe." He'd resisted at first. It was, after all, his
money. He'd earned it and should've been able to spend it
on whatever he wanted to spend it on. But eventually,
without saying anything to her, he'd gone out and bought
the suit. That was the kind of boy he'd been, or rather the
kind of young man he'd become. He listened. So, for the
service she'd decided that he would wear his clothes, what
he'd felt most comfortable in. She selected a pair of blue
baggie jeans and a throwback Dallas Cowboy jersey.

She looked at the rest of his clothes. Shirts and pants
hung neatly on hangers; already color coordinated and
matched up. Maybe she'll let his friends come by and pick
out what they wanted. The rest she'd give to Goodwill.

She stood at the closet for a moment and thought about
his Home-going service. It had been a beautiful service.
She'd had no idea that her son had so many friends. Of
course, the story in the Duraleigh Standard may have had
something to do with the attendance. Still, it had been
comforting celebrating her son's life with so many people.
It had helped to mask her pain, making it almost bearable.
Now…she was alone again.

She steadied herself, closed the closet door, and
walked over to the small desk in the corner near the
window. Papers were stacked in neat columns atop it. She

pulled out the chair and sat down. The newspaper had implied that her son had been the victim of gang violence. There may have been some truth in that. She didn't know the exact details. But she had a good idea who'd killed her son, though she didn't know why they killed him. She knew what he'd been involved in. She and Calvin had done what had needed to be done. Maybe Calvin had wanted out. Maybe they wouldn't let him out. She, herself, had often thought about getting out. But she owed them too much. There was no way out for her short of death. Maybe that was what the Simmons boy had decided on Saturday. But she could never commit suicide. Her husband had fought too hard to live, only to eventually lose his life. Her son had lost his life, having involved himself in something illegal in order to make her life a little better. She owed it to both of them to live. But in order to do so, she'd have to find a way out of her mess.

Father's Disciples was powerful. Too powerful. It involved too many people. She thought about the assistant district attorney, Ben Lovison. He'd been there at the hospital on the day Calvin died. She'd assumed the syndicate had sent him, to gauge her reaction at her son's death, to see what she'd do. She knew now that he hadn't been there for those reasons. She'd found out about the premature birth of his twins. His being there had been purely coincidental. She wasn't certain whether he was a part of the conspiracy. But she did know that Father's Disciples had infiltrated the DA's office, the police department, and most of city hall. She knew that they were all on the syndicate's payroll. As the syndicate's accountant, it was her job to know. She also knew that there was no one in the entire city that she could trust.

As she stood to leave, she noticed a small, white triangular tip under the desk lamp. She lifted the lamp, uncovering a business card. Curious, she picked it up. It was the business card of a FBI special agent.

*＊＊

Tom Ram sat in the front passenger seat of Special Agent
Ernie McDougald's black, government-issued Ford Taurus.
He stared aimlessly out the passenger side window,
vaguely aware of the passing sights on the crowded
interstate. The Ford zipped past the outlet stores that
eventually gave way to Charlotte's tall commercial
buildings, which in turn yielded to the tree-lined streets of
one of the city's residential areas.

He felt like a field agent again and a part of him
relished the feeling. It felt good being out amongst the
troops and not cooped inside the bureaucratic walls of
justice. If only it wasn't under these circumstances.

"Do you honestly think she was in danger?"
McDougald asked as he gripped the steering wheel,
keeping his eyes firmly fixed ahead. The afternoon rush
was over, but traffic was still bumper-to-bumper.
McDougald wore dark sunglasses, although the late
afternoon sun was well hidden behind a cluster of dusty-
gray clouds. The weatherman hinted at rain the past couple
of days, but neither he, nor nature had seemed firmly
committed to the idea. Though deep-gray skies had become
the new normal, not one drop of water had fallen anywhere
in the city the past couple of days.

"I do," Ram answered matter-of-factly. He thought of
the deaths of the two federal prisoners, and those of
Leeson, Storrs, and most recently, Simmons. None of the
deaths had been classic gangland hits, nor had they
appeared to be remotely related to each other. But still, it
was just too damn many coincidences. He had too many
years in law enforcement, too many years of relying mainly
on his gut, to dismiss what his experience and gut told him
now: the Bureau's case against Father's Disciples had
somehow been compromised. Until they found out to what

extent they'd been breached, protecting Sarah Leeson was a no-brainer.

They were on their way to see her now. Since having her snatched up from Duraleigh and safely tucked away in a Charlotte safe house, this would be the Bureau's initial interview of her. It was too risky to bring her inside the field office, especially since the source of the compromise was not yet known. At this point, it wasn't known whether it existed within the Charlotte field office or elsewhere within the Bureau. Either way, no chances would be taken with her safety. The decision to pick her up was made within a small circle of agents and communicated the old fashioned way—word of mouth. No technology was used, no computers, no telephones, nothing. As it stood now, only five agents knew that she was in FBI custody, and two of those agents had expertly moved her out of her house within an hour of getting her phone call, bringing her here to Charlotte. She was a godsend. If something happened to this new and now only, Father's Disciple's witness, Ram would be able to count the list of possible traitor-agents on one hand.

"What information do you think she has?" McDougald asked.

It was a good question and one Ram couldn't fully answer. Originally, he hadn't intended to conduct the interview himself, but since the possible compromise, he'd found himself short of available and trusted bodies. Besides that, he had a sense that time was running out. He had one undercover agent missing and another one that could also be in danger. It seemed Father's Disciples was always a step ahead of the Bureau. He needed Sarah Leeson to talk fast about whatever she knew about the syndicate, and in particular, Mayo Fathers. The Bureau needed a very bright light shone on the organization that had for years operated under the cover of darkness. "I hope it's a lot more than what we know now," he said finally. He paused and then turned his head to look at McDougald. "This is not going to be a good-cop, bad-cop routine. Don't fly off the handle in there. Leeson is probably going to be scared and confused. And right now, we need her, a hell of a lot more than she needs us."

McDougald continued staring straight ahead. "What are you trying to say, chief?"

"I respect your reputation and I know your style. You're very good at what you do. But we're going to have to coax a rabbit out of her hole, and if we go too loud and too fast, she's going to run back and burrow herself so deep, we won't be able to get her out anytime soon. And I fear that we don't have that sort of time."

The upper left corner of McDougald's lip curled upward. "You respect my reputation. I'll take that as a compliment. Alright chief, it's your show. But if you need me to bring the heat, just holler."

A few minutes later, McDougald exited the interstate and turned right onto Edgerton Road. He made a series of right turns before making a left onto Fairmont Street, eventually arriving in front of a mailbox with a rusty-gold marker indicating 1016, belonging to a couple now known as Mr. and Mrs. Robert Stock. He pulled the sedan into the driveway of the modest two-story brick-fronted house. The sedan's headlights blinked twice. Both McDougald and Ram saw the blinds on an upstairs window move ever so slightly. The headlights blinked twice more, and seconds later, the garage door of the house crankily lifted up and allowed the sedan entrance.

After sitting the agents on a plush white couch in the living room, Lauren Stock went upstairs, promising to send down Sarah Leeson. Lauren, a veteran of two previous impromptu Bureau visits, added that she had a lot of work to do upstairs and that the agents would not be disturbed. She also mentioned that her husband Robert, who the agents knew had been an accountant in his past life, wasn't due home for another couple of hours. Presently, Robert was head of security at Bank of America Center.

Twenty minutes passed before Sarah Leeson finally descended the stairs and walked into the living room. She was taller than Ram had thought she'd be, perhaps five-ten, six-foot in heels. He sensed her nervousness. She wore a blue flower-printed dress that fell just below the knees and red house slippers. Her eyes darted from the floor to the ceiling and then in the general direction of her two visitors.

Both men, who'd been sitting, stood simultaneously.

As she drew closer, Ram extended his hand. "Hello Miss Leeson. I'm Tom Ram, Acting Special Agent-In-Charge, Charlotte field office. He nodded toward McDougald. "And this is Special Agent Ernie McDougald."

McDougald extended his hand as well. "Pleased to meet you, ma'am."

She weakly shook both hands one after the one, offering a barely audible, "Nice to meet you both."

"Please have a seat," Ram said.

All three sat down, Ram and McDougald where they were previously—side by side on the couch, Sarah in the loveseat positioned perpendicular to the couch.

After everyone had settled down, Ram cut right to the chase. "I know you have questions," he said to Sarah, "and I'll answer as many of them as possible. But, I must stress that I believe time is of the essence. The information we need from you is more pressing, particularly as it relates to Father's Disciples and Mayo Fathers."

She sat still for a few moments and didn't say a word, her hands crisscrossed upon her lap. Finally, she spoke. "When I found Agent Lloyd's card in Calvin's room, I didn't quite know what to make of it. For a while, I allowed myself to fantasize about my son becoming a FBI agent. It was a nice thought. And he could have been one too, you know. He was smart. He was a good boy." She paused, then, "When his father was dying, it tore something from Calvin, seeing his father wither away like that. A once strong, proud man, reduced to a man shriveling up, messing himself. Calvin couldn't take it. I saw it in his eyes when he looked at his dad. It wasn't a look of pity or even embarrassment. He wanted to take his dad's place. He didn't like seeing his dad helpless, and he himself, didn't like being helpless and unable to do anything about it..." her voice trailed off as she gazed in the general direction of the fireplace, though she didn't appear to be looking at anything in particular.

There was an awkward silence. Ram glanced at McDougald and then back at Sarah. He was unsure of what to say. Then she started back talking, her gaze still somewhere near the fireplace. "Then after he was gone, Calvin saw the stress that the medical bills were having on me and he wanted to help. He looked at me as if he wanted to apologize for his father. As if I was going to blame Pete for our situation. He couldn't handle that." She paused again. "For a long time I convinced myself that my son wasn't into selling drugs. That he was smarter than that. But, there were the new clothes, the new shoes, and money to pay some bills. At first he'd just put the money in an envelope and place it in the mailbox. Then eventually, he just started handing it to me in person. I didn't ask any questions about where the money came from. We needed it. I needed it. I didn't know how to tell him it was wrong. The truth was, I didn't want to. I know that it wasn't his responsibility to stand in his dad's stead, but I needed him to. I needed someone to." Tears streamed down her face. She wiped away at them with the back of her hand and laughed unnaturally. "It's ironic really. My husband spent his whole life paying for things in cash, working hard so that we never owed anybody anything. And then he died, leaving us in a mountain of debt, forcing my son to sell drugs, and me to work for a devious funeral home." Her gaze returned to them as she went from Ram's eyes to McDougald's eyes, before finally settling squarely on Ram's. It was as if she'd finally come to grips about why they were here. "After my husband's death," she said in her same slow, deliberate manner. "The funeral home extended me credit so I could bury him. When I turned in my application for the credit, they saw that I was a C.P.A. and that's what they'd been looking to hire, a certified accountant. They offered me a huge salary and forgiveness of my debt with them. They also paid the mountain of hospital bills. It didn't take me long to figure out why they'd been so generous. I guess deep down I always knew they were into something illegal; but I chose not to think too hard about it or ask too many questions. Naively, I thought the less I knew the better off I'd be." She suddenly stopped talking. The room was quiet again as the three of them sat there in silence just looking at each other.

After a few more moments of uncomfortable silence, Ram leaned forward from the couch. "Miss Leeson, may I call you Sarah?"

She nodded affirmatively.

"Sarah, tell us about Mayo Fathers and his business."

She swallowed hard. "The funeral home business is a front for Father's Disciples' criminal empire. You read about these sorts of things or see them on television and you think there's no way this could happen. You can't hide vast amounts of money. The government is too smart. But that's what the funeral business allows him to do. Fathers has a chain of funeral homes throughout the Carolinas and parts of Virginia. Illegal drugs are packed into the caskets. The caskets are loaded onto hearses which are then delivered wherever they need to go. Most of the syndicate's money is laundered through its funeral home business. Funeral home prices are so outlandish that no one really questions it. The funeral home can sell a casket for a hundred dollars and then list it on tax records as being sold for five thousand dollars. Or it can sell a ten thousand dollar funeral service to a family. Let the family put five hundred dollars down while the funeral home finances the remaining ninety-five hundred. The family makes the payments off the books to the funeral home in cash which the company pockets. The funeral home then pays off the balance on the books with the dirty money as if the family made the payments. But it still keeps the family on the hook." She shook visibly, her eyes trained on her lap. When she finally looked up at Ram, a light mist formed around her eyes.

"Can you prove any of this? Do you have records?" Ram asked.

She slowly nodded her head. "There are records. I record the transactions in notebooks, but they are locked in a safe at the funeral home. I was told that the company had a bad experience with computer records and that they were no longer allowed."

"Did you make copies of anything?" McDougald asked.

"No, I worked in a room alone in front of surveillance cameras. But I never thought about making copies anyway. For what reason would I think to do that? Who would I make copies for?"

"Us," McDougald said fiercely. "You could have made copies for us. Fathers Funeral Home is breaking the law and you're helping them. You should have come to us!"

"And what would you all have done?" Sarah shot back. "Would you have paid my bills? Would you have paid the funeral home back what I owed? Would you have protected me when they came after me? Huh, would you have?"

"It's not our responsibility to pay the bills you racked up. But it is your responsibility to do the right thing. And if you would have done the right thing, yes we would have protected you."

Sarah glared at him. "Like you protected my son?" Her

tears flowed freely again.

"We're sorry about what happened to your son," Ram interjected sincerely. "At this time we're not sure if his death is related to Father's Disciples."

"It's related," Sarah said strongly.

"Then help us take the syndicate down," Ram said.

"How can I do that?"

McDougald shot to his feet. "You're the bookkeeper for one of the most ruthless crime outfits operating today. You've helped these murderous scumbags launder millions of dollars. By your own admission, you have defrauded and cheated thousands of helpless families. You're just as responsible for the atrocities committed by Father's Disciples as if you'd personally committed them yourself. These are things that you're responsible for. I'll put it to you in plain English— you either help us bring them down or you go down with them."

Sarah fell back against the loveseat and curled into a ball. Her face contorted in a fusion of anger and sadness. "You don't have a right to talk to me like that. No right."

Ram went to her and kneeled down beside the loveseat. He patted her gently on her head. He glared back at McDougald. "You're out of line, Ernie. Wait for me in the car."

McDougald looked at him sheepishly. He shrugged his shoulders and left. Ram's eyes followed him as he walked out of the living room. A moment later, Ram heard the front door open and close. He turned back to Sarah and gently stroked her arms. "Sit up, please."

Slowly she sat up and he sat next to her on the loveseat. "He's wrong. You don't have to help us. I realize that you're just as much a victim as the others. We understand the position you were put in. We understand all that you've been through, and we won't add to your misery. But I'm asking, no...I'm begging you. Help us."

For several minutes she said nothing as she focused on

her interlocked fingers sitting on her lap. Just before the silence became unbearable, she asked, "What can I do?"

Ram smiled. "Good, thank you. You can testify against Father's Disciples once we bring them to justice. But in order to do that, we're going to need those records. Are you sure there's no other records kept? No computer records of any sort?"

"Not to my knowledge. As I said, I wasn't allowed to work on a computer. I entered everything manually in notebooks."

Ram frowned slightly, but quickly regrouped. "It's okay. What about the drugs in the caskets and hearses. Are they stored initially at the funeral home?"

"No," Sarah said. "Drugs are never kept at the funeral home. The caskets and hearses pick up the drugs from one location and then deliver them to various places. But, I don't know where."

"Is there anything else you can tell me?"

Sarah didn't hesitate. She looked him squarely in the eyes and told him everything she knew about the payments made to the mayor, the DA's office, the police department, and other various departments in Duraleigh's city hall.

***

Later, when they drove back to the field office, Ram looked over at McDougald. "What part of "Don't fly off the handle" was the most confusing to you?"

McDougald kept his eyes on the road. "I understood you perfectly, but she was getting ready to stonewall. I sensed some indignation coming on. I thought a little switching of the gears was in order."

Ram considered that for a long moment while staring at McDougald. "You're forgiven," he said finally. A half smirk formed across his face before he faced forward again.

"Like I told you before, I know your style and I respect your reputation."

They rode together in silence for a while, hearing only the harmonious sounds of the comings and goings of the various vehicles on the interstate. Then McDougald asked, "What do you make of what she said, chief?"

"Father's Disciples has a nice operation, and it looks like they're getting great cooperation from Duraleigh's finest."

"Do we have enough to get a search warrant?"

"No. Sarah knows a lot, but she can't prove any of it. She doesn't have any records, and according to her, no drugs are kept anywhere on the premises at Fathers Funeral Home or Fathers House. We could run surveillance and follow the hearses when they leave the premise, but if we follow them we'd have to have a reason to stop them. And if we stop them and we don't find any drugs, we could be sued for harassment."

"So we're still at square one," McDougald said.

"Not exactly," Ram said. "We know more now than we did yesterday."

They were quiet again. Then McDougald asked, "You think the syndicate killed that Simmons' kid?"

Ram continued looking straight ahead. "Our findings on his death weren't conclusive."

"Oh," McDougald said. "I bet our UC would beg to differ."

"I know our undercover wonder is some type of genius," Ram said, "but whoever killed Simmons was skilled and careful."

"Maybe. But I don't think any of us believes that kid committed suicide."

"What we believe and what we can prove...," Ram didn't finish the sentence. It wasn't necessary. He knew McDougald understood. For now, the Simmons kid's death would go in the books as a suicide. Despite that, Ram found himself feeling ebullient. Until today, Father's Disciples seemed to be one-upping the investigation every step of the way. Now, thanks to a new, unexpected witness, he had a feeling that the Bureau's luck was about to change.

Chapter 10

Marvelous Killens reveled in his job as Father's executioner. It was his dream vocation, one in which he'd been born to fulfill. He was named after the moniker of one of the greatest middleweight champions in the history of boxing. There had been an expectation that young Marvelous would one day match and eventually surpass the boxing exploits of the legendary Marvelous Marvin Hagler. But fate and a tenuous left hook that had been notoriously slow getting out of the gate doomed any shot at boxing greatness. His last professional fight had been conducted in front of his current employer. It'd ended in Marvelous' victory, but with fifty thousand dollars leaving the relative comforts of Father's treasure cove for the harshly undeserving domain of Big Hand Sam, Father's betting pigeon.

"You lucked up with that hook tonight," Father had said. It was moments after the fight. Father stood in the doorway of Marvelous' dressing room as the fighter had the tape removed from his hands. "We told our fighter all week that your hook was virtually nonexistent and you'd telegraph it a month before delivering it. Tonight, our boy got careless and stopped looking for it altogether. And you nailed him with it. Other more seasoned fighters won't be so careless. But I like your heart. I like your instincts. You sensed blood in the ring and I suspect if the referee hadn't stopped the fight, you would have beaten our boy until the life had seeped out of him. You're a killer—a marvelous killer. Unfortunately for you, the boxing game won't allow you to do what your head and heart most want to do. But I will."

It had been a revelation. A freeing revelation that soon

forever separated both he and Father from the fight game. Now Marvelous stood in the bowels of Fathers Funeral Home, disdainfully listening to a traitor's ragged last breaths. He looked down at the soon-to-be-dead traitor's body. The traitor's skin was ashen as if all the life had already been drained from him. His face was sunk in and his midsection was moving up and down jerkily, slowly, painfully. He'd last spoken over an hour ago in a desperate plea for his life. They had been cowardly words, sickening words. It had made Killens nauseous hearing them. The fool had no pride, unlike the young boy, Cain.

Cain had accepted his fate like a man. He neither begged, nor cried. After Killens had tightened the electric cord around the boy's neck, Cain had held his head high in an almost defiant gesture. Killens admired the young man's resoluteness. He'd witnessed grown men, huge men, rich and well-muscled men, cry like little babies, pleading for their lives, and offering all kinds of vile things in exchange for their lives. Cain had done none of that. As a result, Killens had a marvelous time seeing just how much resolve the young man had. Surprisingly and wonderfully for Killens, it had been a lot. The young man did not give up the ghost easily, though he did not thrash about. He simply held on for as long as he could—twenty minutes. Only the gods knew how he'd been able to last so long. But oh, how Killens had enjoyed every minute of the spectacle. Now, two days later, he could still feel the boy's fight for life and he relished it. He could still hear the last words, spoken through clenched teeth and constricted throat, "Tell my fans I was a soldier." Listening to his last words had been musically riveting. Watching life finally loose itself from the boy's grip had been heavenly, like the sweet first bite of a succulent meat.

Marvelous wheeled the now dead traitor into the retort. The traitor had been a big bastard. The incineration would take nearly two hours. But time was of no factor. Killens had nothing to do until Father placed another order.

Feeling hunger pangs, he remembered the candy bar he'd left on the nightstand in his room. As the burning body began to blacken, Killens went back to his room to retrieve the candy bar, walking past a stone-thick closed door which opened to a cemented tunnel which itself led to the basement of Fathers House.

**

On Wednesday morning, Luther Savannah arose early and scurried over to the chow hall where he quickly wolfed down a slice of toast, scrambled eggs, an apple, and a bowl of Cheerios before hustling over to the administration building. He was anxious to see Butler State Prison's newest residents as they marched into the gray-stone walls of their new home, or more specifically, he wanted his first glimpse at Father's Disciples' newest prison representative—Peyton Lars.

After nearly thirty-three years of incarceration, the last twenty-nine served with nary an infraction, not even a raised eyebrow, Luther was considered a model prisoner and was a respected trustee. It was a position that came with envied benefits, including the one he was exercising at the moment—virtually unsupervised roaming of the prison grounds. Hell, he thought, the guards probably figured that a fifty-three year old black man who'd been locked up for half his life, and who had no family on the outside, wouldn't dare try to escape.

They'd figured right.

He spotted Lars, third in line. I be damned, Luther said to himself. That boy's still on his momma's milk. He was a skinny kid, with a Rastafarian mop of hair that reached down to his shoulders. He didn't look scared, but Luther had seen that type of false cockiness before. For most young punks waltzing into prison walls with pompous attitudes, it would end badly. But for Lars, a Father's Disciple, Luther would be able to set him straight before anything got out of hand.

It had been Father's vision for Father's Disciples to work the prison system from within. As a result of that vision and Father's Disciples concerted efforts, the syndicate controlled several state prisons in North Carolina, including Butler's and a few dozen federal ones across the United States.

According to Father, the ultimate downfall of a crime family was not law enforcement, not a government and its citizens, not even other criminals, but rather it was the crime family itself. Or more specifically, the family's cocky assumption that none of its members would ever get caught running afoul of the law. Consequently none of the great crime families of the past, not the Gambino family, not the Columbo Family, not the Chicago's Sicilian Mafia, none of them, had ever taken the time to prepare for a very inevitable possibility, prison. When the inevitable finally happened—the arrest and subsequent imprisonment of their family's members, it usually meant the beginning of the end of the family's life's work.

In some cases, just the threat of prison had spelled the end as family members afraid of the possibility of a life spent behind bars, had ultimately turn rat and divulged family secrets to unscrupulous law enforcement agents. Arrogance, Father had long decided, was the death knell of the crime family.

But in Father's world, the possibility of going to prison was front and center. He was determined that the threat of prison would no longer paralyze his family with fear. The family, he'd said, would always be there for each other, both inside and outside prison walls. Subsequently, his vision had led to the setup of Father's Disciples' elaborate prison program. "Father's Disciples was a family," Father said, "But make no mistake, it's also a criminal organization. Our very nature is criminal. We will not sugarcoat it. And being criminal means law enforcement is opposed to our very existence, an opposition that will most certainly lead to the arrests of our members, some of whom will undoubtedly serve prison terms of varying lengths, including possibly, lifetime. It would be foolhardy for Father's Disciples not to prepare for such a certainty."

Father made no bones about prison to the family; being locked up was still being locked up. But for a convicted Father's Disciple member it would no longer hold the kind of sway that had sounded the death knell for so many crime families before it. The transition to prison life for a Father's Disciple was going to be made much smoother. His immediate family would be taken care of while he served his time. As for the member, once he orientated into the prison system, he would quickly sync up with other family members already established in the prison. From day one he would experience what it would take other new prisoners, years, if ever, to achieve: protection, connections, and all the creature comforts that stone walls and metal bars would allow. Membership in the Father's Disciples family was going to have privileges. There would be different status levels, depending on what the individual's role had been within the organization. But the family was going to take care of its own, both inside and outside prison walls.

But first a Father's Disciple's prison stronghold had to be created.

To that end, Father had his disciples infiltrate North Carolina's prison system before even the first Disciple had ever been placed in handcuffs. The infiltration had been orchestrated through various volunteer groups, churches, prison ministries, any organization with an aim to serve the prison community. Father's Disciples posed as fine upstanding members of such groups in order to gain entry into the prison system. Once inside, they flooded the system with money, bribing both prisoners and prison officials. They synced up with gangs already established in the prison, promising to aid their family members on the outside. By the time the family's first convicted member, Luther Savannah, had entered the system in 1978, Father's Disciples had an established foothold.

Generally, the prison's intake process took a week. The new prisoners would be tested for their educational levels. The prisoners would be evaluated mentally and classified accordingly, and once an appropriate cell was available, assigned.

Lars's intake process was completed in less than two hours, and prisoner number 1949B68 was already settled in his cell when Luther paid his first visit. The youngster's cellie, a big bruiser named Cleo, was standing in the corner of the cell next to the toilet, salivating. Cleo, serving an eighteen-year manslaughter charge for beating his younger brother to death, had dark bluish-black skin and a clean shaven scalp. Lars lay on the top bunk, looking up at the ceiling as if he hadn't a care in the world.

Cleo glared at Luther as he entered the cell. "Luther, can you believe this kid? He's acting as if he owns the joint. I'm going to love breaking him in."

Luther ignored him and walked over to the bunk beds. "Kid, you alright?"

Lars did not move.

Luther leaned in closer and spoke in a low voice. Lars turned his head to face Luther and whispered his response. The two then exchanged knowing nods and smiles. Lars sat up, and then jumped off the top bunk. "Can I have my bed now?"

Luther said, "Sure thing." He looked over at Cleo and shrugged his shoulders.

"One of yours," Cleo said.

Luther nodded. "I believe he prefers the bottom bunk."

Cleo snarled at Lars before reaching down and pulling the linen off of the bottom bunk, and then tossing it back onto the bed.

"Hey," Lars said. "Why don't you make that bed?"

Cleo took a menacing step toward the kid, but was stopped by Luther's patted hand to his chest. "Easy big fella," Luther said. "I'll explain things to him. He's a neo. Give him a break." Cleo grunted once and left the cell.

Luther looked down at Lars, "Come on, kid. Let's take a walk."

***

Later during the waning moments of the prisoners' afternoon free hour, Luther and Lars stood against the fifth tier railing, looking down at the prison courtyard. The prison was a five-story-high, boxlike structure. There were twenty cells per side, one hundred cells per tier, with armed eyes everywhere, both video and human. The hustle and bustle of institution life was in full swing as the prisoners talked and interacted amongst themselves. The noise was indistinguishable from what one might hear on a busy city street sans the automobiles. Luther said, "We run things in here. But we're not gods. There's an order to things—a protocol."

Lars didn't say anything. But Luther could tell the kid was mulling over what he was being told. He continued. "This is prison. Despite what you might have heard on the outside. Life is hard in here. Now, Father's Disciples will make your time easier, but you got to get with the system. And if you do, you'll be back with your family in no time, getting mad props from the organization. There's no telling how high you'll rise up. Look at it as sort of an initiation. You pass this shit in here, and out there, the sky's the limit for you."

Lars nodded his head and bit down on his bottom lip.

Finally, he said. "So that executive privilege stuff Father talked about was just a bunch of bull."

"Nah," Luther said half grinning. "Executive status is real. You're coming in at a level that it takes niggas years to reach. Among other things, you're talking about first dibs on job assignments. Pick of the litter of the contraband. And in the yard, as the motherfuckers running this place, Father's Disciples have the best location. It's right in the middle of everything—the basketball court, the weights area, the lobby. From our vantage point, we can watch all the yard activity. Can't nuthin' go down, lest we know about it." He stopped for a moment and let his words sink in. Father's Disciples was a powerful group inside and outside the prison system. Sometimes, he guessed, it took a newbie to make one realize just how good one had it. "There's this one group," he said half laughingly. "They call themselves the Chi lows—whatever da fuck that means—their yard spot is right near the outside toilets. Nobody wants that spot. And if the fucking Chi lows had any clout in this place, they wouldn't be there. Some bull?" Luther asked. "Nah it ain't bull. As for you, you get to sit next to me and the rest of the executive heads of Father's Disciples. We're flanked by some of the baddest motherfuckers in this joint. If you didn't have executive privilege, your ass would be on point your entire two-year sentence. Eyes open, constantly roaming, scared shitless. But with us, if you follow the rules, you have no worries."

A look of satisfaction flushed over the kid's face. He was silent for a moment. Then he said, "You got family on the outside? Somebody waiting on you?"

Luther gripped the railing a little tighter. "Not in this lifetime. I'm a lifer. No possibility of parole."

Lars nodded his head, but didn't say anything else.

The blast from a trumpet-like horn ripped through the din, signaling the end of free hour. Luther stood with his back against the railing for a few moments, watching as the newbie strutted off, his head held back as if he was counting the stars. The cockiness of youth, Luther thought before trekking down to his second tier cell.

Chapter 11

The Revival Convention Center was the city of Duraleigh's crown jewel. The five-hundred-thousand square feet of luxurious extravagance was a direct offspring of the marriage between the city's low crime rate and its desire to gain market share in the lucrative convention business. It sat majestically in the city's east corridor, between two four-star hotels. What the city lacked in natural resources, it had hoped to make up for, in part, with the sheer spectacle of the convention center. The architect who designed the center had done so with a goal in mind of extremism meets the future. His design had wowed city leaders beyond their expectations. The place was an architectural, as well as functional, beauty. With its reflective glass walls stretching up to the sun, it looked like a gigantic block of glistening ice. It had over forty meeting rooms, two exhibit halls, several onsite restaurants and stores, state of the art technology, including wireless, voice-to-data transmission, high-definition flat screens and computers in every nook and cranny, and a forty thousand square foot ballroom. It was within walking distance to all the nightlife the city offered, which included additional restaurants, including several that morphed into dance clubs after eleven PM, catering to a livelier sect who maybe preferred a little extra spice to their convention getaways. Since the center's opening three years ago, the city had seen its tourism dollars increase dramatically. The place had quickly earned its keep.

Even though Wednesday morning was a little cooler than the weatherman had promised, Ben still decided to walk the three blocks from the courthouse to the convention center. A gorgeously bright, late-January sun posed just-for-show above him, its long golden rays beaming ineffectively across a diamond-clear blue sky. His suit coat proved as ineffectual as the teasing sun. With his laptop bag strapped across his shoulders, he shivered as he stuffed his hands into his pants pockets and hurried on. The huge digital-clock perched atop the tall Merchant office building alternately displayed the time as ten-forty-five and the temperature as thirty-nine degrees—fifteen degrees lower than the jolly weatherman had forecasted.

He crossed at the intersection of New Bern and Martin street, and continued east on Moorland street. The normally heavy traffic was at a chasm, caught between the stampeding early morning rush and the midday lunch dash. Mayo's conference wasn't scheduled to start until noon, but with the Storrs murder case handed over to the jury this morning, he'd reached a comfortable breaking point in his hectic schedule and had decided to head to the convention center now.

He ascended the center's marbled steps, entered through the revolving glass doors, and went immediately to the wooden concaved desk that displayed the word INFORMATION boldly across the top. A thin, pretty, twenty-something-year old girl, directed him to conference room 3-B, and warned him that he was a tad bit early for the conference as workers were still putting finishing touches to the room.

The conference was entitled State of Duraleigh's Public Safety. It was a byproduct of Mayor Cleveland Becker's annual State of the City speech, and, as one reporter had exclaimed during a lunch with his colleagues, "Just a glorified way for the mayor to shoot additional smoke up his own ass." Unemployment was low. Crime was low. Tourism was high. The city's buckets from its tourism revenue and basic tax base were overflowing. The city was at its zenith. The public safety conference was being co-led by the police chief and the district attorney,

116

both of whom wanted their own share of the limelight and credit for the prosperous times. The keynote speaker, invited by the DA himself, was one Mayo Fathers, founder of Fathers House, an establishment that turned wayward youth who were once potential thorns in the city's side, into very productive members of society.

He found the room and stood for a moment at its entrance, peering inside. Medium-sized circular tables surrounded by four chairs dotted the room. There was a platform at the front of the room, on top of which was a microphone-outfitted podium, and a rectangular-shaped table backed by four chairs. Two ladies, scurried about the room, checking their clipboards, talking amongst themselves, and placing placards on the tables. Sensing his presence, they both looked over at him and smiled pleasantly. He smiled back and entered.

It wasn't long before the room slowly began to fill up with the sights and sounds of civic-minded responsiveness as citizens, clergy, city employees, including several members of law enforcement, community activists, and representatives from several of Duraleigh's various schools and neighborhoods merged together. There was even a generous sprinkling of college students throughout the room.

The first forty minutes of the conference went as expected with the mayor, police chief and district attorney each giving his take on the reason behind Duraleigh's low crime rate. Although each was more than willing to give their respective departments fair share of the credit, each had humbly concluded in their closing remarks that it actually took a concerted effort from all involved, the police, the prosecutors, and most importantly, the citizens. To that end, Etlzer introduced the keynote speaker, fellow citizen Mayo Fathers.

Mayo Fathers was a study in physical contrasts. His appearance at once bespoke a man of limited ability but

limitless means. Though stylishly dressed in a very
expensive Kiton suit, he seemed uncomfortable. He was
slight of build. His complexion was a pasty white. He
meekly approached the podium. His hands tentatively
gripped its edges. He looked around the room as if unsure
of what he wanted to say, or if he hadn't the nerve to say
anything. Then he spoke. His bass voice was rich and
melodious, and with it he immediately commanded
attention.

He started by self-deprecatingly, saying that he didn't
deserve to share the stage with three of the city's bigwigs.
He talked about growing up in Duraleigh believing he was
white and then one day finding out his white skin had been
an illusion. He'd heard tales of how some black people had
been able to pass as white; but he'd never believed it was
truly possible. He talked about how his father's decision to
'pass himself and his family off as white' had shaped he
Mayo as a man and as a person. He talked about realizing
that many minority kids were born without some of the
advantages that he'd been born with, and about how, with
Fathers House, he tried to do his part to remedy that. He
talked about the difference he believed Fathers House had
made in the boys' lives. He then introduced the two Fathers
House graduates in attendance, proudly telling the audience
how both Caleb Dawson and Benjamin Lovison had not
only finished high school, but had both finished law school
and were now a special agent with the FBI and a Duraleigh
County assistant district attorney, respectively. They both
stood and said a few words about what Fathers House had
meant to each of them. When they had finished, Fathers
leaned into the microphone, "You can make a difference in
your community," he said proudly. "These two gentlemen
are living proof of that." The applause was loud and
genuine. When it finally settled down, Fathers thanked the
audience, and he and the two Fathers House alumni
returned to their seats.

***

The first question was directed at Etlzer and came courtesy of a Duraleigh Standard reporter who was seated near the front of the room. "Are you satisfied that the Calvin Leeson murder case has been solved?"

Etlzer frowned. "I respectfully ask that you keep your questions related to today's conference. We've already held press conferences in regards to both Leeson and Cain Simmons."

"Was Cain Simmons' death officially confirmed a suicide?" The question came from somewhere near the middle of the room.

"Yes," Etlzer said, irritably. He didn't elaborate. Instead, he acknowledged a raised hand in the center of the room. A tall man stood and said, "There's a rumor out that the DA's office was aggressively pursuing the idea that there were other people involved in the Leeson kid's death, and that the office had put pressure on the Simmons kid to divulge those names. Any truth to that?"

"No," Etlzer said flatly. "Cain Simmons confessed to getting into an altercation with Calvin Leeson. The altercation ultimately resulted in death. Simmons came to us on his own accord and he said he acted alone. Our investigation revealed that to be accurate. Now with both principles of these unfortunate events dead, both cases are officially closed."

"You're not at all concerned about the way your office handled the Leeson case?"

"No," Etlzer said. "There's absolutely nothing to be concerned about."

A low murmur rose throughout the room.

"What about the county's anti-gang ordinance?" The question came from somewhere in the back of the room.

Etlzer glared in its general direction. "What about it?"

The room quieted as the questioner stood up. He was a short, balding man and despite the January weather, he wore a white short-sleeved button-down shirt, with a solid dark blue tie that he had loosened at the collar. He held a small notepad, which he squinted at through reading glasses that dangled dangerously near the edge of his small point-tip nose. "Earl Beavers, Hendersonville Chronicles," he spat quickly. Hendersonville was located about twenty miles east of Duraleigh. "The anti-gang ordinance outlaws membership in a gang. It bans the wearing of known gang colors. It prohibits group loitering. It..."

"I know what it does," Etlzer interrupted. "I sponsored the ordinance and quite frankly, it's been very successful."

"It's been controversial," Beavers said. "The ACLU has threatened to sue."

"The ordinance has been in effect three years and we've yet to hear from the ACLU. In fact, all we've seen in that time is a dramatic drop in youth violence."

"Until the Leeson murder."

Etlzer grimaced. "Calvin Leeson's death was wholly unrelated to gang violence. It was unrelated because there aren't any gangs in Duraleigh. The youth understand gang membership is against the law. Their parents understand it's against the law. Former gang members who think fondly back on their glory days of yesteryear understand that it's against the law. We've pushed out youth gangs just as we have the adult gangs of those inglorious years of our city's infamous past. The statistics support these findings, which is why Duraleigh consistently ranks as one of the safest cities in America."

Beavers persisted. "Some people say that Leeson's death was, in fact, gang-related, and that the city is covering it up."

"Who are those people?" Etlzer barked. "If they have information contrary to what we have, then they should put it up. Do you have information?"

"Well no," Beavers answered meekly. "I'm just asking questions."

"And I'm giving you answers. I suggest you listen carefully. There is no gang violence in Duraleigh because there are no gangs in Duraleigh. We recently had two of our youths tragically killed with one killing the other and then killing himself. It's tragic. We wish it hadn't happened. But no city on earth can prevent all tragedies, all killings. Our citizens can rest assured that Duraleigh is still the safest city in North Carolina, and according to the FBI, one of the safest in the nation."

"How do the recent events figure into your candidacy for governor?"

"I don't believe they figure at all," Etlzer said. "My record speaks for itself. Did you miss the first part of the conference?" he asked with an immodest grin. Laughter erupted in the room.

***

Ben arrived at Roscoe's at seven-thirty. The place was known for having great steaks, burgers, and well-seasoned, steak fries. As he'd expected for a Wednesday night, it was not that crowded and he was able to find a parking space near the front of the restaurant. Inside, two solitary figures sat at opposite ends of the bar. The bartender leaned on the bar near the thin one and nodded up at the flat screen above his head. A basketball game played onscreen. Ben sidled up to the bar next to the other one, a broad shouldered fella who appeared to be working on at least his second drink. An empty glass was in front of him and he sipped from another glass.

"There he is," Caleb said as Ben plopped down on the stool.

"Sorry, I'm late," Ben said. "I stopped by the hospital

to see my boys." Caleb had stopped Ben after the conference earlier, and suggested that they have dinner and catch up.

The bartender looked his way and Ben shouted his drink order, a Heineken.

Ben indicated the empty glass. "Two at a time?"

"Gets to the blood quicker," Caleb said and downed the rest of his drink. "Mayo told me about the twins. How are they doing?"

"They're doing great. We're hoping they'll be able to come home soon."

"How's the wife? April, right?"

"Yes, April. She's doing well. She came home last week. Her parents are staying with us for a little while. So that helps."

"The in-laws, huh? You get along with them?"

The bartender slid the Heineken in front of him and picked up Caleb's empties. Ben took a long swig from his beer and then swiped the back of his hand across his mouth. "Well I don't hate them or anything. I don't really know them. I guess you could say our relationship is as good as could be expected."

"You guys eating, drinking, or both?" the bartender asked. He dumped the glasses into the sink behind him.

Caleb looked at Ben. "I'm hungry. You want to just order some food here at the bar? Or would you rather get a table?"

"Here's fine," Ben said.

"Looks like we're eating," Caleb said to the bartender. Caleb plucked a menu from the wiry rack in front of him. The bartender stood in front of them with a pencil and pad at the ready. After reading through the menu, Caleb said, "I'm going to go with the Bacon-Cheddar, fries, and another vodka tonic."

The bartender nodded and then looked at Ben.

"I'm going with the New York Strip, well done, steak

fries, and broccoli." He held up his bottle. "I'll be ready for another one of these by the time my order gets here."

"Sounds good," the bartender said. He wrote both orders down on a notepad. He ripped the top sheet off and handed it to a waiter who was heading toward the kitchen. "Take this to the back for me please," he said.

"Sure thing, Willie," the waiter replied.

A few moments later, Willie slid another drink in front of Caleb.

Looking at his friend's drink, Ben said, "You going to be okay to drive?"

Caleb smiled. "Actually, I'm going to be just fine. I came in a cab."

Ben laughed. "Smart." He took another long swig of beer. "What did you think about today's conference?"

"Not much. It was the usual dribble. Mayo was impressive though. The people seemed to love him."

"That they did," Ben said.

They were quiet for the next several moments. Each quietly sipping his drink and absently looking at the basketball game on the flat screen.

Before today they hadn't seen nor spoken to each other since they were teenagers. Back then, the words had come easy. At least they had before they had a falling out of some sort. Ben couldn't recall what it had been about. He remembered Caleb's dad resurfacing and moving the family to South Carolina. It was just after Ben's mother was killed. But he and Caleb had stopped speaking before either of those things had happened. Whatever had caused the former best friends to quit speaking was now water under the bridge. Anyway, they had been teenagers at the time. They could have squabbled over anything. Most likely it had been over some girl that both of them had long since forgotten.

"How's the job?" Ben asked as he drained the last of his beer.

"Great. Yours?"

"I love it. It's busy though. I could use some time off."
He paused, then, "I didn't think the feds ever took time
off."

Caleb grinned. "We don't usually. But Mayo asked a
favor, and I said what the hell. I could use a little rest."

The food arrived and the two ate in silence awhile.
Then Ben said, "You ever think about Fathers House?"

"What do you mean?"

"I don't know. The other boys. Mayo, Miss. Helm."

Caleb chewed his food slowly as if really considering
the question. "I loved Miss Helm. I guess you could say she
was like a mother. But I was only there a couple of years
before my father came back, and I wasn't really close to
anyone there, except maybe you. But Fathers House does
kind of stay with you," his voice trailed off.

Willie slid another Heineken in front of Ben and
picked up the empty. "Thanks," Ben said. He stuffed a
steak fry in his mouth and then looked at Caleb. "Anything
strange ever happen to you at Fathers House?"

"Strange? What do you mean by strange?"

"You remember one of the kids they mentioned today
at the conference, Cain Simmons?"

"The suicide?"

"Yeah, well I talked to him the night before he
supposedly hung himself, and he didn't seem the least bit
suicidal."

"That's not unusual. I've known a few suicides where
a family member or friend of the victim stated that they had
no idea the victim had been suicidal. Sometimes, even the
so called experts miss the warning signs. Sometimes the
victim is just good at hiding their intent. Sometimes you
never know."

"I get that. But, it's not just that. Cain was real
frightened. He told me something weird about Fathers
House, something about the basement."

"Basement?" Caleb said through a bite of his burger. "What about the basement?"

"He said if you were ever sent to the basement, then you wouldn't have to ask about it."

"Okay, humor me. What exactly happens in the basement?"

"I don't know exactly. But whatever happens down there, it is supposedly connected to bad cops and some type of illegal activity. And Father's Disciples."

"What exactly is Father's Disciples?"

"From what I understand, it's a drug cartel."

Caleb burst out laughing. "Are you kidding me? At Fathers House? That young man must have been pulling your leg."

"You think?" Ben said. "He pulls my leg, and then less than twelve hours later he hangs himself?"

Caleb shrugged his shoulders and continued eating.

"He said the FBI was involved."

"In what way?" Caleb asked.

"He didn't say. But I don't think he was making this stuff up. And then there's the matter of Calvin Leeson. I don't buy that Cain alone beat that kid to death."

Caleb looked up from his plate, staring straight ahead. "Is there any evidence to the contrary?"

"There's the extent of the beating. And the fact that Calvin was seen getting into a car with Cain and two other people. But Cain was the only one in the car that was identified."

"What does Etlzer say?"

"You heard him today. Cain killed Calvin and then himself. Cases closed."

Caleb laid his fork across his plate and then turned to Ben. "You want my advice? Follow Etlzer's lead and move on."

"Despite the dead kids?"

"I wouldn't say despite. I'd say because of. The way I

see it, the first you've heard of any of this basement stuff is from a kid that's no longer alive and who had confessed to beating some other kid who is also no longer alive. Where are you going to go with two dead witnesses?"

Ben chewed his food without really tasting it. For a few moments he studied his plate, circling his fork around the broccoli. He took a long pull from his beer bottle. Then, he looked at Caleb. "If the FBI was investigating a supposed crime outfit or gang called Father's Disciples. Would you tell me, provided of course you knew about it?"

Caleb studied his plate. He put the last of his burger in his mouth and quickly stuffed a steak fry in with it. "No," he answered, chewing.

Chapter 12

Ben rang the doorbell at 1907 East Street a third time and waited. There was still no answer. He stepped back on the front porch and took full measure of the house's front exterior. All was still. While heading back to his car after leaving Sarah Leeson's house for the second time, he thought he'd seen a curtain move from within 1907. But if someone was home, clearly they didn't want to speak to him. The house was directly across the street from Sarah's. It was the third neighbor's house he'd tried. He hadn't gotten responses at either of Sarah's next door neighbors. He looked at his watch. It was eight o'clock in the morning.

He'd gotten a White Pages listing for Sarah Leeson and had called her several times in the past week, leaving several voicemail messages. She hadn't returned any of his calls. He'd called again last night after he'd gotten home from Roscoe's only to find that her landline had been disconnected. And this morning, after not getting responses from either of her next door neighbors' houses, he went back to her residence and peered through a few of the windows. Furnishings remained in some of the rooms. Still, he got the sense that Sarah Leeson had abandoned the place.

He stared at the front of 1907 a moment longer and was just about to turn to leave when the front door opened.

***

Emma Tunnel was of feeble body and a gradually deteriorating mind. That was according to her caregiver, Maria Rodriquez. Ms. Tunnel, Maria explained, was ninety-two years old and although her mind had been strong for most of those years, it was slowly becoming a shell of its former self. Ms. Tunnel was increasingly forgetful, moody, and antisocial. An uncomfortable amount of her days were spent in a sort of mental fog where even basic things like putting fork to mouth were an adventure. Some days were better than others. Today was one of the better days. It had been Ms. Tunnel who'd noticed Ben across the street ringing doorbells, and it had been Ms. Tunnel who figured that he was doing so because he was inquiring about the whereabouts of Sarah Leeson.

After inviting Ben into the house and offering him a seat on the couch, Maria excused herself to go make coffee. Ms. Tunnel, having refused assistance from both Maria and Ben, wobbly inched toward the recliner in the living room. She was hunched over as her spine had lost either its will or ability to straighten. Her paste-colored face was a convoluted mass of crisscrossing wrinkles which undoubtedly extended to every conceivable part of her body—from her arms which were painfully visible linking out from a short-sleeved button-down plaid blouse, to her needle-thin legs which were mercifully hidden in a pair of loose fitting burgundy slacks.

Finally, she reached the recliner. She wearily stretched out her hand to grab the arm of the chair and then in a surprisingly quick motion she swung herself around and plopped herself down onto the seat. "Give me a minute," she said, breathing heavily. After a few moments, she said, "You say you're with the district attorney's office?"

"Yes ma'am," Ben said. "I'm an assistant district attorney."

"You a good guy?" she asked earnestly.

"I like to think so," Ben answered in equal earnest.

"My late husband used to say all of them weren't good."

Unsure how to respond, Ben simply said, "Is that right?"

"That young woman is in some trouble, isn't she?"

"Not with our office," Ben said. "I wanted to ask her some questions about her son."

"Her son?"

"Yes ma'am. Her son died recently. Did you know Sarah Leeson and her son, Calvin?"

She scrunched her face, trying to recall them. She slowly shook her head. "Not well enough to comment. I've seen them come and go. They seemed like nice enough people. Was the boy in some trouble?"

"Not with our office, ma'am."

Maria brought in the coffee and set it down on the table. "You take cream and sugar, Mr. Lovison?"

"Yes," Ben said. "About a spoonful of both."

She prepared his cup and handed it to him on a saucer. He took a sip. "It's good. Thank you."

She then prepared Ms. Tunnel's cup of coffee and placed cup and saucer on the end table next to the recliner. "Thank you, dear," Ms. Tunnel said.

"Maria," Ben said. "Did you know Sarah Leeson and her son?"

"Not really," Maria said. "I chitchatted with her a few times about the weather and such. But nothing other than that. I never really saw the son that much. But I was sorry to hear about his passing. I took some food over there last week. She was so sad. I felt sorry for her. Do you suppose she moved?"

"I don't know," Ben said.

"The government took her," Ms. Tunnel offered.

"Excuse me?' Ben said.

"I saw her leave with two men earlier this week. They drove off in a black car, one of those unmarked ones, a government car."

Ben looked helplessly at Maria. "Did you see anything?"

Maria shrugged her shoulders. "No."

"Maria sees nothing," Ms. Tunnel said. "She's not that observant. Unless of course she's watching me. Then, she sees everything."

"I'm only paid to watch you," Maria said. "Not to spy on the neighbors. Besides, you look out that window enough for the both of us."

"I don't spy. I observe. It's called neighborhood watch. It helps keep all of us safe when we watch out for each other."

"Her late husband was a former police office. He taught her how to observe things most people would ignore."

Ms. Tunnel said, "He was a fine policeman too, and an honest one. Thirty years on the force. He would have died on the force if they hadn't forced him to retire."

"That's too bad," Ben said. "But are you sure about the men and the black car? And that Sarah left with them?"

"Very sure," Ms. Tunnel said.

Maria said, "She's been very alert this week. It's possible."

"Stop third-personing me," Ms. Tunnel said irritably. "I've told you I don't appreciate that. I'm right here. And yes, I've been alert this week."

The doorbell rang and Maria excused herself to go answer it. Ben heard her greet a Betty and Paul Samuels, and Mrs. Samuels asking, "How is she today?" Maria replied, "Great. She's even met a new friend." Ben then felt the tingly vibration of his smartphone in his pants pocket. He pulled it out. He'd gotten a text. He swiped his finger across the screen, unlocking it. The text read simply, Jury's back. Hurry! He stood up quickly. "I'm sorry, Ms. Tunnel. But, I'm needed at the office."

Seeing him move quickly toward the door, Mrs. Samuels said, "We didn't mean to rush you off. We were just checking on Emma."

Ms. Tunnel said, "He's not rushing off because of you

Betty. He got a message on one of them smarty-phones."

"Sorry, I didn't get a chance to properly introduce myself," Ben said. He had one foot out the door.

"Mr. Lovison," Ms. Tunnel called out.

Ben stopped and stuck his head back in the house.

Ms. Tunnel said, "The government came back again last night with a truck and moved some of that girl's stuff out."

Chapter 13

At ten fifteen, Ben walked into Jeff Stone's office where he found the senior prosecutor talking on the phone. Seeing Ben enter his office, Stone, who was sitting behind a wide-top oak desk, indicated one of the two chairs in front of it. Ben sat down in the offered chair and waited for Stone to finish his call.

The jury had deadlocked nine to three in favor of acquittal. The impasse had supposedly been cemented the night before. But Judge McMichaels had ordered the jurors to sleep on its decision in hopes that one additional night's rest and its accompanying next day fresh start would help forge a consensus.

It hadn't.

Stone looked remarkably peaceful for a man who'd just lost a murder one case—and for the prosecution, a deadlocked jury was a lost case, although it wasn't a fatal one like an outright acquittal would have been since the defendant could be tried again. In this instance there was no double jeopardy.

"That's exactly what I need for you to do," Stone said, speaking into the phone receiver. He looked mildly irritated. "I don't care if it does chafe your ass. Review the whole investigation. No, I don't want you to retrace your steps. I want you to start the investigation from the..." He paused, mid-sentence, mouth slightly ajar. "Let me worry about that."

Jeffrey Arthur Stone, III, with his tall slender frame, dark hair, and neat, thinly trimmed mustache, had the looks and mannerisms of a fifties era matinee idol. He was a third generation Yale man, a fact that he could casually drop into any conversation within ten minutes. Stephen Ellison, Ben often thought, would get a kick out of him because Stone could trace his heritage back to its original dirt. Stone men were historically high achievers and strongly self-motivated. Though the family owed the majority of its prosperity to its shipping business, they'd also successfully plowed through other fields, such as, medicine, business, and architecture. Surprisingly, Stone was the first attorney in his family.

As Ben sat observing him, he could see Stone's mind at work and he knew perfectly well why he was so calm. He'd seen this scenario played out before. It was classic Jeff Stone. Faced with a legal setback, Stone wouldn't necessarily deem it as such, but rather he'd view it as a mere hiccup on the road to justice, and justice was his primary goal. He sought it, fought for it, and believed in it, sometimes blindingly so. But it was because of that commitment to justice that Ben so admired the man. It wasn't about wins or losses to the veteran prosecutor. It was always about right coming out on top. If the jury had rejected his argument, then Stone would surmise that he'd been making the wrong argument. That something had been missed somewhere, hence the need to go back to square one, hence the need for calm rational thinking and rethinking.

What had the jury seen that he had not seen, would be his question of the day. Now was not the time for anger, or blame, or second guessing. They needed a comprehensive review of the facts of the case and, if necessary, an exhaustive search for additional facts. If after these steps were completed, and Stone then determined that he, heaven forbid, had either been drastically mistaken the first time around, or a guilty man had somehow managed to pull the wool over the eyes of the jury, then and only then would there be anger, blame, and second guessing.

Stone slammed the receiver down in its cradle. "Well, that was a fucking surprise," he said. "I admit I totally miscalculated the impact of not having found any fingerprints on that hammer. Locked apartment, loud argument, and a murder weapon left at the scene. And nine of the jurors couldn't see past the fact that Storrs' prints weren't on the murder weapon, as if he couldn't have wiped them off. Reasonable doubt bit us in the ass today."

"So what now?" Ben asked.

Stone didn't answer the question immediately. "And Reverend Storrs. I have to say, she was a very good witness for the defense. The jurors ate that omen shit up."

"Are you going to try him again?"

Stone leaned back in his chair. "That was Detective Johnston on the phone. He's a little miffed because we're going to go back to square one on this one. Said he's got new cases to deal with. But I don't care. We're going to start from scratch. It's going to be like we just discovered the body. No preconceived notions. And if after that we're led back to Deacon Storrs. Then yes, we'll try his ass again."

***

The meeting was to take place at one of Duraleigh's regional libraries. The one located near Martha's Village, an eclectic collection of knick-knack stores and clothing and jewelry boutiques. Locally it was known as "the old white folks'" side of town. Ironically, Marks Library had been named after Roosevelt Marks, the city's first and so far only, black mayor. Marks died in 1983, ten years after leaving office.

The library itself was a cozy little place and was; as libraries tended to be, full of books, periodicals, and a heaping dose of quiet. A prudish looking woman with pale skin and hair coiled into a knot directed him to the periodicals which were near the children's section. He grabbed the latest Time magazine and then took a seat at a table, positioning himself so that he would have a good view of the library's entrance.

After about five minutes, a voice belonging to one of the special agents stationed across the street filtered in through his Bluetooth and advised him that the undercover agent was on his way inside the library and had not been followed.

He spotted the young UC as soon as he walked inside and walked toward the children's section. Procedure called for him to do exactly that, then read a book or work on the computer for about twenty minutes or so, before he was to casually head over to the periodicals where he would rendezvous with an agent for a briefing. Ordinarily that agent would not have been Ram. But things had changed drastically since the start of the investigation of Father's Disciples.

Ram watched as the UC sat down by a computer terminal, dropping his book bag down by his feet. He was a very convincing hood-kid. He projected the confidence and arrogance of a young thug. He was wearing an oversized pair of baggy blue jeans and an extra-large white T-shirt with cartoonish lettering on the front—RIP Cain. His Air-Force-Ones sneakers were a spotless white and fashionably unlaced. Ram could even see the sparkles from the small diamond studs he sported in each ear. Everything was perfect, except of course for one thing, which was the reason why the library had been selected as a rendezvous point in the first place. Kids from his hood rarely, if ever, visited Marks Public Library, making it highly unlikely that anyone from the world he'd successfully infiltrated would witness the clandestine meeting between Jamal "Prodegee" Morris and Acting Special Agent-In-Charge Tom Ram.

Special Agent Cedric David waited exactly twenty-two minutes before he turned off the computer terminal, picked up his book bag, and walked over to the periodicals. When he reached the section of newspapers and magazines, he took a moment to survey the area. There were three tables in the section, all able to accommodate up to four persons. Two of the tables were already at full capacity with children trying to stifle giggles and avoid the librarian's glare while pretending to read a book or magazine. A long figure sat at the remaining one.

Agent David quietly set his book bag down at Ram's table and then sat one chair down and across from Ram. He pulled out a textbook, notebook, and a pencil from his book bag, and then placed the book bag in the chair next to the one he was sitting in. He opened both the notebook and textbook. He pretended to read from the textbook while writing in the notebook. He looked the part of a studious hood rat. After a few moments, while outwardly appearing to focus on his writing and studying, he spoke in a hushed voice. "Sir, I wasn't expecting you. What happened to Thompson?"

Ram's gaze never left the Time. "We've had to pare down a bit. It seems we have a leak somewhere in the Bureau."

"Serious?"

"Very. But we think we've found the source. You say you've got another possible connect?"

"Yeah, his name is Maalik Jackson. He's eleven."

"What does he know?"

"Probably not as much as Cain. Maalik was newly inducted, about four weeks ago. At first he wouldn't talk to me about it. But Cain's death really shook him. He's scared."

"What has he shared so far?"

"He said he witnessed someone being tortured to death."

Ram shuffled uncomfortably in his chair and turned a few pages of his magazine. "Where?"

"In the basement at Fathers House. That is also where

the kids meet and are told where to get their supply of drugs to sell." David glanced up at him and then back at his textbook. "Fathers House is as we'd suspected. Except not all the boys are dealing in drugs. It's only the basement boys."

"The basement boys?"

"Yeah, it's what we call the boys sent to Fathers House's basement for punishment. Uncle Mayo, that's what Mayo Father prefers that we call him, basically divides the boys up essentially between the do-gooders and the ne'er-do-wells, at least as far as he sees them. If you've consistently gotten in trouble at school or with the law he sends you for a brief stint in the basement as some sort of punishment. Usually it's about a two week stay. You basically live in the basement for those two weeks, sleeping, eating, everything. Every moment of every day, except when you're at school."

"What goes on down there?" Ram asked.

"I don't know. Other than the torture session he saw, Maalik won't talk about it. And with Cain any talk of the basement and drugs had been off limits. I've tried to get myself sent down there. I've acted up in school, played hooky. Even let Miss Helm find some weed in my belongings. But Uncle Mayo won't send me down. He says I'm too smart. I think it had something to do with Cain. Now that Cain's dead. We'll see."

"Who does Mayo Fathers think he is," Ram asked incredulously, "Some sort of god?"

"Seems that way."

"And Mayo Fathers is the only one who determines who gets sent to the basement?"

"From what I can tell, yeah," David answered.

"Does he supply them with the drugs? Does he physically give it to them?"

David looked off for a moment and then looked directly at Ram. "It's possible. But I don't think so. They get the drugs from a different location. I don't think any drugs are ever at the house."

Ram frowned at him, before casting a cautious glance about the room. No one was paying any mind to the whispered confab between the hood kid and the middle-aged white man. "You don't think Mayo handles the drugs?"

David shook his head, and then started back writing in his notebook. "As far as I can tell, Uncle Mayo's only involvement with the basement boys is to sentence them to it. His house routine pretty much stays the same while the boys are down there, and when they get out, Uncle Mayo spends less time with them, not more. It's like from that moment on, they're perpetually in his doghouse. He doesn't treat them badly or abuse them or anything like that. But his attitude towards them definitely changes. It's like he's less connected to them. I don't think he's the one supplying them with drugs, but I'm working to confirm that."

Again looking at the Time magazine, Ram nodded. "But you've got to be careful. We've lost contact with our other UC."

"There are two of us?" David asked.

Ram, feeling eyes on him, looked to his right. The prudish librarian had moved to a nearby computer terminal and was looking over the top of her glasses in their direction. He nodded silently in response to her unspoken request for lowered voices. He turned back to the Time magazine, pretending to read it as he spoke just above a whisper. "Our plan was to use two agents to try to infiltrate Father's Disciples from the bottom. It was you going in through Fathers House and a special agent named Tony Burns who was to get in through the street side. We didn't want either of you to know about the other. If one of you was compromised, he wouldn't be able to jeopardize the other."

"Makes sense," David said. "But what happened to

Burns?"

"We're not sure exactly. About a month ago he failed to show for a briefing. And we've since lost all communication with him."

David looked at the textbook and then at his notebook. He started writing again, before suddenly stopping to look up and away as if he was considering some challenging problem. Ram knew that he was, actually, although not of the educational variety. Finally, he asked, "Could Burns have been your leak?"

It was a good question and a possibility that Ram had already considered and dismissed because the leak had to have access to the FBI's computer system, a feat which could only be accomplished by using a FBI-issued PC or laptop. For obvious security reasons, the Bureau cut all physical ties to its UCs. "We ruled him out,' he said without going into any further detail.

But he didn't have to, David answered his own question. "Right, it would have been impossible for him to get into the system while undercover. What do you think happened to him?"

Ram said, "I have a few theories, none of which bode well for our case. But we're hopeful he'll turn up."

"What's his undercover name?"

"Nas Robinson," Ram said.

David dropped his pencil and looked off to the side. "Damn," he said under his breath.

"What?" Ram asked.

David looked mournfully back at the special agent-in-charge. "He's dead."

***

When the briefing was over, Ram remained seated at the table for about twenty minutes after Special Agent David/Jamal Morris/Prodegee had left the library. Ram felt a tinge of guilt. He was sending a child back into a den of wolves. But then again, David was no ordinary child.

That was what a former colleague of his—Sandy Dale from his Bureau recruitment days had told him seven years ago when she'd first brought the then eleven year old David to see him. "He's a child prodigy," she'd explained. "He already has an Ivy League law degree." At that time Ram had been nine years removed from recruitment, having moved into the area of counter-intelligence/terrorism where he had already received a couple of commendations, including one signed by the Director himself. "It shows he's bright. Okay, extremely bright," Ram had told her. "But eleven is eleven."

With an understanding look, Sandy replied, "That's why I brought him here to see you because that's what they'll say. They'll dismiss him without even bothering to see him or talk to him. But you won't make that mistake. You've been involved in recruiting. You've seen the diamonds-in-the-rough. The ones who couldn't pass the eyeball test for shit. But you'd developed a knack for finding young men and women who go on to make excellent field agents. You were willing to look past the exterior. That's really all I'm asking that you do now. Talk with him."

Ram had talked with David, quickly finding out that Dale had been right. The young genius was no ordinary child. And it wasn't just the accelerated brain power. The boy had spoken with an authority well beyond his years. In fact, the youngster had pitched himself, outlining clearly why he should be allowed to join the Bureau. Ram had been enthralled and soon found himself making the same sell-job on the Director that Dale and the lad had made on him.

"He's not your ordinary child," he'd told the FBI director, echoing Sandy's words. "He has an advanced Ivy League degree. He's a child prodigy who wants to become something other than the next Beethoven."

The Director had listened patiently and when Ram had finished, he said predictably, "He's eleven. And he looks eight."

"I know," Ram had said. "But despite tough felony penalties for dealing drugs on or around school grounds, elementary-aged children are a fast growing segment of both drug-dealing and using. What we've been doing thus far basically amounts to chipping around the perimeter, and it hasn't exactly been wholly effective. We need to think outside the box here." He paused, and then added, "And a child shall lead them." It was cornball, meant to lighten the moment. But it somehow worked. The Director seemed to soften. So Ram had continued, basically and unabashedly plagiarizing the impassioned plea David had made to him. And it'd sold, working just as well on the Director as it had on him, even sans David's cited examples of the success of wunderkinds in the arts, and other professions, particularly in the athletic realms of swimming, golf, and tennis. Cedric David was soon undergoing FBI training at Quantico. Though he wouldn't officially become a Bureau employee until he reached the age of sixteen, the Director did waive the requirement that he be at least twenty-three years of age before he could become a special agent.

Ram glanced around the library. Children were reading, poking each other, talking amongst themselves, smiling, being children. The Bureau was employing a different strategy in trying to take down Father's Disciples. A strategy that involved cutting the syndicate's feet off while simultaneously chopping off its head. It was a gamble using Special Agent David to try to bring down a ruthless drug syndicate. It was, after all, his first major assignment. But when it came to trying to protect the innocence of children, all options needed to be on the table.

Chapter 14

Father's office was tucked in a corner of the basement of the funeral home. It was an almost barren room. Its only furniture was a large, walnut desk, and a single, low sitting, armless chair in front of it. The white, cement walls were bare except for the forty inch flat screen television hanging on the wall behind the desk. Noticeably absent was a chair behind the desk. The desktop was polished, showroom ready. It was void of any signs of having ever been used. It had no frayed edges. There were no stacks of papers. No container of pens. No pictures of loved ones.

Caleb shifted uncomfortably in the low sitting chair. Although he'd spoken with Father on a semi-regular basis throughout the years, he hadn't actually seen the man in over ten years. A sinking feeling mired in his gut as if he'd been summoned to the principal's office. Thirty minutes after the time he'd been told to be there, the flat screen came to life.

A computer-generated image of a human head appeared on the screen. It reminded Caleb of the old television series, Max Headroom. He looked curiously at the image, wondering, What gives? Oddly, the image seemed to glare back at him. After a moment, it spoke. "Did you get the information on Sarah Leeson?" The voice was stilted, computer-enhanced. But there was no mistaking who it belonged to. It was Father.

"Why this setup, Father?" Caleb asked. "I haven't seen you in a while. I was hoping…"

Father cut him off. "Did you get the information I requested?"

"No. The file has been firewalled. I can't get in."

"Is that standard procedure?"

Caleb bit his lower lip and slowly shook his head. "I don't know. I don't normally backdoor my way into cases I'm not directly involved in. But if a firewall's there now, it means they suspect a breach."

"Can they trace it back to you?"

"I don't know."

The computer head flickered across the screen. "Is there any other way to find out if the feds have Sarah Leeson?"

"Not outside of personally asking one of the agents involved with the case."

"What do the feds know about Father's Disciples?"

Caleb stared hard at the screen. The old man apparently wanted a summary of the information he'd already provided. The Leeson woman's disappearance was obviously very troubling. He wondered what she knew. "Well," he began slowly. "According to the file, at least from the last time I've been able to access it, the information they have at this point is very sketchy. They suspect Father's Disciples is a high powered crime syndicate operating up and down the eastern seaboard. They believe the syndicate is headed by Mayo Fathers and is being run out of Fathers House and Fathers Funeral Home. They also think McCain and Bledsoe are part of the power structure. They suspect some type of link between the syndicate and Duraleigh's city hall, including the mayor, the police department, and the district attorney's office. They suspect that children as young as seven and eight years old are being recruited into the syndicate through Fathers House. Other than the suspected head of the syndicate, and a few believed-to-be members, it's not known how the syndicate is organized or exactly how many members it has. There were five potential witnesses. Two were convicted felons, Billy Daniels and Nathan Smith. Separately and unknown to the other, each had contacted the Bureau through their attorneys. It was through them that it was first learned of a possible link between the Duraleigh police and Father's Disciples. Both convicts were cooperating and were trying to negotiate lighter sentences, when each was killed in separate prison incidents, seemingly unrelated to Father's Disciples, but highly suspicious nevertheless.

"The other three witnesses lived in Duraleigh. Cindy Storrs approached the Bureau. Both Calvin Leeson and Cain Simmons were identified by an undercover agent. All three were killed in separate incidents seemingly unrelated to Father's Disciples. Storrs was killed in a domestic dispute by her husband. But a jury recently deadlocked on that theory. She claimed to be an accountant for the syndicate and that she had records of how its money was laundered. She claimed to have knowledge of all the public officials on the syndicate's payroll, including high ranking officials in city hall and the district attorney's office. She also claimed to have an outline of the syndicate's organizational chart. She was killed before she could deliver on the promised goods.

"Should I rehash Leeson and Simmons?"

"No," Father said.

Caleb leaned back in his chair. "Well, that's it then. At least the part of it that was in the file through last week. I don't know when the firewall was set up. I hadn't tried to access the file again until after you called me Wednesday night. And of course I was never able to find out the identity of the undercover agent who I suspect had approached both Leeson and Simmons."

Father said, "We've learned the identity of the undercover agent."

"How?"

"Torture. We had him in our custody. We'd thought he was an outsider trying to encroach on my territory. He confessed his true identify just before he died."

"Who was he?" Caleb asked.

"His undercover name was Nas Robinson. But actually he was Special Agent Anthony Burns. Did you know him?"

"Yeah," Caleb said. "He was a good guy." He paused. "If the Bureau learns of his death, they're not going to stop until Father's Disciples is wiped off the face of the earth."

Father laughed. His computer voice sounded packaged and unnatural. "If the feds want Father's Disciples, they can have Father's Disciples."

Caleb had no idea what he meant, and at the moment, quite frankly didn't care. He felt glued to the low chair, unable to move. The television screen with Father's computer head still visible seemed a thousand miles above his head. Tony Burns had been a friend, and Caleb, through both his actions and inactions, had contributed to Tony's death. He'd always understood that his choices affected others, albeit indirectly. But Tony, that was a direct hit.

Chapter 15

The normally crowded and intensely busy Duraleigh Police
Department was in the midst of an unusual pocket of calm.
It was what the officers likened to being in the eye of the
storm where for a brief time the phones weren't ringing
incessantly, the number of drop-ins by people either with or
without valid reasons had ebbed, and there weren't a
million little emergencies all begging for attention at once.
It was a moment to be enjoyed and savored like the last
piece of pie, because when it was over—it was over, and all
hell was likely to break loose at any given moment.

Leo Johnston looked indolently through the Storrs file.
As part of his own personal middle-finger at the D.A.'s
office after yesterday's conversation with the chief
prosecutor, he'd purposely delayed even thinking about the
Storrs murder case or the deadlocked jury. As a result, it
wasn't until now, late Thursday afternoon, that he finally
got around to fulfilling Jeff Stone's bullshit request for him
and Roberts to...what was that again, start the case from
scratch.

His start from scratch would be a cursory review of his
initial interview of Deacon Storrs. He found it downright
insulting that the People had not only blown what should
have been an easily winnable case, but also had the
audacity to request him and Roberts to rework the case
from the absolute beginning. "As if you'd just discovered
the body," Stone had said. Instead of reviewing his own
failed tactics, Stone appeared to be laying the blame for the
loss at the feet of the detectives.

Johnston, a twenty-two year veteran of the police
department, had a perfectly symmetrical rotund body that
looked as if he'd swallowed an inflated balloon. He was

wearing a well-fitted dark blue suit that moved where he moved and gave where he gave. A hint of woodsy-scented cologne misted about him. He was sitting at his desk in the medium-sized cubby area he shared with his partner, Roberts. Their semi-circular desks were situated at opposite ends of the cubicle and were, as was their body dimensions, a study in contrasts. Detective Joel Roberts was lint-thin and his desk was, as usual, an unfettered mess with papers, files, picture frames, and all types of family memorabilia jockeying for space atop it. His side of the cubicle's walls were stick-pinned with various sticky notes, several sheets of papers with listed phone numbers, and yet more family pictures. His limited shelf space was overcrowded with a directory, an English-to-Spanish dictionary, and several books, including one on North Carolina Laws as well as one entitled Tactical Homicide Investigations. Johnston, on the other hand, generally kept his desk clutter-free with only his laptop and maybe one or two of his current files getting any desk-space at a given time. His side of the cubicle's walls was bare. His shelves were empty. There were no pictures of any sort. Not of family. Not of himself.

With a pair of headphones hugging his ears, he put the Storrs interview DVD into his laptop's D-drive. From the menu, he considered a moment before selecting the first frame— may as well start his cursory review of the video at the beginning.

With the video rolling, he leaned back in the swivel chair, interlocking his stubby fingers behind his head. He plopped his meaty legs across each other atop his desk next to the Storrs file. He heard his voice filtering through the headphone, identifying himself and Deacon Storrs, and then citing the interview's date and time.

"Are you aware this interview is being recorded?" he was asking Storrs on the video. Only the back of Johnston's wide body could be seen on camera as the lens had been focused mainly on Storrs.

A small tape recorder had been placed in front of Storrs who was sitting opposite of Johnston at a small rectangular table. He was facing the video camera that had been installed on the back wall behind and above Johnston. Storrs looked haggard and in need of a shave. He ran his hands through his bushy lot of hair, and then used the back of one of those hands to wipe his running nose. "Yeah," he answered, dropping his head.

"Is it being done so with your permission?

Again, his answer was a short clipped, "Yeah."

Johnston, hoping his voice sounded sympathetic, said "I am sorry about your wife. But can you tell me what happened?"

Storrs lifted his head, but still mostly avoided eye contact. "I don't know. I was asleep on the couch. I got up around six in the morning and went into the bedroom where I found her. She was…she…," he gasped. His head flopped backward. "Oh my God!"

"Take your time Mr. Storrs. Can I get you anything? Some water? Coffee?"

After a moment, Storrs sniffled and appeared to regain his composure. "Some water, thanks."

Johnston got up and moved off camera. Seconds later, the sound of water being poured into a glass could be heard. Johnston reappeared, sliding a glass of water past the tape recorder, toward Storrs.

Storrs grabbed the glass and held it wearily for a moment before taking a sip.

"Okay," Johnston said. "You wake up. You go into the bedroom and find your wife. In what condition did you find her?"

Storrs put the glass down, and then sucked in a deep breath, slowing exhaling it. He shook his head as if trying to ward away the memory. "I hadn't noticed at first. I started to lean over her, intending to kiss her. Then I saw that she had her head under the covers. My wife never sleeps that way. She never puts her head under the covers. I thought, man she must've really been mad at me. Then the outline of her body under the sheets caught my attention. It was positioned kinda funny. It was crazy, but for a moment that twister game came to mind. Then my heart got heavy. I started heaving. I couldn't catch my breath. I slowly pulled the covers back." He gasped again. "Blood. There was blood all over the bed." He bit his fist.

There was silence on the video as Johnston sat watching and waiting for Storrs to continue. He was observing Storrs as he had from the moment he'd arrived at the crime scene. It was no secret that husbands and wives were historically the primo suspects in the murder of their spouses. And Johnston himself knew the murderous rage someone could feel toward a person that they'd once promised to cherish and hold until death did them part. But in Deacon Storrs' case, historical reasoning wasn't needed to make the husband the odds-on favorite. His own words and actions were doing just fine.

Per Deacon as told to the murder scene's first responders, he'd found his wife's body in their marital bed. Per at least two of his neighbors, he and Cindy Storrs had had a ferocious argument the night before. Per also the first responders, Deacon Storrs had to unlock the front door to let them in. There had been no signs of forced entry into the house. Not through the front door. Not through any window in the third floor apartment which were only two—one in the master bedroom where the body was found and the one in the living room. And the frigging cherry on top, the de facto ace in the pocket was that the obvious murder weapon—a bloodied hammer was found at the scene.

At the time of the interview, Johnston was sure that the hammer would come back with Deacon Storrs' prints all over it, though it eventually hadn't. But what he'd wanted during the interview process was Storrs' confession and quick closure to the obvious case. He'd wanted an end to

Storrs' charade as the grief-stricken husband. For once, he would have liked to hear the husband say, you know what, the bitch just nagged me one time too many. She finally crossed the line. She pushed me over the edge.

So, Johnston had waited, truly hoping to hear something along those very lines. It was ten minutes before Storrs had spoken again and when he had, confession had been the furthest thing from his mind.

"I don't know what could have happened," he began slowly. He looked up at Johnston. His facial expression was one of wretchedness and confusion as if he really didn't have a clue as to who had bludgeoned his wife to death. Johnston hadn't initially pegged the old boy as an actor. But apparently, Storrs was far more gifted than the detective had given him credit for and no doubt far more prepared. The ignorance defense wasn't one Johnston would've necessarily used for himself if he'd decided to kill his old battle-ax of a wife instead of divorcing her, but it seemed Storrs was willing to give that dubious defense, the good old college try.

"Okay," Johnston said. "Let me ask a question. You said you went into the bedroom where you found your wife," he paused a moment as Storrs nodded affirmatively. "Do you and your wife normally sleep apart?"

The question seemed to bring about more anguish. Storrs' head dropped again. Then he slowly raised it, looking at Johnston squarely. "No, no we don't. We had an argument early in the evening. I got mad and left the house. I got back kind of late. I'd been drinking and just decided to sleep on the couch."

"What had the argument been about?"

"I'd rather not say."

"I kinda rather you did."

Storrs sighed. "I don't know. Usual stuff. Money."

"Alright, money. Too much? Not enough?" What?"

For the first time Storrs looked agitated. "What is this

about? My wife's been murdered. You guys should be out
trying to find the killer, not harassing me about…" He
dropped his head again. Judging from the jerky movements
his body was making, he was either crying or going for the
Oscar.

Johnston waited, and then after several moments, said,
"I'm sorry that you view this as an inconvenience to you, or
maybe even unnecessary. But trust me; I've been doing this
sort of work for over twenty years. This is a necessary evil,
so to speak. But rest assured that even as I sit here talking
to you that there are men out trying to find your wife's
killer."

Eventually, Storrs appeared calm again. "I'm sorry."
He hesitated a moment and then started talking slowly,
barely above a whisper as if he was divulging a secret.
"Lately, we'd argued more and more about money. But,
we'd been doing okay. You know. We weren't in any
serious debt. We had a little saved and were on track to get
a house. But Cindy thought things were moving too slow.
She wanted bigger things, nicer things, and she didn't want
to wait for them. I'm a mechanic. I work for Jackson's
Mechs. It's a chain of mechanic shops owned by Albert
Jackson. I make pretty decent money. And Albert was even
considering me for a partnership. You know, for some time
in the future. But like I said, Cindy wasn't a wait-for-the-
future type of gal."

"She started to nag you about bringing in more
money," Johnston interjected.

"No. She didn't need to nag me about that because she
was already bringing it in. Since she was the one handling
our finances, I hadn't noticed it at first. But then I started
seeing things. Small things at first, a new coffee table, new
end tables. Some new dishes. Stuff like that. She'd tell me
that she got a deal at a consignment shop or flea market or
something. So I'd let it slide. Wouldn't press it. She was
happy and there was peace in the house for a while. But

then her wardrobe started to look too good. I mean I'm not a fashion expert, and I couldn't tell you with any certainty the cost of a stitch of women's clothing, but she was starting to look expensive, more expensive than a store cashier and wife of a mechanic should look."

Johnston asked, "Did you ask her where she was getting the money?"

"No," Storrs answered. "Not at first. Ironically, it wasn't until she bought a gift for me that I said anything at all. It was a fifty inch HDTV. It was in the living room when I got home from work. Man when I saw that TV, I just about lost it. I demanded that she show it to me. Show me the credit card I assumed she'd secretly gotten. She said there was no credit card. Said she paid for it in cash. I asked her where she got that kind of cash. She refused to tell me. Said it was none of my business. My wife now is talking to me like that. When she said that, all kinds of things started going through my head, and I wanted to hit her. I admit that. I started thinking about sugar daddies and some fool beating my time. And I wanted to…but I didn't. But she knew I'd wanted to. And it scared her. It scared her so bad that she fessed up and told me everything. But what she told me just didn't make sense. I couldn't wrap my head around it. She…" Abruptly, the sound clipped off and the screen went to black.

Johnston sat up straight. His feet dropped to the floor, pulling the headphones off his ears. He pulled out the headphone plug and hit a key to fast forward the video, which only served to bring up additional black screen. He stopped it and hit the reverse button, speeding back over previously viewed blackness until he came to the point in the video where picture and sound had suddenly ended. He hit play and the same scenario played out again. Storrs saying "I couldn't wrap my head around it. She…," and again there was no sound, just blackness.

"That's just great," he mumbled to himself. He popped

out the D-drive tray and retrieved the DVD. He studied it, turning it over in his hand. He wasn't an expert on DVDs, but this one didn't appear damaged in anyway. There weren't any scratch marks, at least not noticeable ones. He returned the DVD to the D-drive and replayed it, fast forwarding to the spot of the stoppage. It was the same thing. The end of his interview with Deacon Storrs was gone.

Again he took the DVD out of the laptop. Except this time, he returned it to the jacket folder on the inside of the Storrs file. He flipped through the folder's contents and found the interview transcript.

"Well I be damned," he said when he realized that the part missing from the video was also missing from the transcript. What in the hell was going on?

At that moment, Roberts walked in and went straight to his own desk. He was carrying a cup and a box of Bojangles chicken, the smell of which stirred Johnston's stomach.

"Joel, I think somebody's been tampering with the Storrs file," Johnston said.

Roberts sat down at his desk and took out a chicken breast. He bit into it, and then while chewing, said, "What do you mean tampering with?"

"The end of my interview with Deacon Storrs has been blacked out, and the corresponding part of the written transcript is also missing."

After swallowing, Roberts said, "I'm sure there's a logical explanation for that."

"Yeah? What would that be?" Johnston asked.

"I'll riddle you that if you riddle me why you care all of a sudden. The prosecutors fucked up. Remember? Wasn't that what you were pissed about yesterday? Because they wanted us to revisit it. Or scratch something or other." He shook his head and took another bite of his chicken. "Geez, if someone had tampered with that file, it sure didn't hurt that guy any."

Johnston was silent for a moment. Joel was right. If the file had been tampered with in hopes of increasing the odds of Storr's conviction, it had failed miserably. If that was in fact why it had been tampered with in the first place. Finally, he said, "I guess you're right." He closed the Storrs file. "But humor me anyway. What's the logical explanation here?"

"Well speaking logically, let me ask you. Have you ever viewed that entire video?"

"No, I can't say that I have."

"Exactly. Think about it. When do we ever view those things? We do the interviews, take our notes, and most times we just use the video as a backup."

"What's your point?"

"That there could have been a malfunction or problem with the video from the start, a problem that could have been present when we sent the video over for transcription."

"Right," Johnston said, following Roberts line of reasoning. "Meaning the transcriber would have only written what she'd seen on the video, meaning the mismatching transcript is no evidence that the file had been tampered with. Okay. That works for me. I'll chalk this up to a technical glitch. I'm going to table the scratching for now. Already I've spent far more time on this than I'd intended to. The smell of that chicken has reminded me I'm hungry."

Roberts sipped from his cup. "I doubt anything ever has to remind you of that."

"Very funny little man. I'm going home. Probably grab me something to eat on the way. I'll be back in a couple of hours unless something comes up."

Roberts waved him off, and then took another bite of chicken.

He'd eaten inside the restaurant, feeling somewhat silly at having made it a point to say to Roberts that he would grab something to eat on the way home. As if Roberts didn't know—he was a detective after all. Although it wouldn't take a detective to figure out that Lt. Leo Johnston preferred eating his chicken and biscuit amongst strangers to eating them alone in his empty house. It was a sad state of affairs when he thought about it. Big Leo Johnston, the very one who unapologetically had always spent more time at work than home, and who had, for at least nineteen of the twenty-two years he'd been married to her, said the meanest, vilest things about his wife. Sometimes he'd spoken in jest, but more often than not he'd said the words with the sincerest wish that they would take on the same physical capabilities as sticks and stones.

But truth be told, he missed her. And even if it wasn't the kind of missing born from a loving place, he still felt it nonetheless. He'd always told himself that he couldn't wait for the day of his release, the day that he and his battle-ax could finally put an end to the charade. They'd known three years and two children into their union that it was ill-fated, and that the two of them weren't compatible. It was funny, he'd thought often in the three months since the divorce was finalized, but neither of them had actually ever spoken those words. Nor had they ever had an agreement, spoken or otherwise, to stay together for the benefit of their two boys. But that was what they'd done. It was but two short months after their youngest had graduated from high school. She waited for Johnston to complete his twelve-hour shift and arrive home in his usual nonchalance.

"I'm leaving," she'd said in a matter-of-fact tone.

He'd simply said okay just as casually, as if she'd said that she was on her way out to buy a carton of milk.

He kept the house. She took about everything of any importance in it, including the king-sized bed that amazingly they'd continued to sleep in together all the years of their loveless union. He'd likened their agreement to her getting to eat all the filling out of a cherry pie, leaving him with only the crust. The winner of such an arrangement depended upon whether one liked the cherry filling or the crust. Perhaps it was him, perhaps it was her, or perhaps it was both or neither of them. In any event, it was done.

What he hadn't counted on, in all the years of riding out his marital sentence, was the jolt he felt from the rapid reduction in speed from the family-fueled sixty mph to the decidedly pedestrian zero mph of a newly divorced and overweight bachelor.

As he'd sat in Bojangles, eating his meal, he'd felt somewhat relieved by the emergence of reservations concerning the Storrs file. Any other time, he would have been pissed at himself for even remotely thinking about a case that had so recently been out of his mind and sitting comfortably closed. But now, any thoughts were more welcomed than the thoughts of self-pity. And he much preferred his detective voice holding court in his mind, instead of the sound of his cynical self, irritably repeating over and over, "Be careful what you ask for because you just might get it. Be careful what you ask for because you just might get it."

His reservations concerning the Storrs file were quite simple really, and were most likely nothing to get his dander up about. Roberts' theory about the file was just as good as any and was probably correct, he supposed. But he still couldn't help but think that the file had somehow been tampered with, though he couldn't imagine by whom and for what reason. And Roberts had been right to ask him why he cared anyway. Because at the end of the day it was only Storrs' words that were missing and Storrs was ultimately guilty as hell. No harm, no foul, right?

Except that something didn't seem right.

He'd considered calling Jeff Stone to see if Stone still had the copy of the interview video that he Johnston had sent to the D.A.'s office. But then, he'd decided against that. If the tampering had been done before the copy had been made, then Stone would only have what he Johnston had, half an interview and half blackness. Besides, welcomed reservations or not, at the moment he wasn't feeling any love toward the D.A.'s office.

Back in his car, he picked up his cell phone, dialed the jail and was told that Storrs had made bail the day before. He looked at his dash clock. It was seven-thirty. It wasn't too late to pay the newly released murderer a visit.

As he drove to Storrs' apartment, he tried to pick up from memory the part of the video that was now missing. However, his mind was not as accurate and user-friendly as a DVD player. He couldn't go to the exact point in his memory bank where the video had abruptly ended. He couldn't even now recall the gist of what Storrs had been trying to say. At that time, he'd already made up his mind that the so-called grieving husband had been trying to feed him a load of crap, and thus he'd tuned the wife-killer out. If a defense attorney could've read his mind then as well as now, then he knew the counselor's next words were sure to be, "Ah ha, I knew it! A rush to judgment!"

But he was unapologetic for any of his premeditated findings of guilt. Partly because he understood that he was only human and that as such he was occasionally susceptible to forming early opinions and making snap judgments. To fault him for doing so would be to fault him for being human. But mostly it was because he had over twenty years experience being a homicide detective and he trusted that experience to temper any human tendency to rely only on the initial take of any situation. But any homicide investigator worth his salt would be foolish to totally dismiss his or her initial gut feelings because more often than not, those feelings would be spot-on.

At Storrs' apartment complex, he parked next to a vehicle with a dented driver-side quarter panel, missing left rear wheel, and an orange sticker warning of the vehicle's looming tow date stuck to its windshield.

He knocked on Storrs' apartment door and waited. There was no answer, but he noticed a very slight pressing on the door. He took out his badge and held it up to the peephole.

After another moment, the door opened slowly. A young, skinny girl, perhaps in her late teens or early twenties stood before him in the doorway. She was carrying one toddler in her arms while another one draped her leg. "He ain't here," she said.

"Who ain't here?" Johnston asked.

"My man Billy, that is who you're here for, ain't it?"

Johnston smiled. "No, I'm not. I'm looking for Deacon Storrs."

The girl seemed relieved and almost managed a smile herself, but just as her lips turned up to form it, her attention was quickly diverted to the toddler draping her leg. Evidently the little one's fingernails were digging into her leg. She slapped down at his hands. "BJ, I've got to do something about your nails. You're piercing my skin." BJ dropped his hands and looked sheepishly up at his mother.

Both children, Johnston noted, seemed well behaved and remarkably close in age and looks. "Twins?" he asked.

"Yes," the girl answered. "Fraternal. One boy, one girl."

"They're adorable."

This time she managed a full smile. "Thank you," she said. "But, I don't know a Deacon Storrs."

Of course, he thought to himself. It was a rented apartment. Storrs had been locked up a year while he awaited trial. "He used to live in this apartment," he said. "How long have you been living here?"

"About six months," she answered. "You can probably

ask Mr. Wilson down the breezeway. Seems he's been living here since forever. He probably knows him." She pointed him in the direction of Wilson's apartment, and then closed her door.

Murphy Wilson hadn't quite made since forever, but he had been living in his apartment over twenty-five years. He was eighty-seven years old. He and his wife had moved in the apartment after his retirement from the postal service. The former homeowners no longer wanted the responsibility of maintaining a property, and neither wanted to live solely amongst old people. His wife had been dead for ten years now and he still missed her dearly. He told Johnston all of this in nearly an hour of conversation.

Johnston suspected that the old man was lonely and wanted the company, and so he obliged him, feeling glad that he did so. Hearing Wilson talk about how much he'd loved his wife and how much he'd missed her, actually made Johnston feel less lonely.

Wilson had also told him where he could find Deacon Storrs. It was now a little too late to go over there, he decided. But tomorrow was another day.

Chapter 16

His boys were coming home.

He sat up on the edge of the bed, letting the realization sink in. He'd received the great news from April who'd called him from the hospital. "They've both reached their target weights of four pounds," she'd said excitedly, basically paraphrasing what the doctor had informed her. She'd added, "Now is a good time to transition them into their new home."

It was great news and yes, he was happy. But to be honest, there was a touch of uncertainty mixed in with the happiness. His boys were coming home. Two beautiful new beings that were going to be completely dependent upon him for their mere survival. They were coming to his house, their home. The hospital was honestly going to let that happen? Shouldn't they know better? They were really going to entrust him with the care of two newborns? Two premature newborns? Didn't they know that his boys would need no less than the steady hand of an experienced caregiver? Of which he definitely was not. And neither was April for that matter, he added. He looked back at her. She lay still, comfortably enjoying the sleep of confidence and nonchalance. And why not? She could no doubt call upon natural motherly instincts that were probably present in all women, ready to be activated at a moment's notice when and if they desired to call upon them. He leaned back and pecked her on the check. She did not stir. He kissed her lightly again on the forehead. She shuffled slightly under the covers, but stayed comfortably in the throes of peaceful, unworried sleep. Rub it in, he mouthed silently as he got up and left the bedroom.

He walked down the hall to the nursery and flicked on

the room's overhead light. He looked around the room and then rested his eyes on the two cribs that lined the back wall. He'd spent a whole Sunday afternoon putting those cribs together. Yes, he'd put them together. Sure, he'd merely followed the directions. But still, putting them together hadn't been a simple task. The instructions had suggested that two people should assemble the cribs. Yet, he'd done so by himself. By himself! That was something, wasn't it? Sure, it was. It's what men did. It's what fathers did. They put things together. He began to feel a vestige of usefulness. Maybe putting things together could be his thing: bikes, model planes, anything at all. Maybe in his boys' eyes he'd be some sort of hero, someone who could create something, anything, out a pile of loose boards and screws. Maybe in his boys' eyes he'd be some sort of MacGyver. Not that they'd know who MacGyver was. Still, he could be that guy, that put-it-together guy. April would say, "Leave that for your father. He'll put it together when he gets home." And the boys would wait patiently for him to get home and afterwards they would witness his skills at turning nothing into something— little jagged cardboard pieces into completed jigsaw puzzles, metal frames and chains into rideable bikes, a mess of wires into working videogame consoles, piles of wood into furniture, anything at all. Yep, that could be his thing. Amazingly, he began to feel a little better. Maybe this fatherhood thing would not be such a bad experience after all. No doubt it was going to take some time. But he was ready for the challenge if the twins were.

Standing just inside the nursery's entrance, he admired the room awhile longer. April had decided to decorate it in a wild animal motif. Cartoonish lions and tigers adorned the walls. A large stuffed giraffe was centered between the two cribs both of which were outfitted with animal print sheets. Cute room, he thought before turning the light off. Cute and ready to accept the Lovison home's two newest occupants.

He left the room and headed downstairs to the kitchen. He made some coffee, and then walked— cup in hand, through the living room to the front porch, grabbing his jacket from the coat closet along the way. It was the second February weekend. Despite yesterday's warm weather mirage, the southern winter was beginning to reassert itself. The air was cool, crisp and there was a thin layer of ice atop the grass. Oblivious to the cold, he sat in one of the two white rocking chairs that April had snatched from the clutches of a fellow flea market bargain seeker. He sipped his coffee, gently rocked back and forth, and thought about games of catch and talks of birds and bees.

***

The vibrating cell phone danced noisily on the nightstand. With his eyes closed, Etlzer sleepily felt around for it before snatching it up. He squinted at the little screen. It was four o'clock in the morning. The call was from Father.

"Etlzer," he said in a muffled bark.

"They have Sarah Leeson."

He sat up in the bed. He was awake now. "Confirmed?"

"Yes," Father said.

"Now what?"

"We'll do as we discussed."

Etlzer swallowed hard. "To the T?"

"To the T," Father confirmed.

Etlzer glanced over at his wife. Her face was partially covered by a night-mask. She was sleeping peacefully. A light whispery snore escaped her lips. "Is this the best way?"

"It's the only way, Governor," Father said and then he was gone.

Etlzer lay back on the bed and stared hard up at the

ceiling. "Damn," he said quietly.

Chapter 17

Monday, February 9 was a symbolically perfect day for a funeral—cold and gray.

It was two weeks and two days after Cain Simmons' untimely death and he was finally being laid to rest. The Homegoing Celebration was to take place at three o'clock at the Fathers Funeral Home chapel. At twelve-thirty, the funeral home's parking lot was already near capacity. Jim Crouch, after circling for a bit, finally found a spot near the back of the lot and backed his Honda into it.

As a veteran Duraleigh Standard reporter, this was not the first Homegoing Celebration for a black teen that Crouch had attended. The most recent one had been for thirteen year old Ebbie Lewis, who'd been struck down two months ago by a drunk driver. Crouch's resulting story, intended to humanize the victim of such a horrific, callous and totally avoidable act, had been well received and was nominated for a media award. If the information he'd received about what was supposed to take place at today's funeral was accurate, he anticipated no less than a Pulitzer.

As he watched a line of eight cars enter the parking lot and circle around looking for parking spaces, he realized that his instinct to arrive early for the funeral had been spot-on. He'd attended the erstwhile rapper's show two weeks ago and had witnessed firsthand how popular the young man had been. Today's event at the very least promised to be a shoulder to shoulder crowd.

Unable to find parking spaces, cars began lining up behind parked cars. He watched a dizzying array of teenaged boys many with gold-capped teeth, glistening earlobes, and heavily tattooed arms quickly exit the cars and head toward the entrance to the funeral home. There wasn't a suit or tie amongst the bunch. There were a few scattered collared button downs, but most wore T-shirts, a few of which had R.I.P. Cain printed across the front.

As the last of the teen mob entered the chapel, a new contingent of cars, expensive late models flowed solemnly into the parking lot. The cars sailed to the back and single filed it right in front of the last row of cars, the one in which Crouch was parked. He was boxed in, but he was in no hurry to leave. He watched as suits and ties got out of this set of cars. He snapped a couple of quick photos of them with a small zoom lens digital camera. There were a fair amount of platinum-grilled teeth and studded earlobes amongst this group. The funeral's clientele had definitely upgraded. As he grabbed his notebook and pen and got out of his Honda, he felt certain he was witnessing confirmation of the unsolicited and untraceable email he'd received last night from 'A concerned citizen,' alerting him of the forthcoming transfer of power that was to take place at some point before, during, or after the funeral, a transfer of power in a criminal outfit aka a gang. A gang that District Attorney James Etlzer less than two weeks ago had insisted did not exist in Duraleigh.

**

After the last of the mourners had filed into the funeral home's crowded chapel, Leo Johnston found a spot to stand along the back wall. Though the funeral home looked rather large and impressive from the outside, it was still somewhat of a surprise to him that it contained a chapel very much the equal in size and aesthetics of any church he'd ever known. It had a plush-looking pulpit, sizable choir stand, and about twenty rows of cushioned benches.

It appeared Cain Simmons had been a little more popular than Johnston had realized. Every nook and cranny of the chapel was crammed with mourners, an eclectic mix of young and old, and black, brown, and white. Light sniffles intermixed casually with the soft organ music that oozed from the walls.

After about five minutes, the man he was looking for—Mayo Fathers entered the chapel from a side door near the front of the building. During the past week, Fathers had proved as elusive as a leprechaun's pot of gold. Johnston watched him take a seat on the front row right next to the deceased's mother. He wore a dark-colored, Italian-looking suit that was probably worth about two months of a cop's salary.

Johnston reached into his right breast pocket and pulled out a small flash drive. He looked at it, turning it over slowly in his hand before returning it to his pocket. It had belonged to Deacon Storrs' wife Cindy. It contained figures, a lot of them. Supposedly the figures were related to Fathers Funeral Home's side businesses: money laundering for a drug syndicate and bribing public officials. There were no specific names attached to the payoffs, just incriminating abbreviations like M.O., D.A., and P. D which according to the letter Deacon Storrs had given to Johnston, stood for mayor's office, district attorney, and police department. Deacon Storrs had given the flash drive to him last week as proof that someone else had reason to want Cindy Storrs dead.

When he'd gone over to Reverend Ethel Storrs' home last week to see her son Deacon, an overwhelming feeling of calm had come across him. It was as if he knew that when the door to her home opened, he was going to get some type of revelation, a revelation that would demand to be accepted. It was unlike any feeling he'd felt before. He couldn't explain why he'd felt it then, but it almost hadn't mattered because when Deacon Storrs had opened the door and found Johnston standing there, he'd started to slam the door in the detective's face.

"No," Ethel Storrs had said when she saw what her son was about to do. "Let him in. God is still protecting you."

Deacon stepped back and allowed Johnston into the house.

"Thank you," Johnston said. "I know this visit is unexpected. But I need to ask you a few questions."

"I don't see why," Deacon said. "You won't believe my answers."

That was a fair enough statement. When Johnston had first interviewed Deacon Storrs he did believe the man was guilty as sin. And the evidence as seen through Johnston's eyes or any rational person's eyes seemed to support that rush to judgment. The battled, bloodied body, no signs of forced entry into the home, a murder weapon—though without fingerprints, it had all pointed to the same conclusion and everyone, save nine jurors, had arrived at that conclusion. "I know you probably don't believe me," Johnston said. "But I really do want to find your wife's killer."

"It's not me," Deacon said matter-of-factly.

"Well, that's why I'm here."

The house smelled like a bakery with its pleasantly fused assortment of aromas from several kinds of baked goodies.

"I have some shortbread made fresh today," Ethel Storrs said as she offered him a seat on a plastic-draped antique high back. "I'll bring it out with some coffee."

"I hope it's not a bother," Johnston said.

"Not at all," Ethel Storrs said. "I've made plenty. Now you boys sit and talk while I go fetch it." She looked at her son and tilted her head toward a fat-legged flower print couch that was also covered in plastic.

Deacon, moving with the speed and grace of a petulant child, followed his mother's direction and sat down on the couch.

"Good," Ethel Storrs said and she left the room.

"Well," Deacon said.

"Look, I can understand the reason for your hostility toward me. I get that. But it's not going to help your case now. You were not acquitted of murder. The jury was hung which means the DA can simply try the case again with twelve different people who could see the case differently. You could still end up going to prison for life."

"Or I could walk," Deacon said defiantly.

"You could," Johnston agreed. "But either way, your wife's killer would still be free."

Deacon flipped his head back and slouched back on the couch. He sighed. "There's not a whole lot to be done about that. The person responsible for my wife's murder is powerful. He's connected."

"That's why I'm here," Johnston said. "During the first interview you mentioned a person's name. When I went back to review your taped interview, that portion of the interrogation had been removed. I couldn't remember the name initially. But now I do."

"Removed, huh?" Deacon said. "Just like I said, he's connected. I'm not going to get involved in this, which was why my attorney did not bring up his name in court."

"You brought it up before," Johnston said.

"I'd just found my wife brutally beaten to death and you guys were focusing on me. I threw out another possibility. Besides, you hadn't wanted to believe me then."

"I'm listening now."

Deacon straightened up and glared at Johnston. "Before you didn't believe a word of what I said. Now, you come in here, tell me that part of my original interview has been removed, and you want me to talk about the man who has the power to doctor police evidence while it is in police custody, and to kill whomever he wants dead. Well no, I won't do that. If you want this man, you've got to get him on your own."

"What about your wife? Don't you want justice for her?"

"Getting myself or my mother killed won't bring her any justice."

Ethel Storrs came back into the room. She set the tray of shortbread and coffee down on the coffee table. "Deacon, you have something that will help Detective Johnston and you're going to give it to him." She turned and faced Johnston, looking deeply into his eyes. "I trust him."

"But Mom, these people play for keeps. You saw what they did to Cindy. I won't let that happen to you."

Still eye to eye with Johnston, she said, "Son, you know I'm not worried about any mere man. God protects me just as he protects you. We've prayed and now it's in the hands of the Father." Ten minutes of awkward silence passed, but eventually Deacon got up, left the room, and brought back the flash drive.

Cindy Storrs had spoken to her husband and mother-in-law beyond the grave. Shortly before her death, she'd given Reverend Storrs a letter which she requested be read only in the event of her death. In the letter, she revealed the existence of a flash drive she'd stored in a safe deposit box at First Merchants Bank. The letter claimed that the flash drive contained incriminating evidence against many Duraleigh public officials. The letter also warned them not to trust anyone in Duraleigh's city hall, including the police department and district attorney's office. It had been that generality of the letter that had prevented Deacon and his mother from discussing the flash drive with anyone in law enforcement. But Reverend Storrs made an exception in Johnston's case. She said she did so because they were going to have to trust someone sooner or later, and God had revealed to her that Johnston was that someone. If true, the contents on the flash drive would expose the biggest scandal in the history of the city, possibly the state. And though it didn't name any officials specifically in regards to payoffs and bribes, Johnston didn't think it would be hard to follow the money.

The same rationale behind Deacon Storrs and his mother's decision to not go to law enforcement with the flash drive was also behind Johnston's decision not to discuss its existence with any of his colleagues. Any and every one could be on the take. He decided he could trust no one and that it would be better to confront Mayo Fathers directly. If the flash drive contained an accurate account of what was going on in Duraleigh, then such a confrontation would likely bring any dirty officials right to his doorstep.

Chapter 18

Marvelous Killens had never disagreed with Father on anything. And for good reason, he never had to. Father was an absolute visionary genius. He saw things that ordinary people, such as Marvelous, were incapable of seeing. Father's thought process was on a different plane than mere mortals. It was almost extraterrestrial. It was why he was a leader and people such as Marvelous were followers. It was the natural order of things as far as Marvelous was concerned, and quite frankly, he wouldn't have it any other way.

But today he decided that Father was wrong. Dead wrong. It was blasphemous thinking for sure, the kind of thinking that could get a person killed. Hell, he was tempted to put a bullet to his own head right then and there. But it was thinking that deserved to have its day. After all, Father was getting along in years. Was it beyond the realm of possibility that he could have some mental slippage? Not much mind you, not enough to make him the equal of underlings, but just enough for him to make less than perfect decisions. Father would never admit to that. And of course, he would never have to. Marvelous would make sure of that. If necessary, he would always cover any of Father's potential shortcomings. No one would ever know if Father had lost a step.

Not even Father would ever know.

Sitting in front of the monitors in the Fathers House basement, Marvelous straightened up in his chair and glowered at the video feed coming from the chapel. As he watched all the principles in Father's plan enter the chapel, the sense of foreboding dread he'd felt earlier overcame him once again. Father's plan just didn't feel right.

Something was going to go wrong.

But there wasn't a whole lot he could do about it, sitting there in the basement. He should be in the chapel executing Father's plan, not watching it unfold on some goddamn TV. Why Father would tap Morant for such an important task was beyond his comprehension. Morant simply was not ready. The youngster was going to fuck this up, Marvelous could just feel it. Besides, the kid had already shown his greenness a month ago when he'd botched the Leeson kid's death. Surely, Father couldn't have forgotten about that. Damn it. Slippage! Why did Father have to grow old?

But Father was a genius, Marvelous repeated to himself as if reciting a mantra. He'd always seen things that others could not see. That he, Marvelous, could not see. And there was no denying that. Father had seen Marvelous' truly extraordinary gifts before Marvelous had, even before Marvelous' own father had. Maybe Father had seen that same something in Morant. And, Marvelous admitted to himself, Morant was a cold-blooded killer, which was indeed a gift. The mistakes the kid had made in the Leeson situation weren't due to squeamishness or lack of nerve. They had been purely technical mistakes. The young gun had simply been unpolished. Nothing, Marvelous realized, that a little more experience couldn't correct. This, he reasoned, could have been Father's intent all along, to gain the kid more experience in the fine art of killing. But still, for Father to do so at the expense of a beautifully crafted plan seemed uncharacteristically foolhardy. Besides, Marvelous did not trust Morant. Morant was a dirty cop. And by nature, Marvelous didn't trust any cops, clean or dirty. And he particularly didn't like anyone who was capable of swearing allegiance to two opposite sides.

Father's plan was pure genius. How else to describe a plan which essentially faked the death of an entire organization? Father called it, Operation: Self Destruct.

Elements of it he'd said had been put in place since the early days of Father's Disciples. According to Father, the downfall of any great organization, whether criminal or not, was not due simply to bad fortune, hostile takeover, or even the incompetence of its leadership at the top. As potentially devastating as these factors were, Father surmised they were not an organization's greatest threat. That, he said, was the leadership's unwavering belief that the organization itself would never fail, that it would continue to go on to infinity, which was an implausible reality. All organizations face an ending at some point in time. But it was only the ones with leadership that recognized that cardinal truth that would be able to impede the ending as long as possible, and enjoy what appeared to be everlasting prosperity.

Father said that even the leadership succession plans, which so many organizations had put in place, were not indications by their leaders of the possibility of the organizations' demise. Rather they were simply an acknowledgement of the frailty of the leaders, themselves, as human beings. These so called leaders believed that their organizations would continue on even if they had to under the stewardship of new blood at the top. It was an unwise and wholly arrogant assumption.

But Father had long declared that Father's Disciples would not make that mistake, at least not while he was at its helm. As the organization had grown in statue, power, and influence, so had his obsession with the various ways it could meet its downfall. He had contingency plans in place for hostile attempts by rival gangs, mutiny by its own rank and file members, and even though criminal enterprises rarely experienced rough financial times due to economic downturns, Father was equally prepared for such situations just the same.

But what Father was most prepared for was what he felt was the organization's number two threat, law

enforcement. For as he put it, law enforcement's number
one reason for existence was to find and eliminate
organizations such as Father's Disciples. For the leader of
such an organization to think otherwise was imprudent.

Father understood that law enforcement would stop at
nothing in order to accomplish its goals, including turning
an organization's members against each other. A technique
they'd used effectively in the past to bring down many
criminal empires.

Prison, Father had explained to Marvelous, was a real
possibility for anyone whose way of life ran afoul of the
law. Again, it was foolhardy to think otherwise, and
irresponsible not to prepare for the possibility of stints of
varying lengths in prison. Another mistake that Father
determined that Father's Disciples would not make.

Obviously, Father had explained, the most effective
remedy against prison was to never get caught in the first
place. But failing that, Father had decided that Father's
Disciples would do everything in its power to keep its
members charged with crimes out of prison. This goal was
often accomplished through the bribery of police officers,
prosecutors, and even judges. Father also understood that
bribery wouldn't always work and that attempting to escape
from justice was sometimes unwise or impossible, making
incarceration inevitable. That is why he'd expanded
Father's Disciples' reach inside prison walls and thus made
the organization as formidable inside of prison as it was on
the outside. There was no abuse of Father's Disciples by
inmates or prison officials. And organization members had
as many outside creature comforts inside prison walls as
could be smuggled in. Because of Fathers vision, law
enforcement's threat of prison had been dealt a serious
blow, and in a lot of instances, it was rendered virtually
impotent.

In the history of Father's Disciples there had not been
an instance of its members ratting out the organization. If

law enforcement was going to bring Father's Disciples down, it would need to do so without the assistance of any of the organization's members. Still, Father understood, it would not keep law enforcement from trying. And in trying, one day they could very well succeed. And if they did, he was determined to be ready. Again, his wisdom had proved unparalleled. Law enforcement had kept trying and this past week it appeared they had succeeded. And as a testament to his vision, Father was ready. Hence, Operation: Self-Destruct was put in motion.

But the plan, which was meant to give law enforcement the illusion of the organization self-destructing right before their very eyes, was in danger of not going off because of Father's questionable decision to give Morant a major role in its implementation.

And Morant…what the fuck! Marvelous leaned in closer to the monitor. He saw Mayo Fathers taking his seat. Oh, how that man could be related in any way to Father was a wonder of wonders, he thought, as he scanned the other monitors, looking for Morant.

The kid was nowhere to be found! Damn, it was just as he'd thought. Morant was going to fuck this up!

A chill shot through Marvelous as he saw the other two members of Father's Disciples' so called power triumvirate, Lucas McCain and Jermaine Bledsoe, take their seats on the third row on the left side of the chapel facing the front while their soon-to-be killers sat behind them on the forth row. "Damn," he muttered again as he looked intently at the monitor. Morant should now be sitting in the front row on that same side. Marvelous checked his watch. It was five minutes to three. The whole thing was supposed to go down in fifteen minutes and Morant, that sniveling piss-ant, was missing.

Ten minutes later, when Morant had still not shown, Marvelous opened the top left hand drawer of the desk on which the monitors were located and pulled out his .357

Magnum. He checked the chamber. The gun was fully loaded. Popping the chamber back into place, he headed out the room. It was clear that he was going to have to take care of Mayo Fathers himself. Something Father, for reasons known only to him, obviously hadn't wanted him to do. Otherwise, Marvelous would've been assigned the task in the first place. Slippage.

He left the basement through Fathers House and exited out of its front door. He walked briskly down the covered breezeway to the funeral home. After taking care of Mayo according to Father's plan, he was going to plant a cap in Morant's ass for good measure. Slippage or not, in the future Father would not be given the chance to entrust that boy-cop with important responsibilities. Talented, cold-blooded killer or not, the kid was too unreliable to ever be useful.

Marvelous glanced over at the parking lot. It was full and most everyone appeared to have already gone inside the chapel. After seeing movement out the corner of his eye, he dipped his head below his shoulder, and hurried down the far side of the funeral home. He reached the back of the building and then moved quickly to the exit door.

He checked his watch again. Two minutes until show time. He paused at the door for a brief moment. If the door was locked, Father's plan was as good as screwed. There would be no way for Marvelous to get inside quickly enough to shoot Mayo Fathers right after McCain and Bledsoe would have been shot.

Gently he twisted the doorknob. He was in luck. It turned completely counterclockwise and he heard the sweet metallic sound of the cam being released. The door lurched open.

One minute to show time.

The door opened right into what was essentially the front of the chapel where the pulpit was located. Inside, he heard the minister's request for everyone to lower their heads for prayer. No one paid much attention to him as he entered the room and took a spot along the sidewall.

Thirty seconds to show time.

He took out the Magnum and waited.

Ten…nine…eight…

He took a deep breath and then heard… Pop! Pop! Two shots.

And as Father had predicted, no one in the chapel knew exactly what was going on.

After the firecracker like sounds, someone yelled, "Damn!" And panic quickly ensued which would have been Morant's cue had he been in place. But now, it was up to Marvelous. With gun drawn he headed across the front of the chapel toward the other side where Mayo Fathers sat on the front row. It wasn't until Marvelous had reached the spot where the casket was that he saw the problem. It would have been a small thing in the grand scheme of things. But it loomed large when someone was attempting to execute a plan that was depended upon timing.

Marvelous was a left handed shooter and thus held the Magnum in his left hand. The casket was to his left. In order to get a good shot at Mayo Fathers he would either have to switch the gun to his right hand or move to a position in front of the casket.

He made his decision quickly and moved to get in front of the casket. But evidently his slight hesitation was all that a previously frozen-in-place Mayo Fathers had needed to assess the situation. Perhaps sensing that his life was in danger, Mayo jumped to his feet and turned toward the nearest exit.

Marvelous aimed the gun just as Mayo had gotten to his feet. Even though pandemonium had broken out all around him, Marvelous heard not a sound. It was as if he was in an airtight vacuum, just him and his intended target. The Magnum, his weapon of choice for so many of his executions felt a part of him as if he'd been born with it in his hand. At the sight of his target, his finger as reflexively as a yawn, cocked the trigger.

Marvelous did not feel the bullet rip through his own arm, piercing into the right side of his body. He had no idea anything was amiss until he started falling just as he'd squeezed off a shot. Before hitting the floor and taking his last breath, he saw Mayo Fathers fall awkwardly through the exit door.

***

The sound of gunfire and the ensuing panic that had erupted in the funeral home chapel had sent Johnston hurtling to his knees and scrambling for cover behind the nearest bench. He'd been a homicide detective for so long that he'd grown used to arriving at the scene after the dust had settled. Now he was smack in the middle of the action as it unfolded. Despite the screaming voices and the cattle rustling-like sound of people scurrying for cover, Johnston could still hear the beat-box thumping of his own heart.

The gunplay had started so suddenly that he barely had enough time to draw his own revolver. And when he had, the first thing that had caught his attention was the bald behemoth at the front of the chapel aiming what appeared to be a .357 in the direction of where Mayo Fathers sat. Acting instinctively, Johnston had cocked his weapon and aimed it at the behemoth, yelling at the big fella to drop his weapon.

The behemoth hadn't even bothered looking in Johnston's direction.

But with so much chaos going on, Johnston wasn't sure if the big fella had ignored him or simply hadn't heard him. But it soon hadn't mattered, because another shot was fired, striking the behemoth through his right arm. The bullet appeared to rip through the arm, going straight into his torso. The big man held the gun steadfast in his left hand and still managed to fire off a shot in Mayo Fathers' direction before dropping to the floor like a boulder.

Johnston couldn't tell if Mayo Fathers had been shot or not. He'd seen Fathers stumble toward the door, but in the ensuing mayhem, he couldn't tell if the old man had been hit by the bullet or if he'd tripped over something.

Now scrunched behind the bench, with a few other low-lying, trembling bodies, Johnston closed his eyes, trying to visualize what was happening. After a few moments of relaxed breathing, he tried to recall the number of shots fired. He remembered hearing four, with the last one coming about three minutes ago. He opened his eyes and slowly raised his head, surveying the landscape. He saw a few dozen heads bobbing above the benches, none of whom looked dangerous. The possibility of an orchestrated hit suddenly occurred to him.

His mind sequenced the action. The first shots had come from somewhere to the front and left of him. The behemoth had gotten off the third shot, and then the forth shot which had ripped through the behemoth's arm and torso appeared to have come from the same direction as the first shots had. But where had the first shots gone? And who, pray-god, had done the shooting? And why?

Johnston didn't believe that the behemoth had fired first, although he wasn't entirely certain. The shots had seemed to come from the rows to his left which would have been to the behemoth's front. When he'd heard those first shots, Johnston had looked in the direction he'd thought they'd come. But the ensuing panic had made it impossible to make out what was happening. People were already scrambling about, and he couldn't make out if one of them had done the shooting.

With one knee planted near the head of a scared little girl and his gun still drawn, he slowly stood up and scanned the room. Upfront, the casket had been knocked over. The reverend cowered behind a lectern. People who had been unable to escape the chaos had dropped where they'd stood, seeming perpetually frozen in a childhood game of one-two-three-red-light. People crowded in the aisle and a few had made it to the exit where they were bunched back like a tub of water being forced through a straw. After a few moments, some of them started to rise.

"Stay down," Johnston ordered.

The heads went back down hastily.

Luckily, the Simmons boy's casket had been closed. Otherwise, the body may have spilled onto the floor. The discovery of which may have set off an emotional outburst. The chapel had the collective feel of a deer in headlights. Scattered muttered cries rose and fell before birthing a din which soon synchronized into a sound akin to harmonious chanting.

"Is everyone okay?" Johnston called out.

"A couple of people have been shot over here." The voice came from the rows to the left and front of Johnston. He looked up and saw a man of about forty years in age. The man wore a brown patched-elbow sport coat and blue khaki pants. The beginnings of a full beard outlined his face from ear to chin. "I think they're dead," the man added. "I've dialed 911 and requested an ambulance." He held up a cell phone and shook it in Johnston's direction. "Some people ran out that door up there." He pointed to a door up front to the left of where the casket had been before it was knocked to the floor.

Johnston suddenly remembered his own cell phone clipped to his belt, though he didn't reach for it, instead he looked in the direction of where the man pointed before focusing his attention onto the man. "Who are you?" Johnston said.

"Jim Crouch. I'm a reporter for the Duraleigh Standard."

"Those people you saw hightailing it out of here, were they the shooters?"

"Yes."

Johnston stepped over the little girl and made his way over to Crouch. "How many shooters?"

"Counting that big fella up there, four. Two of them sat on this side and they shot those two," He pointed at the two bodies slumped over the benches a couple of rows in front of him. "There was another man who came out of that restroom over there," he said pointing to a door to his left. "He shot that big one just after the big fella had shot at someone on the front row. Everyone then took off for that exit up there."

"Did you get a good look at their faces?" Johnston said.

"Not really I was seated behind them." Crouch said.

"Not really?"

"Well, I didn't see their faces at the time of the shooting. But I had gotten here earlier. I think the shooters were part of the group of young men that had gotten here early too. I got an alright look at them. If I saw some photos I may be able to pick them out."

"Okay," Johnston said. "I'll need you down at the station."

"Is it safe to get up?" Someone asked.

Johnston looked to his right in the general direction of where the voice came from. The chapel was now a crime scene. But there didn't seem to be any additional immediate danger. He looked back over to where the bodies were slumped over a bench. All the rows behind it were a skewed and empty. Evidently, the people who'd been seated behind the shooters had high-tailed it as far away as possible once the gunplay had begun. It was going to be impossible to determine who had seen what. Although he realized that even if there was a potential witness or two to the actual shootings, it may be a challenge getting someone to come forward. "Yes, everyone get up slowly and make your way to the exit. If anyone cares to make a statement on what they saw, stick around."

Johnston walked over to the bodies. The men had fallen frontward over a bench; their butts were protruding out as if they'd been getting ready to moon someone. Johnston leaned over the bench. Their heads had been nearly blown off. Blood was spattered all around.

He headed for the exit where Crouch had said the shooters had gone through. With gun drawn, he opened the door and peeked out. The door opened to the outside. It was the side of the chapel on the opposite end away from Fathers House. The sun still hid behind a mass of gray clouds. Johnston looked to his left, and then to his right. To his left led to the parking lot which was the rear of the funeral home, but the entrance to the chapel. On the right, Holston Street appeared abandoned. He doubted seriously if the shooters were waiting around to confess. Either direction offered a trouble-free escape route. Sirens could be heard from a distance, getting louder by the moment. He holstered his gun and went back inside the chapel.

An acrid mix of gunpowder and blood hung in the air. Though most of the mourners had made their way out of the building, a few of them still milled about inside the chapel. But Johnston doubted that they were waiting to talk to him. He decided to wait until the cavalry arrived before he went through the potentially useless motion of questioning anyone. If tradition held, the reporter would be the only witness willing to say he'd seen anything; everyone else would suddenly become Helen Keller-like. No one here was likely to take the chance of getting themselves or their loved ones on the radar of cold-blooded killers.

He walked closer to where the behemoth had fallen. The man's legs were splayed like a puppet that had been suddenly dropped to the floor. Johnston turned toward the pulpit where Reverend something or other had scrambled to his feet. He looked at Johnston and nodded at the fallen casket.

"Yeah, that'll be okay," Johnston said.

The reverend eased down from the pulpit and tapped the shoulders of a few of the men who'd hit the floor near the front of the room.

"Don't touch him," Johnston said, nodding toward the behemoth. "Just pick the casket up."

The reverend nodded in agreement, and then he and three other men girded themselves on either side of the casket. After a couple of grunts, Cain Simmons' casket was set back upright.

Standing over the fallen behemoth, Johnston mimicked the big man's aiming of his gun at Fathers. He pointed his index finger in the direction of where he'd remembered Fathers falling backward. There was no body on the floor. The whole front bench had been cleared. Evidently, Fathers hadn't been hit and was among those who'd been able to get out.

Johnston mentally traced the bullet's supposed trajectory. There, he said to himself when he spotted a small hole in the front bench's crease-corner. The behemoth's aim had evidently lowered after he'd been shot. Johnston, surmising the bullet's continued path, looked over at a lower portion of the wall to the side of the bench. Another hole. The bullet had gone through the lower wooden trim on the wall.

After examining the hole in the wooden trim, Johnston walked over to the exit and pushed open the door. Unlike the one on the other side of the chapel, this door was not an immediate exit to the outside. It opened to a hallway. On one end of the hallway appeared to be additional rooms. On the opposite end was a door which likely led to the outside.

Johnston walked down the hall in the direction of the rooms. Light sprayed out from the first room on his right. He pulled out his revolver and approached the door slowly. He leaned his head in the door. It was a conference room.

Empty. The next room door was closed and locked. He looked down at the bottom of the door. There was no light coming from the room. He knocked on the door though he doubted if Mayo or anyone else was in the room. There was no answer. There were four remaining doors down the long hallway. They were alternately open and empty or closed and locked. He reached the end of the hallway at the door with the rectangular glass window.

The door opened on the side of the funeral home that connected to Fathers House. He looked up at the house. It looked as if it had been recently whitewashed, especially noticeable in contrast to the grayness of the day. He stared at the house for a long moment. Mayo had retreated home. He was sure of it. Just as he was sure the would-be killers had taken off in the direction of Holston Street on the opposite side of the funeral home. Siren-blasts snapped off suddenly as police cars and ambulances slammed to stops in the parking lot in front of the funeral home. Johnston heard the onslaught of rapidly opened and slammed shut car doors. The cavalry was here, he thought as he holstered his gun once again. He fished his hand in his front pocket and felt the cold hardness of the computer flash drive. Maybe after almost being killed, Mayo Fathers would be more susceptible to some hard questions. He returned the flash drive to his pocket and headed down the breezeway to Fathers House, leaving the now calmed mayhem of the funeral home.

Chapter 19

Later that Monday evening, Tom Ram sat behind his desk in his home office. His fingers intently drummed the edge of the large, custom made maple desk. The desk, patterned after one owned by a previous FBI director, was the centerpiece of his home office. Some people would look around in his office, particularly at the portrait of the President of the United States on the wall and the two flags flanking the desk, and think it strange that his home office could twin for any government office. They would assume he was either a crazy workaholic who couldn't separate his personal life from his career, or he was just plain crazy. But they'd be wrong on both counts.

He wasn't a workaholic and he wasn't crazy. He was ambitious. His goal was to one day become the Director of the FBI. It was a lofty goal and one not completely within his control. But if the current or a future president was going to see him as a director-type, then Ram himself would have to see it as well. Patterning the lifestyle and habits of past directors helped Ram to see himself in that way. He studied their career paths, the way they dressed, their hobbies, whatever he could find out about them. Even wearing the same type of drawers they wore wouldn't have been out of the question, if he could be reasonably certain of the type of drawers that they had worn. Ram was convinced that the easiest and quickest path to success was the path already proven successful.

But looking, acting, and dressing like a director of the FBI was only part of it. He also had to think like one. He had to think like a leader. And to that end, what would a director who would have been at this point of his career do about the recent developments in the Father's Disciples case.

For five years, the case had moved along at the pace of a handicapped snail. And though the Bureau had historically taken as much time as needed to investigate cases, with some being on the vine for a decade or more before baring any fruit, the powers-that-be had gotten a little antsy on this one. They'd wanted results yesterday and for good reason. Allegations that the corruption involving Father's Disciples had reached the federal level had been disturbing and were potentially embarrassing for the government.

Father's Disciples had always seemed to be one step ahead of the Bureau's investigation. Information about the syndicate had been anything but free-flowing. Witnesses had been killed even before they'd become official witnesses. And the supposed leader of the syndicate, Mayo Fathers, was the salt of the earth if his reputation in the syndicate's home base of Duraleigh, North Carolina was to be believed. But with the procurement last week of Sarah Leeson as a witness, Ram had felt the Bureau's luck had changed. That belief had been further deepened by the recent discovery of Caleb Dawson's clandestine activities for Father's Disciples. Those two events added with today's funeral home murders of two members of the syndicate's leadership, McCain and Bledsoe, along with the attempted murder of Fathers, painted a picture of a syndicate imploding.

But thinking as a director, Ram would not underestimate his adversary. Father's Disciples was a formidable opponent. It had infiltrated the Bureau and lord only knew what other government entities. Ram also knew that Father's Disciples still held the upper hand. The case against it hadn't been fully fleshed out. And thanks to Dawson, all the witnesses against it, except one, had been eliminated. And besides, Mayo Fathers had survived today's attack, which meant the syndicate had survived. And Ram couldn't shake a rising and nagging feeling. What if the whole thing had been planned? What if all the recent events were just elaborate ploys by Father's Disciples to get the Bureau off its trail? It was that possibility that curdled Ram's blood. If Fathers was that devious of a leader and had been willing to kill his own lieutenants to rid the syndicate of the Bureau's attention, then the Bureau was dealing with a truly demented, evil being. And one who apparently knew no bounds.

Ram pushed back from his desk, stood up, and stretched. His thoughts turned to Special Agent Caleb Dawson. Last week, the Bureau's IT people had been able to trace the electronic footprints from a classified file to a computer accessed by Dawson, who as recently as last week had attempted to access the Father's Disciples' file. Though Dawson had a high security clearance, he wasn't authorized to access the Father's Disciples case file.

As a result of its findings, the Bureau had asked Dawson's permission for a search of all the computers he had access to, including his personal computers. To throw off suspicion, they'd also made it known that several other high-clearance agents had agreed to a search of their personal computers. They were to be routine searches and not for anything in particular. The searches were simply due to the nature of the agents' security clearances. Dawson surprisingly had agreed to the search right away. Evidently, he had assumed that his hard drives had been successfully scrubbed.

He'd assumed wrong. It had taken the IT experts less than two hours to find evidence of the security breach on two of Dawson's computers. Dawson had apparently found a way to use his personal computer to access the Bureau's system. A feat that the Bureau had previously thought was undoable.

Ram sat back down at his desk and started back

drumming the edge of it. As of now, Dawson was not advised of their findings. Far as he knew, the search of his computers had been routine and hadn't relinquished anything of note. And Ram was going to let him continue to think that. It would be pointless to bring Dawson in now. He could lawyer up and deny the Bureau an opportunity to find out how far the syndicate's tentacles had reached. In addition, there was Ram's nagging feeling that despite recent events, news of Father's Disciples' death was greatly exaggerated. Leaving Dawson alone at this point may bear fruit. The syndicate may attempt to contact him, or him, it. It may be the only way to find out if Father's Disciples was staging its last days strictly for show.

Ram's cell phone's musical ringtone chimed in with his finger drumming.

He thumbed the SEND button. "Ram here."

After listening carefully, he said, "Take them to Flantos. I can be there in an hour."

***

The ranch style house was located about forty miles east of Duraleigh in the boondocks of Clayton County. Fronted by two acres of neatly barbered bright green fescue and a sentinel row of tall pine trees, the house, solely owned by the US Government, had been occupied for the last ten years by Billy Ray Flantos.

Flantos, a short, sweet-faced man with weather-tinted skin greeted Ram at the front door. "Tom, it's been way too long."

"Which is a good thing," Ram said as he entered the house. "It means you're safe and out of the reach of those pedophiles you helped put away."

"Where is everyone?" Ram asked Flantos.

"The agents are in the kitchen," Flantos replied. "The boys are in the family room. Follow me."

He led Ram to the family room. Maalik Jackson sat on a green sofa, furiously pecking away at a handheld gaming device. Prodegee, aka Special Agent Cedric David, sat beside him, nonchalantly flipping TV channels with the remote. Prodegee looked up when Ram and Flantos entered the doorway. Ram nodded at Prodegee who in turn stood up and said to Maalik, "I have to use the bathroom. It's my turn when I get back."

"Bet," Maalik said without looking up

Prodegee left the room. Flantos stood at the doorway for a moment and said to Ram proudly, "That's my PSP he's playing."

"No kidding," Ram said. "I have one too." He reached into his inside breast pocket and pulled out the gaming device.

"You're a gamer?" Flantos said, smiling.

"Bona fide," Ram said.

"Go figure," Flantos said before turning to the doorway. "You should come by more often. Play some games. And bring some friends."

"Sure thing," Ram said. Though they both knew that was just idle chatter. After today, he wouldn't see Flantos again unless the self-proclaimed gamer was in immediate danger or the FBI had a similar urgent need. Two scenarios Ram hoped would not occur.

He turned his attention to Maalik. Ram had brought his PSP to break the ice. He had read Prodegee/Agent David's report on the boy. He was eleven years old. He lived at Fathers House. And for the last month and a half or so, he'd been pushing drugs for Father's Disciples. As Prodegee, Agent David was slowly gaining his trust. But the process was too slow moving. Maalik had yet to divulge the details of the connection between Fathers House and Father's Disciples. The Bureau knew that several of the boys who lived at the house were involved in the organization's illicit drug trade. But not all of the boys in residence were.

Prodegee had been living there longer than Maalik and he hadn't been solicited to join. In fact, he'd received the cold shoulder from the ones he'd confirmed were dealing drugs, other than Cain Simmons, and Simmons was now dead. They would sell him drugs, but they would not "hook him up with a job." Initially, the Bureau hadn't known if the boys' selling drugs were inconsequential to living at the house or that they sold drugs because they lived at the house. Prodegee's investigation had confirmed the latter, and right now they had enough information to make a few bottom rung arrests, but not enough to take out the whole bottom. The Bureau needed more knowledge of the infrastructure, a complete layout of the organization from bottom to top. And now with the Caleb Dawson situation having unfolded and the special agent having a known connection with Fathers House, Ram had a new possibly farfetched but nonetheless troubling question: was Father's Disciples breeding criminals?

"I have about fifteen games on the hard drive and a couple of movies," Ram said as he sat down beside Maalik and turned on his PSP.

Maalik continued playing the game and muttered something that Ram couldn't quite make out. He was still in his funeral gear: a sharp, black suit with a red tie, fat-knotted at the top. His hair was neat, closely cropped, no cornrows. Except for his two diamond studded earlobes, he could pass for a young junior executive intern for a Wall Street outfit.

"I find myself playing mostly puzzle games lately, although from time to time I'll get into one of the shooting games." He scrolled through the games on his PSP. But mostly he watched Maalik who was still furiously tapping away at the handheld.

After a moment Maalik said, "I ain't no snitch."

Ram leaned away from him. "Whoa! Who said anything about snitching?"

Maalik kept tapping away. "I ain't stupid, man. Why else would you guys snatch us up and bring us here. I don't see anyone else here. That cat that lives here. He's cool and everything, but it looks like he's been snitching. So, ya'll want us to say something too."

Ram turned off his PSP and placed it on the coffee table, and then looked at Maalik. "Well, do you have something to say?"

"Nah man. I ain't got nuthin' to say." His little fingers kept expertly banging away at the device's small control buttons. Rapid gunfire and screaming human voice sound effects could be heard coming from the device. Whether that was good or bad, or whether the game was being won or lost was indeterminate as Maalik showed no emotion.

"Three people were killed today. And unlike the characters on that game you're playing, those three aren't going to get a chance to come back to life and start over. It's real life for them. Game over."

Maalik stopped tapping for a moment, and then started back. "That's hood life, man."

"No, son," Ram said. "That's Father's Disciples' life. Two of those people were important members of an organization where you're just a foot soldier. And if the Disciples can't protect their leaders, how are they going to protect you?"

"I don't need no protecting. Like you said, I'm just a foot soldier. Killing me wouldn't amount to much."

Ram leaned back against the couch. "Yeah, maybe you're right. Killing you probably wouldn't amount to much to a rival group. But what if it wasn't a rival group? What if it was one of your own? What if Father's Disciples killed Father's Disciples? What if family is killing family for whatever reason or no reason? Just because they can."

Maalik stopped tapping and slumped back against the couch. He rested the handheld in his lap and looked up toward the ceiling. A stream of tears slid easily down his face. But he didn't say anything.

For the first time since Ram had entered the room, Maalik looked like a kid. There was a box of tissue on the end table to Ram's left. He reached for it, pulled out a couple of tissues, and handed them to Maalik. "Talk to us, son. We can protect you."

Maalik grabbed the tissues from him and wiped his face. Then just as suddenly as it had appeared, the sadness that gripped his face evaporated and transformed to indifference. He looked at Ram and slowly shook his head. "As far as I know, you're one of us. And this is a test. So either way, I'm good as dead. But I'm going to be able to look the executioner in his eyes and tell him, I ain't said shit."

***

Fifteen minutes later, Ram sat at the kitchen table of the US government owned, but Billy Ray Flantos occupied, ranch house. Special Agent Cedric David sat across from him. "No way," Ram said.

David pushed away from the table and stood up. "But sir, respectfully, we don't know anything. It's too soon to pull the plug."

"It's also too dangerous. Need I remind you that three people were killed today? Three."

"I know that, sir, which is all the more reason for us to go back in. We're getting close to something. I can feel it. Those shootings today are because we're getting close."

"We don't know that. It could have been a rival gang. Impulse killings. We'll assess it. But in the meantime, we're pulling you out."

"And what will you have to show for my time there? A few low level dope pushers. Something the locals could have gotten on their own. Nothing showing the connection between the bottom and the top. No information on alleged murders or missing people. No viable information on dirty police officers or dirty city officials. We don't even know where they keep the drugs. Basically, we have a whole bunch of nothing. And if today's murders were just some planned mirage for our benefit... " his voice trailed off.

Ram drummed the kitchen table with his fingers. "Then, we'll keep watching and waiting."

David leaned on the table toward Ram. "That's manpower and dollars. And you know we're running on short supply of both. People want major results. Not a photo-op."

"Watch it," Ram warned.

"I'm sorry, sir," David said. But he wasn't backing down. "It's just that we're close. I know it. Let me and Maalik get back in there. He's not going to talk here. But he'll talk to me. Out there."

"That boy is in no condition to go back into anything. He's scared shitless. And I don't think he's going to talk here, there, or anywhere. He holds not snitching like some badge of honor."

"Maalik's tougher than you think. He'll go back. And he'll talk to me," David said.

"Yeah, and rat you out as a snitch."

"He won't do that. He's my friend."

"He's loyal to Father's Disciples."

David sat back down in the chair and sighed. "No, it's not about Father's Disciples. It's about belonging to something, having somebody watch his back. It's about family with him. Something he hasn't had. I think today shook him up a little bit. But he liked Cain. And since I was close to Cain, now he trusts me."

"Still, it's too dangerous," Ram said.

Sir, we have to try. Otherwise, my undercover work so far was a waste of my time, the Bureau's time, and the taxpayers' money. I was made a special agent for a reason. This is what I was trained to do. Put me back in. Let's finish the job."

"Somebody may have seen you guys being whisked away."

"Probably, but it wouldn't be the first time cops have harassed innocent people. Take us back. If we need to, we'll cuss you out in front of the house. We'll be okay."

For a few moments the only sound was the staccato beats of Ram's fingers on the wooden kitchen table. Then finally he said, "Two weeks."

"Cool," David said smiling. "That's all I'll need."

Chapter 20

Six hours after the shootings upstairs in the funeral home's chapel, Father's initial anger had waned and he was no longer upset that his instructions for today had been so severely altered. His current attitude was attributable to his natural being for he was an adaptable being. Father considered himself a formless entity, a shapeless form with malleable characteristics which allowed him to adhere to the realities of any situation, good or bad. He was the quintessential lemonade maker, a natural over-comer of circumstances, as well as a visionary planner. Good things will continue to happen to people who always plan for the inevitableness of bad things happening to them. It was his long-winded response to the question 'why do bad things happen to good people.' For Father, who was the farthest thing from 'good people' as there ever was, the answer was quite simple: bad things happen to good people because bad things happen…period. And the sooner so called good people realized that and planned accordingly, the better off they'd be. And the sooner they'd be able to get on with their lives regardless of whatever lemons life threw at them. That was Father's creed. It was the fabric that ran through his life. So even in the throes of that initial anger, he knew he would eventually arrive at this state of calmness, assess the current situation, and chart a new path forward. He knew it because mentally he had already prepared to have to do so.

He was prepared because he understood that he worked with vessels that were unlike him. These vessels were prone to mistakes and some had either an inability or lack of desire to learn from them. As a consequence, Father understood that these imperfect vessels would potentially fail him at the worse possible times and would be more often than not, the reason he would need such a creed. And though the punishment for those failures would be quick, violent, and sometimes final, the presence of the failures in and of themselves was never surprising. There would be the initial frustration and anger on his part, but there would also be a realization that a plan B, an adjustment to the previous well-conceived plan, would ultimately be needed.

He'd already phoned his displeasure to the only surviving imperfect vessel responsible for the reprehensible turn of today's events. Fortunately for that fool, Fathers red hot temper had been controlled by the influx of policemen roaming about upstairs. He'd figured rightly that they'd eventually search every ounce of the funeral home under the pretense of looking for the killers. The search led them down here to his office. Of course, they were unable to locate the secret room within the office, and in which he'd been sitting on the single bunk bed and watching them on a monitor. But in the unlikely event they'd been able to find the secret room, and thus, him; he would have been the perfect picture of ignorance. He would not have resembled the man who moments earlier had threatened the imperfect vessel, Morant, with death for having so egregiously fucked up. And Father, not one to make empty threats, would have had Morant killed, quickly and in a most violent way. Instead, since the police were literally within steps of him, he'd simply ordered Morant to go home where he was to stay until further instructions. And now since Father's cooler head had prevailed, Morant would not only live to see another day, but as a result of the death of Father's top lieutenant—Marvelous Killens, he'd also have a new role within the organization. Some would call it a miscarriage of justice that the person responsible for killing Marvelous Killens would be the person to take Killens' place. But to Father, it was simply lemonade-making. Besides, if

Marvelous himself hadn't been a foolish imperfect vessel and had done as instructed, he'd still be alive.

Now, what to do about his brother, he asked himself as he watched the monitor and saw Mayo enter his office and sit down in the low sitting chair in front of the desk. Reflexively, Father started to hit the switch which would bring his computerized image to life on the flat screen in the office. But he stopped, suddenly remembering that would be unnecessary. His brother knew exactly what he looked like. They were, after all, twins. Instead, he flipped the switch to the left and the wall retreated within itself, uncovering the recess. Father stepped out of the room and walked to his desk. He reached under the desk overhang and pushed a button. The wall slid smoothly back into place.

Mayo looked up. His face was drawn and he looked tortured which was not at all surprising. After all, he'd barely escaped death. He dropped his head. "What's going on brother? Do you want me dead?"

Father chuckled unnaturally. "Dead? What would make you say such a fool thing?"

Mayo looked up again. "That was your henchman shooting at me. He aimed at me. I looked in his eyes and he wanted me dead. There was no doubt. If he hadn't been…"

Father cut him off. "Exactly, if he hadn't been shot first, you'd be dead. Who do you think shot him? Morant shot him, one of my boys." He leaned over the desk, looking down on his brother. "I don't know what had gotten into Marvelous. But he was not acting on my orders."

"Then what's going on? Is somebody trying to move us out? Bledsoe and McCain were killed, and Killens was gunning for me."

"I'm looking into it," Father said calmly. "It's nothing for you to worry about."

Mayo stood up and started pacing the room. "That's

easy for you to say. No one's gunning for you. No one's seen you for over ten years. It's my ass on the line. It's my face out there."

Father glared at him. "Yes," he said, speaking slowly, deliberately. "It is your face out there. You're the face of a business that was dead. You hear me. It was dead. Until I saved it. Until I brought it back from the dead."

"Ill-gotten gains, drug money," Mayo said with an edge.

"Who gives a damn how it was done? It was done. After you and our so-called father had nearly destroyed it, it was me, the cast off, who saved our inheritance."

"You blame me, don't you?" Mayo asked. He walked to the front of the desk, facing his brother. "You blame me for what Dad did."

"Blame you. No, I don't blame you. I know that's what you think. I know that's why you turned Fathers House into some sort of halfway house for fatherless boys. But you can't be my daddy any more than you can be theirs. What's done is done. I don't even blame him. Our father was weak. He was a coward. But I know he didn't reject me. He rejected my skin." He held both his hands up in front of his face, turning them slowly. His hands, like most of his body, were a piggish pale splattered with blotches of blackness. Vitiligo had eroded most of his pigmentation. "It's funny; this disease has nearly erased the one thing that made my father hate me. I'm almost as white as you now." He walked around the desk and put his arm around Mayo's shoulder. "Stop beating yourself up. Your daddy's dead. I've moved on."

His brother's touch comforted Mayo. But he didn't believe their father had been a coward, misguided perhaps, but not a coward. But he wasn't going to argue the point. It was just the two of them now and the past was the past. "Alright," Mayo said. "But there is one other thing. A Detective Johnston came by to see me after the shootings today. He said he has proof that Fathers Funeral Home is into drugs, money laundering, and bribing public officials."

Father squeezed his brother's shoulder. "Stop worrying. If the detective had something, they would've shut this place down and he would have arrested you. He has nothing. At least nothing that can be substantiated. What you need to do is rest. Go back to that big house, climb into bed, and go to sleep. Tomorrow will be a better day."

Mayo took his brother's advice and left the office, trudging back to Fathers House through the underground tunnel that connected to the house's basement. After he'd left, Father once again tapped the button under the desk overhang, opening the door to the secret room. He preferred the Spartan room to Fathers House. He lay down on the bunk bed which was lined against a side wall. Looking up at the ceiling, he cursed the spirit of the worthless imperfect vessel Marvelous Killens. If not for Marvelous, that weak, spineless brother of his would now be dead.

Oh well, there was always plan B.

Chapter 21

Two weeks after moving into their new digs, the Lovison twins—Corey and Casey, made their second road trip. This one was to a routine checkup at Dr. Shepherd's office. The six of them, April, Ben, Patricia and Stephen Ellison, and the twins, had initially crammed into one of Shepherd's examination rooms. But Shepherd, needing a little more room to maneuver and sensing grandma and grandpa were just as concerned about the twins' examinations as were the parents, decided to conduct the exams in his office which provided everyone a little elbow room.

"I still can't believe how small they are," Stephen Ellison said as he peered over Ben's shoulder at Casey. The baby, inching toward dreamland, was nestled in his dad's lap. "You think they gained any more weight?"

"I sure hope so," April said in a near whisper. She sat in the chair beside her husband, holding Corey against her bosom. "I'm hoping they gained at least a couple of pounds."

"I don't know," Stephen Ellison said. "They both look small enough to slip through an eye of a needle."

"Never mind, Stephen," Patricia Ellison said. "They're fattening up." She reached down and scooped up her grandchild from April's arms. "Slowly, but surely."

After relinquishing control of Corey to her mother, April reached for Casey. Stephen Ellison leaned toward Ben, watching as his son-in-law handed the infant over to his mother. "Sure they are, Pattie," Stephen Ellison said. "I'm only teasing."

Ben looked impatiently at the empty leatherback chair behind the desk. He checked his watch. It was a quarter past ten. Where's Doc, he wondered. Shepherd had excused himself moments after getting them settled into his office. That was thirty minutes ago. After handing Casey over to April, Ben leaned back in the chair and yawned. He was dog tired and he was having a hard time concentrating on anything. Since the twins moved in, he'd been operating on an average of two hours of sleep a night. The twins had atrocious eating and sleeping habits, preferring to do both at odd hours of the day and night. Feeling restless, he rose from his chair, stretched, and walked over to a wall collaged with pictures of crying babies, smiling babies, indifferent babies, babies alone, and babies with one or two parents. He stared absently at the wall and sighed. Stephen Ellison quickly commandeered the just vacated seat, and leaned toward April and reached for his grandson.

April jerked backed involuntarily. "Let me put him in the carrier."

"I can do it," Stephen Ellison said defiantly. "If I'm going to help out with these little mosquitoes, I may as well get used to it now."

Reluctantly, April leaned over and placed Casey in his grandfather's arms.

"That's my little grandson," Stephen Ellison beamed. "That's my little mosquito."

April stared at the two of them for a moment and then she stood and walked over to join her husband at the wall. She hugged him from behind, resting her head between his shoulder blades. "You feel tense," she said. "Are you okay?"

The truth— he was sleep-deprived, anxious about being a first time dad, and thoroughly perplexed about Father's Disciples. Information on the syndicate had been limited, only what he'd gleaned from the Duraleigh Standard's account of last week's funeral home shootings. Mayo Fathers, who'd almost been killed during the shootings in what the newspaper had reported as gangland type carnage, had stonewalled him. Caleb hadn't returned any of his calls, and Etlzer had been out of the office the whole week, campaigning for the governor's office. Everyone else in the DA's office seemed as clueless as he was about Father's Disciples. And he still had no idea what had happened to Sarah Leeson. Although he was becoming increasingly convinced that her disappearance was somehow related to Father's Disciples, a crime syndicate that wasn't supposed to exist in Duraleigh. But he didn't say any of that to April. Instead, "Yeah, I'm fine."

"Sorry, folks," Shepherd said, moving as quickly into the room as a seventy-something year old doctor was apt to. "Saturdays are usually a madhouse around here, mainly because I'm one of the few doctors who still keep Saturday hours. Anyway, let's get a look at those babies."

The exams took less than twenty minutes, and surprisingly, and thankfully, both of the twins slept through the weighing, measuring, and poking. And both of them, to the delight of all the adults present, had gained some weight during the past two weeks. Casey, a pound and three quarters, and his brother Corey, two full pounds.

Shepherd sat behind his desk, watching as April and Ben settled the sleeping twins into their carriers. "The babies are healthy and are developing nicely," he paused and waited for April and Ben to return to their seats in front of his desk. "But what about you two, is everything going okay?"

"Yes, we're fine," Ben answered quickly. "Maybe a little tired, but..." he stopped as Shepherd's cheery expression changed suddenly to one of concern. Ben followed the doctor's gaze to April. She was crying.

"Baby, what's wrong?" Ben said. He placed a hand on her thigh, patting it gently.

Patricia Ellison, who was sitting at a table near the back of the office, admiring her sleeping grandbabies, looked up. "Darling, are you okay?"

Stephen Ellison said, "What's the problem, pumpkin?"

April pulled a tissue from her purse and dabbed lightly at her eyes and nose, "I don't know. It's just...everything. I'm just...." She stopped, unable to put into words exactly what had caused the tears.

"What you're feeling is perfectly natural," Shepherd offered soothingly. "You're going through a significant life experience. It was the pregnancy, then the births, your hormones, breast feeding, no sleep, motherhood...it's a lot. And a lot of advice coming from all over, but no one living your exact experience the way you are, and you can feel alone. Some mothers feel guilty and become depressed because they had fleeting moments when they wished for the single life again."

"The baby blues," Patricia Ellison said. She walked over to her daughter and hugged her, kissing her lightly on the forehead. "I had it for several months."

"The point is," Shepherd continued, "that even though it may feel like it, you're not alone. Talk to your family, talk to me. And don't think that therapy is a dirty word. If you need to talk to someone professionally, do so. I have some great referrals. Let someone know how you're feeling. Don't hold anything in. These feelings, if ignored or left unchecked can develop into something more serious." He smiled reassuringly. "But, you're going to be okay."

April nodded her head agreeably. "Thank you, Dr. Shepherd."

Ben held his wife's hand, squeezing it gently. "Are you sure you're okay?"

April's face flushed red and she smiled awkwardly. "Yes, I'm alright. I guess I just needed to get that out."

After a few moments, Dr. Shepherd reached under his desk and pulled out a digital camera. "I hope you folks don't mind, but I have a long standing tradition. I need one picture of the babies and the family for my wall."

Patricia Ellison looked at the wall admiringly. "These are all pictures of babies you've delivered?"

"Just about," Shepherd said proudly.

***

Ben was overly attentive the rest of the day and barely let April lift a muscle. He felt guilty that he hadn't noticed how his wife had been feeling. He'd been so wrapped up thinking only of himself, his job, and his uncertainties, that he hadn't paid any attention to her. He had assumed that she was some type of superwoman, able to magically adapt to a situation that was new to her as well. He was not going to make that mistake again.

That evening he prepared dinner—fried chicken, corn on the cob, and mashed potatoes from scratch. Afterwards, as April pumped a few bottles for the twins' overnight feedings, he cleaned up the kitchen. Around nine o'clock, with help from his in-laws, he put the twins down for the first of their nightly catnaps. On their third one, sometime after three o'clock in the morning, he met his mother-in-law in the hallway. She was hurrying to the nursery, carrying two of the breast milk bottles April had prepared earlier. Seeing Ben, she said, "I have it dear. Go on back to sleep."

Ben smiled, "Thanks anyway Mrs. E., but you only have two hands. There are two hungry babies in there, you know."

"I guess you're right," she agreed.

The twins' synchronized yelping was silenced as soon as the bottles hit their lips. Each of them attacked his bottle with a passion. Thankfully, it didn't take long for the return of full bellies and blissful quietness.

After putting the twins back into their respective cribs, both he and Patricia Ellison paused, standing over the cribs, admiring the twins as they settled deep into slumber. After a few moments, Ben turned and walked into the hallway. Patricia Ellison followed him, pulling the door to the nursery partially closed behind her.

Ben proceeded onward toward the master bedroom he shared with April. After he'd taken a few steps, Patricia Ellison called out to him in a voice a tad above a whisper. "Wait a moment, Ben."

He stopped, and turned to face her.

"I know you feel guilty about what happened today. But it's not your fault. Many women feel that way after childbirth. It happens. There's not a whole lot the man can do."

"Thanks, Mrs. E. But it's not why she was crying that I feel bad about. It's that I didn't notice how she'd been feeling. It was like I was here, but I wasn't here. You know what I mean. I don't ever want her to think that I'm not here for her or my boys. I'm going to be here."

Patricia Ellison touched his arm gently. "She knows that. And Stephen and I know that. You're a good man. But you're human too, and you need rest. I'm going downstairs to finish reading my novel until the twins wake up again, and when they do I'll handle it alone so you and April can sleep in. No need for the whole house to be out of whack in the morning."

"Are you sure? I don't mind doing it," Ben said. "It's two babies."

"I'm sure I'll manage. Besides, Stephen will be up and he can help me. I'm sure April and you both could use the extra rest."

He yawned though he no longer felt like sleeping. In another hour or so, he'd be up anyway. "Thank you, but you know, I feel like going for a run."

"At this time of night? You don't think it's too cold?" she asked.

"Nah," he said, heading back to the bedroom to change into his sweatpants. "The cold will revitalize me."

At four o'clock, a half-moon held court in a cloudless sky as darkness still claimed the morning. He stood on his front porch, rolled his neck and stretched his legs. The morning was still and cold. He glanced east, and then west, before deciding to go west. As he ran down the street past the houses, he noticed a few of them had on porch lights, but all the interiors were dark. He imagined their occupants snuggled in their beds, clinging to the dreams of a sleep soon to be over. He didn't know many of his neighbors, but he'd seen most of them come and go. Many were two-parent homes. He wondered if the children in those homes felt safer with their fathers around. He wondered if he would make his boys feel safe.

He rounded a curb and headed down a different street. A couple of streets over, a dog barked twice and stopped, returning the morning to an unusual quiet. Even his footfalls sounded muffled as if he was running on foam instead of pavement. He ran up and down two other streets, and then, feeling his fingers getting a little numb from the cold, decided to head back home. Out the corner of his eye he saw a figure approaching him. Without breaking his stride, he turned his head and squinted into the darkness. To his surprise, it was Caleb.

"You could have simply returned my calls," Ben said. "You didn't have to stalk me."

Caleb said, "The stuff the kid told you about the basement was true."

Ben stopped running. "What?"

Caleb ran on a few steps, then stopped, turned around, and walked back toward him. His breathing seemed a little labored. "It happened to me. It was after my father left the first time. My mom had sort of flipped out, and I went to live at Fathers House."

"Yeah, that was before my mom died," Ben said. "We both were in the afterschool program, and then your dad left, and you went to live at the house. I remember that. But this other thing, the basement, when did that happen?"

"Not long after I moved into the house. I got into some serious trouble. I wanted to help my mom out. I thought if I could just make some money I'd get my family back. I got busted, and Mayo said if I wanted to stay in the house I had to go to the basement for a while. That's when I was introduced to Father's Disciples."

"Where was I?" Ben asked.

"You were still around. We just kind of stopped talking. I got into different things. You were still a good student."

"So were you," Ben said. "Looks like you still turned out okay."

"That's not important right now," Caleb said. "What is important is you."

"Me? What does any of this have to do with me?"

"Father's Disciples is very powerful. Its leader is very powerful, very influential. The syndicate basically runs your fair city, the police department, the DA's office, even the mayor. The Bureau started investigating it a few years ago. When Father's Disciples got wind of that, they killed potential witnesses, including Cain Simmons."

"So he was killed," Ben said under his breath.

"Yes, he was," Caleb said. "None of the deaths were officially linked to the syndicate, but it made the Bureau that much more determined to bust it up."

"But what does any of this have to do with me. I didn't know the syndicate existed."

"I know. But your boss did. Etlzer is in the syndicate's pocket. Its leader controls him."

"Its leader? Mayo?"

"No, his brother. He's called Father."

"His brother, I didn't know..."

Caleb looked around nervously. "Listen, I don't have time to go into everything. I came here to warn you that you're being set up."

"Set up? How? By whom?"

"Father's Disciples and Etlzer. They're trying to throw the Bureau off Father's Disciples' trail by throwing them a few sacrificial lambs. They got indictments on you, a couple of city hall officials, and two or three police officers. They're planning to serve them sometime today."

Ben sat down on the curb. His mind was spinning. None of this made any sense. He looked absently down the street at the houses and saw a few lights flicker on. "Today is Sunday," he said finally as if it should make a difference.

Caleb stood over him. "I know this is fucked up. And I wish there was something I could do. I just wanted you to know beforehand, before they crashed through your door."

Ben's mind drew a blank. All his thoughts—of April, the babies, Etlzer, Mayo, the setup, the indictments rushed together, canceling each other out. He brought his hands up to his head, gripping it, squeezing it within his palms. "Why are you telling me this now?"

Caleb swallowed hard. "I don't know. Maybe, I should have told you this a long time ago. Anyway, there's one other thing."

Ben looked up at him. "What?

Caleb looked his friend briefly in his eyes, before focusing on a spot somewhere on the curb next to Ben. He took a deep breath. "It's about your mom."

***

He didn't have long to wait.

Mrs. Ellison cooked a nice breakfast, but Ben meandered through it, wondering the whole while about the indictments. When would the feds serve them and just how exactly was he going to explain it all to April. He'd thought his life was set. He had a good education. He had April and two sons. He was a homeowner for Christ sakes! He'd done all the right things in life. He hadn't felt sorry for himself when he'd lost his mother. He didn't wallow in self-pity because he didn't have a father. Yet here life was again, throwing him under the bus. Life had taken his mom and his dad. Now it seemed it wanted him too. The knock at the door interrupted those thoughts.

As he looked through the peephole, his eye widened. It was James Etlzer standing on his front porch backed by what appeared to be a small army.

He opened the door. "Jimmy, what's going on?"

A stern voice shot out from Etlzer's right. "Benjamin Clyde Lovison?"

Ben ignored the voice and stared hard at Etlzer. "What's going on, Jimmy?"

Etlzer turned to his right, in the direction of the voice. "It's Lovison." Then he faced Ben again. "Don't make a scene. You knew this was going to happen. You knew we would catch up with you eventually."

The stern voice started up again, yapping something about Ben exiting the house peacefully. It then broke into a recitation of his rights as Ben turned to it. He was a tall man, muscular with a dark and shiny bald scalp. A gold FBI patch was stenciled boldly on the left breastplate of his dark blue jacket which was zipped all the way to the top. Another voice with equal fervor started reciting the state's list of grievances against him. "You are being charged with bribery, dereliction of duty by a public official, public corruption, conspiracy, influencing witnesses, racket…"

"Are you kidding me?" Ben shouted at Etlzer. "Are you freaking kidding me?" The rights and charges he'd heard moments before echoed about in his head. This could not be happening. It was not possible.

He heard his baby boys' cries from above and behind him, seemingly growing louder by the moment as if descending from the heavens. He turned and saw April, holding one of the twins near the bottom of the steps. Mrs. Ellison looking dumbfounded was at the top of the stairs, holding the other. He focused on his wife. "It's not true baby! It's not true." He turned back to Etlzer. "You tell me what's going on, Jimmy."

"I would advise you once again of your right to remain silent," Etlzer replied coolly before adding, "You'll be held at Butler State until you're able to post bail."

"What the dickens is going on here?" Ben turned his head again and saw his father-in-law emerge from the kitchen. April and her parents froze where they stood, open-mouthed and confused. The twins' wails reverberated off the walls of the house and settled into the cold morning.

Ben felt himself go numb, and then his legs buckled.

Chapter 22

The advisory promised that the press conference would start at three o'clock, sharp. It was now 3:17 and so went another government promise. Jim Crouch huddled in the cold with about fifteen other members of the media— print, broadcast, and internet in front of the steps of the Duraleigh County courthouse. The advisory promised breaking news concerning the arrests of some government officials. Speculation and gossip amongst the press ran rampant. Some suggested another shoe had dropped in the Department of Transportation scandal from a few months back. To date, the director of the department, Jamison Pittman, had been the only one indicted in the scandal and his trial had commenced last month. But someone rightly pointed out that the Department of Transportation case was a state matter being handled by the Attorney General's office. The press advisory that lured this current bunch of news hounds had come from the DA's office, meaning it was likely local Duraleigh officials who'd allegedly crossed over to the dark side.

The doors of the courthouse swung open and District Attorney James Etlzer, with four others nipping at his heels, rushed out the building like Kentucky thoroughbreds out the starting gate. Etlzer went immediately to the microphone outfitted podium at the edge of the steps. "Before we get started," he began, "let me introduce the others here. To my immediate right is Tom Ram, Special Agent-In-Charge, FBI, Charlotte. To his right is Chief of Police, Phillip Lawless. To my immediate left, standing in for Mayor Becker who is currently out of town on city business is deputy mayor, Alan Greenberg, and to his left,

Adam Banks, special prosecutor with the Attorney General's office. All four men nodded importantly and stood back. This was clearly Etlzer's show. "It's with mixed emotions I stand here today," Etlzer said solemnly. "While I celebrate the efforts of my investigatory team in uncovering widespread corruption within our city, it is always a sad day when we discover that some of our colleagues have decided to breach the trust and faith that our citizens rightly demand of us. To be sure, the investigation is still ongoing and therefore beyond the list of names of those indicted today, the amount of information that we can share at this time will be limited. I will say that the investigation had commenced about two years ago from a tip received in our office from a concerned citizen. The investigation was a joint effort by my office and the Duraleigh police department. We've since learned that the FBI had also launched an investigation and due to the nature of the allegations, their investigation was being conducted without benefit of any local authorities.

"In your media packets you'll find copies of the indictments. Those indicted include, an assistant district attorney, Ben Lovison, two officials from city hall: assistant city manager, Van Pistilli and city accountant, Walter Grant, and two police officers, Mike Molson, and Bain Freeman. Okay, now I'll take your questions."

A rush of questions attacked him at once. "Whoa," Etlzer said and threw up his hands, "one at a time." He pointed to a blond female reporter near the front. "You."

"Thank you. Lauren Goode, WRAT. Is the FBI's interest because of a link to organized crime?"

Etlzer shot a short, but noticeable glance toward Agent Ram before leaning into the microphones, "I'm sorry. But that would fall outside the limited information we're able to provide at this time. So, no comment."

"Are you anticipating civilian arrests? Goode asked

hurriedly.

"Again, I'm sorry," Etlzer said. "At this time, no comment." He smiled awkwardly and then pointed to Crouch.

Crouch briefly consulted his notebook. "Jim Crouch, Duraleigh Standard. Two weeks ago at the Public Safety conference, Ben Lovison was being touted as a success story. In light of the indictments, was it appropriate to have showcased him?"

Etlzer didn't miss a beat as if he'd anticipated the question. "As I said at the beginning, it's always sad when our colleagues choose a different path, an illegal path. Ben Lovison was someone I had a lot of hope in, a lot of confidence in. I hired him. And initially he showed a lot of promise. So, of course I was disappointed to have to investigate him for possible wrongdoing. But in this country, we're innocent until proven guilty. And we're definitely assumed innocent during the investigatory phrase. So, as his participation in the conference clearly showed, and you'll continue to see as this case unfolds, there was no rush to judgment."

It was Etlzer's last elaborate answer as he responded to the remaining questions with a curt "no comment."

As Crouch headed back to his car he had the nagging suspicion that he and the others had been duped into providing background optics for Etlzer's photo op. The little information they'd gotten could have just as well been delivered via a press release. Oh well, he thought as he got into his Honda and cranked it up, Etlzer was running for governor, this most likely wouldn't be the last time he'd try to use the media for a free campaign commercial.

As Crouch drove away from the courthouse, his thoughts turned to Mike Molson, one of the indicted. Crouch had done a few ride-alongs with Molson for a series of stories Crouch had done on the police department. He'd considered Molson a friend and even had dinner with the young cop and his wife, Melissa. Molson had been on the force for less than three years. Crouch wondered how in that short time, he could have gotten himself involved in what appeared to be deep rooted corruption. Then, as he approached a red light, he suddenly remembered the letter.

When Etlzer returned to his office he found a nervous Robert Cole pacing back and forth. Etlzer ignored him and walked right past him to his desk and sat down. He loosened his tie and leaned back in the chair.

Cole stood in front of the desk. "I've worked on many cases involving Father's Disciples. What's going to prevent this from falling back on me or the others?"

Etlzer closed his eyes and interlocked his fingers nonchalantly across his chest. "The paper files no longer exist and their computer versions all show Lovison as the primary. If the feds insist on seeing them, that's what they'll find. But I don't think it'll get that far. Ram seemed confident that we've uncovered the conspiracy. He's even asked for our assistance in taking down Father's Disciples."

"But what about Ben," Cole asked nervously. "He knows which cases he's worked on."

Etlzer smirked lifelessly, "Ben Lovison will be dead before morning."

Chapter 23

Ben sat alone in his cell. He had been moved to Butler
State Prison, supposedly for his own safety. He was told
that the officials at the Duraleigh County Jail could not
guarantee the safekeeping of two Duraleigh police officers
and an assistant district attorney on such short notice.
According to the people that claimed to know, the inmates
over there would be biting at the bit to get at anyone in law
enforcement. It would be a feather in an inmate's cap. Not
to mention the ultimate revenge factor since anyone ever
accused or convicted of anything always blamed either the
victim, circumstances, or the fucked up wheels of justice
for his predicament. And no one represented the wheels of
justice more acutely than a prosecutor.

Ben looked around the small cell. A dull-gray steel
toilet squatted in the corner, uncomfortably close to the
dinner tray a guard had bought in moments earlier.
Unwanted, the sickly looking apple, biscuit, baked chicken
thigh, and the jaundiced-colored mashed potatoes were left
untouched. He hadn't eaten anything since nibbling at the
breakfast Mrs. Ellison had cooked that morning. He wasn't
hungry.

Suddenly he felt himself losing his breath. An anxiety
attack. He put his hand over his chest and tried to take in
some deep breaths. But his breaths came quick and sounded
stunted like something partially caught in the suction hose
of a vacuum cleaner. He'd been locked up about twelve
hours and the room had gotten to him. It was an almost
colorless room. Although there were different colors in the
room, they all appeared gray to him. The cement walls
were actually gray. But the bars, though badly in need of a

paint bath, were mostly beige. The blanket covering the bed was a type of faded army green. Still, it all looked gray to him. Eventually his breathing returned to normal. He lay back on the single bunk, his eyes open, but unseeing.

He'd spoken briefly with April by phone a couple of hours after his arrest. He could feel her tears through the phone and it took all his resolve not to match her tear for tear. He'd never known her to lose it like that. She had always been a picture of strength. He remembered her stoic expression and how composed she'd been when the twins had made their unscheduled arrival. Her demeanor had helped him remain calm. Perhaps, he thought now, she'd been so calm because it had been her body, her situation. Maybe she'd felt a little more in control in that environment. Sure the twins had dictated the terms of their release, but they still had needed their mother's full cooperation. April, undoubtedly, had still felt a measure of control of her body. And since this current situation was way outside the realm of her body and outside the realm of her control maybe that had been the motivation for her tears. Maybe she was feeling now as he'd felt during the birth of his boys. Helpless, an outsider watching nature do what it do. What it had done since the dawn of mankind and would continue to do whether he'd been in the midst of it or not. Now April was most likely feeling like the outsider. She was caught in the middle of a situation where the rules had been set, the game was underway, and she had no idea how to proceed. She had no control.

But what she didn't know, and he couldn't allow her to know, was that he also had no control. His life was spiraling out of control all around him, and he had no clue how to stop it. Nothing made sense. He was sitting in this jail cell with a ridiculously high, five million dollar bail for doing his job. There was something wrong with the picture. Definitely something he wasn't getting. But what? Mentally, he'd gone through all his prior cases. There'd been plea agreements, but nothing highly unusual. How was Etlzer able to convince a grand jury to indict him? What evidence had he used?

"Lovison, you have a visitor." The mumbled voice came from outside his cell. Ben looked up and saw a chubby guard standing there, slightly wobbling from side to side as if his feet hurt. It was not the same one that had brought the food.

"I was told I couldn't have any visitors," Ben said.

"It's your attorney," the guard replied. He eyed the untouched food. "You done with that?"

Ben stood up and walked toward the cell doors. "Yes."

"Fourteen!" The guard yelled. Almost immediately the steel-barred door slid to its right with a metallic yelp. To Ben, the guard said, "I wouldn't advise passing up any meals. Even if you're not hungry, you need to get something in you. There ain't any late night refrigerator raids here."

"Thanks for that. I'll keep it in mind," Ben said. He felt the shortness in breath returning. He breathed in deeply and tried to summon up positive thoughts.

He was led beyond the visiting area and down a well lit hallway of semi-darkened rooms with closed doors, thick glass up top, prison-steel on bottom. "These rooms are strictly for attorney-inmate visits," the guard explained. "Of course, we don't have many of those on Sundays."

Soon they were standing in front of one of the doors. The room was the only fully lit one in the hall. Ben could see Frank Vass sitting inside the room alone at a table. The guard opened the door and allowed Ben into the room. "I'm afraid I'm going to have to lock you in," he said after Ben had crossed into the room. The guard closed the door after him. Ben heard the metallic clink of the lock cylinder falling into place.

Frank stood. "Ben, are you okay?"

Ben walked toward him, extending his hand. "I'm fine,

Frank. Thanks for asking and thanks for taking my case."

They shook hands like long lost friends. "No need to thank me. When I saw the press conference on the indictments, I was hoping I could get involved. So, I was glad when I got the call from your wife. I don't know all what's going on, but I have my thoughts."

"My wife, how is she?"

"Considering what you're up against, as well as can be expected. I went to your house where I met her and your in-laws. Your five million dollar bail has got them all on edge. I got the impression that your father-in-law has the means to pay it. But the sheer amount of it is giving him some doubts about you, which obviously is causing some tension in the house."

"I know," Ben said. "We hadn't been the closest and now this."

They sat down on opposite sides of the table. Ben clasped his fingers together and looked solemnly at Frank.

Frank said, "I saw you a few weeks ago getting on the elevator at the courthouse. I called you but I don't think you heard me."

Ben smiled uneasily. "Oh yeah I remember. I heard you and saw you, a little too late I'm afraid. I had so much on my mind at that time that I didn't quite recognize you or your voice until the elevator doors started to close. I thought to myself, man, that was Frank Vass."

"I figured as much," Frank said. "I found out later that your twins had been born prematurely that same morning. I saw them at the house. They look great."

"Thank you. We're blessed."

Ben had met Frank Vass during a mock trial competition during law school. They went to different schools and thusly were on opposite teams. Frank, a third-year man had been thoroughly impressed by the obvious courtroom talent of first year law student Ben Lovison. Frank's team ultimately won the competition, thanks in large part to Frank's own considerable courtroom skills. Afterwards, Frank had to meet the young man who had stood toe to toe with him, almost pulling out the win for his own team. The two met again years later in a real courtroom. The stakes were a little higher; a man's freedom had been at stake. But both of their skills proved as formidable in a real courtroom as they had in the mock trials. And again Frank came out victorious as well as impressed with Ben's courtroom talent. They'd shared a drink afterwards, and though the relationship hadn't grown to that of best buds forever, there had been born a mutual professional respect.

"I'm innocent," Ben offered unprovoked. "I don't know anything about any corruption or bribery, and I knew nothing of Father's Disciples until about a month ago."

"I believe you," Frank said matter-of-factly. "But why don't you start from the beginning and tell me everything you know."

Ben told him about Calvin Leeson, and about Cain Simmons and what the teen had told him about Fathers House and Father's Disciples. He told him about the conversation he'd had with Caleb earlier that morning, confirming Cain's story and the teen's murder, and about Ben being set up. (He didn't tell him about Caleb and his mother's murder. He wasn't ready to deal with it.)

Frank listened intently without interrupting, occasionally nodding his head and writing in his notebook. When Ben had finished, Frank said, "I talked to a reporter who'd attended the press conference. He said Etlzer had refused to say if there was any link between those indicted and Father's Disciples."

Ben sighed and then suddenly remembered what Frank had said at the start of the visit. "You said before that you had your thoughts, what did you mean?"

Frank leaned back in his chair, dropped his pen, and rubbed his chin. "I'll get to that. But first, tell me about you and Fathers House."

Ben paused, tilted his head, and looked at Frank curiously. "Well," he began slowly. "There's not much to tell. Fathers House provides an afterschool program for boys and also serves as a home for wayward or otherwise homeless boys. I played there as a kid. And I lived there for about five years, after my mom was shot and killed."

Frank said, "I've heard rumors through the years, mostly from defense attorneys that some individuals connected with Fathers House were receiving sweetheart deals from the DA's office, slaps on the wrist so to speak."

Ben slowly shook his head. "I wouldn't know anything about that. But I can assure you that Fathers House never came up in any plea deal agreements that I'd been involved with. I can only recall about a handful of cases with boys associated with Fathers House. On some I recused myself, others I handled, depending. But I handled all my cases fairly." He paused. "There was one case I handled recently. It was with a kid by the name of Peyton Lars. I checked his case history and apparently I had worked an earlier case with him. I don't recall it all. But apparently he was living at Fathers House at the time. I hadn't mentioned it. At least no mention of it was in the file. It had been his first offense. He'd gotten probation. But honestly, I wouldn't have handled his case any differently had he lived anywhere else."

Frank jotted down notes, but didn't comment.

Ben said, "Does that mean anything?"

Frank continued writing for a moment before looking up. "I don't know. I'll look into it." He wrote something else in his notebook, and then, "What kind of man is Mayo Fathers?"

"He's a good man," Ben said. "He took me in. He encouraged me to finish high school, go to college and to law school. For most of the boys that live in that house, he's all they got." He paused. "Look, I don't have the answers. I don't know of any connection between Fathers House, Mayo Fathers, and Father's Disciples. But it's hard to imagine Mayo being involved."

"So, you believe in this character Caleb told you about, Father?"

"I don't know." He looked squarely at Frank, searching his face, his eyes, his mannerisms, anything for a sign of possible doubt at what he Ben had said. He knew what Frank was thinking. How could he not know anything? He'd played and lived at the house. He'd worked for years in the DA's office. How could he possibly not have had a clue about what supposedly went on evidently under his very nose? It was the same question Ben had asked himself, but one he hadn't been able to answer to his own satisfaction. He could only imagine what all was going through Frank's mind. However, if it was doubt, the counselor wasn't letting on. His face showed no emotion. It had the same kind, concerned expression that had first greeted Ben when he was led into the room by the guard.

Just before their silence reached the threshold of uneasiness, Frank said, "Look, somebody's going through an awful lot of trouble to show not only your awareness of the conspiracy, but also that you're neck-high in the middle of it."

"We have to start with Etlzer. He's the reason I'm sitting here."

"Okay, but it's possible that Etlzer's not pulling the strings. My thoughts are that he may very well be a puppet himself. He's getting all shined up for a governor's run. After Attorney General Butch Waters' heart attack, Duraleigh's DA has been the odds on favorite to be the next governor."

"Well, it would have to be Mayo Fathers," Ben admitted reluctantly. "And his brother." That possible truth was hard to accept. But he had to face facts even if he didn't understand them. He'd thought Mayo had been a

Godsend, helping him in his time of need, encouraging him to make something of his life. But apparently, it had all been smoke and mirrors.

Vass said, "That's a hell of a conspiracy theory. But if true, I can see how Waters is in their back pocket. Either way, we're going to have to get you out of here."

"You think I'm in immediate danger?"

Frank looked at him incredulously. "State prison, Five million dollar bail."

"My family," Ben said.

"They're okay. I have people watching your house."

"Who?"

"Trust me," Vass said. "They're safe. But you're not. Your first court appearance is scheduled for tomorrow morning at nine o'clock. It would be great if you could post bail tonight. But if not, I'm sure I can get the bail reduced tomorrow which is probably what Etlzer and his cronies will figure as well."

"You think someone will try to kill me before then?" Ben asked. It was a wild assumption. But one he couldn't entirely dismiss. After all, a five million dollar bail was unreasonably high. Any rational judge would reduce it, which meant it took an irrational one to set that amount in the first place. Logic dictated he'd done so for a reason. And as Frank pointed out, he was sitting in state prison and not the Duraleigh county jail. Though he couldn't quite figure out why that was particularly important. Surely, if someone wanted him dead and had the means to make it happen, the goal could be accomplished just as well at the county jail.

Frank didn't answer his question. Instead, he said, "I've requested that the warden place you on suicide watch."

"Suicide watch? Wouldn't that give my would-be assassins a plausible explanation for my potential demise?"

"It would," Frank agreed. "But it would also put you

under constant surveillance. Hopefully, that'll keep you safe until we can get you out of here."

***

The elimination of the assistant district attorney had been meticulously planned and immediately put in motion. The honor would be shared by a couple of inmates in D-Block, 19701949B and 19451966C, known to the outside world or at least in their former little corners of it as Zach Weaver and Rico Evans. Both were a couple of two-bit hustlers doing long-term prison time on drug convictions. They weren't affiliated with Father's Disciples on the outside, but pulling off Lovison's killing would not only get them into the group on the inside, but would also give them unique status amongst the prisoners. Inside prison, prosecutors were lower than the scum of the earth.

"You ready, Zach?" Rico asked. He lay on his back on his bed, looking up at the underside of Zach's bunk.

"Can't wait," Zach said. "Remember I get the kill shot. I'm going to stab him right through his heart."

"I'm going for his throat," Rico said confidently. "It'll be a symbolic message to all those lying prosecuting bastards. You lie in court; you'll get your voice box ripped right out."

There wasn't anything particularly funny about his gruesome remark, but the both of them laughed so hard that someone yelled for them to shut up.

Chapter 24

Mike Molson's lapse in judgment had occurred during his second year on the force. It had been late night around 11 PM. A blue sedan made an illegal right-hand turn. The sign next to the traffic signal was clear—no turns on red. Molson blue-lighted the sedan and the driver pulled over immediately. There were two occupants in the car—the driver and a passenger in the front seat. They were both African-American males and appeared to be in their late teens to early twenties. Molson only intended to check the driver's license and registration, and then let the driver off with a warning. There was hardly any traffic. The no-turn-on-red sign, though enforceable twenty-four hours a day, was really meant for the afternoon traffic when pedestrians were more apt to be crossing the street at that intersection. Problem was the driver's license to drive had expired and additionally, Molson detected a hint of marijuana in the car. A search of the car found several packaged baggies of weed and $10,000 cash. It was a major drug bust. Or it would have been. Before Molson had realized what happened. The weed and the blue sedan were gone and he was back in his patrol car, going in the opposite direction, $10,000 richer.

He had no explanation as to why at that time, that precise moment, he'd succumbed to temptation. He was an honest person. He'd been an honest cop. He'd told himself right after the incident that it would be the one and only time. But as it turned out, the blue sedan's driver and passenger were couriers for Father's Disciples and the stop had been an orchestrated test to see if they could flip a cop, Officer Mike Molson in particular. The $10,000 turned out to be the first of his "bonus" money to continue to do as he'd done that night, and evidently what some Duraleigh officers had long done—look the other way.

Now as he lay on his bunk in his jail cell, he thought about his two young sons. They didn't deserve a morally corrupt father. He hoped that they'd understand that he hadn't always been this way. He was a good man once and they were good boys. He thought about the recording he'd made of his explanation of that night as well as his confession of subsequent nights when he'd known exactly what he'd been doing and why. The recording was included on a SD memory card he'd hid at the Duraleigh police department. The memory card was for his boys and would be his final salvo. It included information that could help bring down Father's Disciples. He hoped that one day when the hurt from him not being there had subsided, his sons would forgive him and even find a measure of pride in him.

The jailer brought him the two aspirins he'd requested earlier, along with a cup of water. He put them both into his mouth, sliding them in with the pill he'd just pulled from his navel, He quickly downed the water. Immediately he felt his throat clogging up as if it had been stuffed with rags. He grabbed his neck and started gagging. He flashed a terrified glare at the jailer who himself was wide-eyed with shock.

"Something's happening here," the jailer yelled. "Open the damn cell! He's convulsing!"

* * *

"I'll take you to the basement."

At first Prodegee didn't think he'd heard right. Especially since all he'd heard from Maalik during the past week was how much Maalik didn't want to talk about the basement. How he hadn't wanted to talk about anything. Prodegee had begun to think that maybe Ram had been right. That Maalik was in too fragile a state right now to be of any use. The boy had been almost catatonic. He'd been barely eating, barely sleeping, barely talking. Barely anything.

Prodegee was sitting on the couch in the family room. He turned his head slightly to his left and looked intently at Maalik who was standing in the doorway. The television was tuned to the Cartoon Network. An episode of Scooby-Doo played disinterestedly. It was 8 o'clock, Sunday night. Miss Helm's 'me-time hour' as she called it. The older boys took that as an opportunity to escape the premises for a couple of hours.

When he finally realized what he'd heard, his first instinct was to ask the stupid question—what made you change your mind. But common sense quickly prevailed. What did it matter why a led horse started drinking? So long as he drank. So, he stood up and walked to the doorway toward Maalik. "Alright, let's do it."

The key slid easily into the basement door lock, Maalik turned it while simultaneously twisting the doorknob. After a metallic click, Maalik pushed the door open. He hesitated and looked back over his shoulder at Prodegee, as if to say, last chance to change your mind. Prodegee shrugged his commitment and stepped past him onto the basement top landing. Maalik held onto the door, slowing its momentum as it swung back closed. "I took this key off Uncle Mayo's keychain," he said.

"Won't he miss that?" Prodegee asked.

"Maybe," Maalik replied indifferently as he scooted past him, heading down the stairs. "Follow me."

"Wait a minute," Prodegee said, "What if he comes back early from that church thing?"

"It won't matter. He never comes to the basement."

"What are you going to show me?" Prodegee asked.

"The Book," Maalik said.

"What book?"

"The Book. The executioner read from it just before he killed Nas. That agent guy told me that I belonged to an organization that killed its own and that we weren't really a family. He said that they killed Calvin and probably Cain. If that's true, then the Book will have Calvin's and Cain's names in it, and those other cats that got killed at the funeral."

"And if it does?" Prodegee asked.

"Then, I want out."

Prodegee's eyes hadn't adjusted to the dark yet and he could barely see. He moved tentatively behind Maalik down the steps.

A double row of dimmed ceiling lights greeted them when they reached the bottom landing. Maalik took a few steps and then stopped in front of a glass wall. He pointed to it. "That's where Nas was killed."

"How do you know the man that killed him is not here somewhere?"

"I told you. He was killed at the funeral."

"Are you sure? You said Nas's killer wore a mask."

"He did. And he was huge. What're the odds of two dudes that large being in the same area code. That was the same cat."

The glass door wasn't locked. They entered and Maalik walked right past some metal looking thing in the center of the room, straight to the back table where an overhang lamp provided the only light in the room. The Book was the only thing on the table.

Maalik flipped it over and started breezing through the pages from back to front. After a moment, he stopped flipping pages and started sliding a thin finger down one of the pages. The finger froze on a spot. Prodegee leaned in and squinted at the name under Maalik's finger.

His eyes widened and his mouth opened, but before he could utter Cain Simmons's name, someone flipped on the overhead lights.

Johnston waited about twenty minutes after the agent had entered the hotel room before knocking on the door.

"Yeah," A deep voice from the other side barked.

Johnston held his ID up to the peephole. "Detective Johnston, Duraleigh PD."

The door opened. "Yeah."

"May I come in?"

Ram waved out his arm, allowing Johnston into the room. "What can I do for you, detective?"

"I have some information that you may find useful."

Ram closed the door. "Concerning?"

Johnston glanced around the room. It was a typical hotel room. A couch, a bed, and a refrigerator. There was a laptop on the table and a chair slightly pushed away from it. Ram had already kicked off his shoes. "Father's Disciples."

"Interesting," Ram said. He pointed to the couch and Johnston walked to it and sat down. "How did you know where to find me?"

"I followed you from the press conference."

"That was over five hours ago."

"Yeah, well, I kinda followed you the rest of the day."

"Why me?"

"Because I can't trust anyone in Duraleigh," he reached into his jacket pocket and pulled out the flash drive, "with this."

"What is it?"

"A flash drive."

"What's on it?"

"Maybe you should just plug it into that laptop over there."

Ram took the flash drive from him and walked over to his laptop. "Where did you get it?"

"Deacon Storrs. It belonged to his wife, Cindy. She'd kept it in a safe deposit box."

Ram put the flash drive into one of the laptop ports.

"Why didn't you take this to the DA?"

"Like I said, right now I don't trust anyone in Duraleigh. I don't know who's clean or who's on the take. If the DA is truly one of the good guys, you can share that flash drive with him, have a real pajama party. Right now, I feel better with that in your hands."

Ram tapped a couple of keys on his laptop and sat back in the chair. For the next several minutes he said nothing. Johnston could see images of computer data bouncing off the FBI man's ever widening pupils. Thirty minutes in, Ram uttered, "Mmm, interesting." An hour in, he started smiling. "It's financial statements," he said finally. "They go back all the way to 1986." Still staring intently at the laptop monitor, he added, "Father's Disciples is run like a Fortune 500 company. These are balance sheets, income statements..." he paused again. "There are copies of the funeral home business's income tax statements here." He looked up and motioned for Johnston to join him at the table. "Look here," he pointed at the laptop monitor. Johnston leaned over his shoulder, peering at the screen. Ram continued, "The funeral business is essentially just a part of Father's Disciples, the corporation. See here. According to a witness we have in custody, this amount here listed as a long term asset is actually the syndicate's drug money. And according to her, the money is also hid in the funeral services provided as well as here." He pointed to the screen again. " Under these long term capital outlays for equipment, embalming equipment, computers, software, building improvements, etc., They even list the payoffs as liabilities and if you click here, it takes you to a breakdown of the payoffs—the police department, mayor's office....it even lists when the payments were made. There are no names, but with the way it's listed here, it shouldn't take much effort to track where the money went. We'll get our financial experts to sort it all out. But with the witness we have in custody and this information..." he didn't finish, chuckling as he stared excitedly at the screen.

The information on the flash drive was plentiful; Ram couldn't concentrate on any one thing. He was like a kid let loose in a candy store. "Wow!" he said excitedly as the fast moving data on the monitor continued reflecting off his pupils.

After Johnston left, Ram eventually collapsed back in his chair, wondering how fast he could get Sarah Leeson in front of this information and which judge would be more receptive to signing search warrants for Fathers Funeral Home and Fathers House on this fine Sunday evening.

Chapter 25

After Sunday chow, Peyton Lars headed back to his cell. He kept his eyes fixed to the floor, avoiding eye contact with anyone. Today had been a tough mental day which is how he described any day when the memories of the attempted sexual assault dominated his thoughts, almost crippling him. He tried pushing the thoughts out of his mind. But as always, his efforts were futile. The nearly successful assault still gripped him.

Outside prison walls, tales of inmates being raped in prison were always met with shrugs as if it was to be expected. He'd also heard the tales and he too had believed it probably happened more times than not. But he never imagined it could happen to him, especially with his connections to Father's Disciples. Despite his imaginings and his so called connections, the unthinkable had almost happened,

Even now, four weeks later, he still had trouble believing Cleo's unmitigated gall in attacking a Father's Disciple, and in his own cell even. But he had. It had been only a week after Lars had entered prison. Cleo had obviously been still upset over their initial encounter and had decided one night to apply his own brand of justice for Lars' perceived disrespect for prison customs. The big man had waited for Lars to drift to sleep when he climbed onto his back, easily subduing him, and effortlessly pulling his shorts and drawers down to his ankles.

Lars would never know how Luther had known that Cleo had planned to attack him on that particular night. What had almost happened to him was something he never wanted to discuss. And Luther seemed obliged to honor the unspoken request. To this day, he hadn't mentioned anything about it. He'd even had Cleo dealt with under the table and removed from the cell. Luther undoubtedly had some string-pulling ability. Or perhaps it had been Father's Disciples coming to the rescue a day late and a dollar short. Still, there was no doubt in Lars' mind who he owed. It was Luther. Not Father's Disciples. Not the guards. It was only Luther.

After returning to his cell, he sat down on his bed. Chow, as usual, had been unfulfilling. He reached under his bed and pulled out a box. It was filled with potato chips, cookies, crackers, and bags of noodles, compliments of friends from the outside. He eyed the old metal heater lined up against the wall. Thanks to a cold front that eased in today, the old heater hummed with life. Looks like a hot soup evening, he thought as he plucked the bag of noodles out of the box. Next, he grabbed a plastic spoon and a metal bowl, and then he slid the box back under his bed. As he prepared his meal, he wondered, not for the first time, how to repay a man that had essentially saved his manhood.

This time the answer came to him so quickly that he wondered why he hadn't thought of it sooner. Subconsciously the answer had been born a couple of weeks before. After the attack he'd taken to spending as much time with Luther as allowed. Most of it spent in the older man's cell. It was there that Lars had noticed all the pictures and newspaper clippings of the assistant district attorney who was obviously someone very special to Luther. The wall montage chronicled the assistant DA's life from birth to adulthood. It was the kind of showcase that would be set up by either a love-starved fan or a parent. Lars strongly suspected the latter, and he had the added benefit of knowing that the assistant DA was now Butler's newest, albeit temporary, resident. And if all went according to Father's plan, he would not see the light of day.

His creation started bubbling on the old heater. He dipped his spoon in it, scooping up a bit. The taste was as good as could be expected given the circumstances. He stirred the soup some more and tasted it again, and then laid the spoon next to the metal bowl.

He lay back on his bed, savoring the morsel of soup swishing about in his mouth and the notion of how he was going to be able to return a solid.

***

Ben was clearly not built for incarceration. Though he was from the hood, he was by no means hardened. He'd been in only one fistfight his entire life. And that had ended with him throwing a blind punch which had luckily landed on his adversary's lip, busting it. It had been a lucky punch that had served him well the rest of his school career. His adversary had been a well-known and respected bully, who, surprisingly to Ben and most likely himself, had been terribly afraid at the sight of his own blood. After the punch, which had been witnessed by several of Ben's sixth-grade classmates, the bully went yelling and crying to the nurse's office. From that moment forward, Ben had had no problems from the bully, or anyone else for that matter.

But prison would be different. One punch whether thrown blindly or strategically was not going to cut it. He would have to learn to defend himself, to watch his own back. He would not be able to count on the kindness of strangers to help him. Not in prison. Until he could get out of here, he would have to be careful. He would have to avoid any and all contact with the other prisoners. And pray to God that his bail would be lowered or his father-in-law would have a change of heart and get him out of here.

At nine o'clock, he saw an inmate standing at his cell door. It was still a couple of hours until lights out. His cell door rolled open. The man walked in, carrying pillows. Ben scrambled to his feet. "Who the hell are you?"

"You're going to have to come with me," the man said.

"I'm not going anywhere with you," Ben said.

The man took a tentative step forward. "It's not safe here. Not on this cell block. Not tonight."

"I'm on suicide watch," Ben said.

"And how's that working out for you?"

"And you can take me to a safe place? Here in this prison?" Ben asked suspiciously.

"For a little while, yes," the man said confidently. "Hopefully you'll make bail before too long."

Make bail, Ben thought. How did this man know his situation? Regardless, this could be a trick. Ben looked beyond the man into the hallway. "Where's the guard?"

"It's a shift change. But having you here is little out of the norm. We have to hurry."

Ben stepped back. "I'm not going anywhere with you. I don't know who you are. I don't know what you want."

"The name's Luther Savannah," the man said. "And I don't have time to explain further." He took the pillows over to the bed and placed them end to end under the covers, making it look like a body. He turned to Ben and reached into his pocket and pulled out a photograph. He handed it to Ben. "Maybe this will help explain things."

Ben looked at the photograph, and then looked at Luther. Ben's jaw dropped open. "Damn."

Ben looked from the cell wall, to Luther Savannah, and then back to the wall. It was quite literally a shrine to him. There were pictures of him from toddler all the way through to his ninth-grade year. There were also newspaper clippings from his high school days, ones featuring his athletic exploits and ones which had his name amongst many, highlighted so as to stand out. The newspaper clipping from eight years ago, announcing his being hired as an assistant district attorney was also there— framed and set a little apart from the others. It was obviously a source of pride.

Luther was standing near the doorway of his cell, watching as Ben studied the wall. "I dreamed about this moment many times," Luther said. "What I'd say to you. How you'd react. Of course, in my dreams I'd received a pardon from the governor and was set free. I imagined you well-to-do enough to hire me on as a handyman. After several weeks of working hard and being responsible, I'd gradually gain your trust. We'd start talking more and more. Eventually, I'd tell you about my life. How I'd made some bad choices, landing myself in prison. I'd tell you how my biggest regret was not being there for my family— my girlfriend and my son. I'd say when you've been sentenced to life in prison without the possibility of parole, you have to make some hard choices. Do you tether your family to what essentially will be a corpse? Or do you set them free? Free to pursue happiness and to live their lives to the fullest without the burdensome requirement of being family to someone who could only take, never give. But really that wouldn't be exactly true. Your mom stayed in contact with me. She sent me pictures of you, until…until someone took her away from me, away from us."

Ben turned around to face him. He knew who had taken his mom away. But he was not yet sure, despite the visual testament of adoration displayed on the cell wall that this man was who he was claiming to be. Calmly he said, "In your dreams, what exactly was my reaction?"

Luther smiled awkwardly. "Well even in my dreams you'd be upset. But eventually you'd see my point. How I didn't want you to see your old man like this, locked up like an animal. How I didn't want you to think that somehow this was your destiny. That we were a cursed lot or this was hereditary. In my dreams, eventually, you forgive me."

Ben walked closer to Luther and looked him square in the eyes. "Well. This is real life. No fairytales here. Right now I don't know whether to hug you or strangle you, or simply ignore you. You see, I'm not sure you are who you say you are."

Tears welled in Luther's eyes as he said, "I am…"

Ben held up his hand, preventing Luther from continuing. "Stop. Whether you are or not, I'm not ready for this. So why don't you just tell me how you knew my life was in danger, and how it is that I'm allowed to be here with you."

Luther swallowed hard. "Okay. Fair enough. Peyton Lars told me what was going on."

Ben remembered the name. "The Lars kid. He just accepted a plea deal a few weeks ago. Drug trafficking."

Luther nodded his head. "Lars, like me, is a member of Father's Disciples. He was being used to help set you up. His job was to talk to the grand jury. According to him, he was to accuse you of having offered him a sweetheart settlement in exchange for sexual favors. When he'd refused, you railroaded him, landing him here."

"Not a word of that's true," Ben exclaimed.

"I know," Luther said. "He admitted it to me. I kept him from being raped in here and he felt like he owed me something. When he was in my cell, he saw your pictures on the wall and figured you were close to me."

"So Father's Disciples wanted me dead?" Ben asked.

"Yeah."

"Any idea why?"

"No,"

"But, you were able to stop it?"

"For now."

"Doesn't that put you in danger," Ben asked.

"I'll be alright."

Ben looked off for a moment, and then faced Luther once more. "But this is still prison. How were you able to come get me? How am I able to be here?"

Luther nodded. "Yes, this is prison. Make no mistake about that. I've been locked up over thirty years. I've made more friends than enemies. Most of the guards respect me, the honest ones anyway, because I help keep the peace around here. So, I called in a favor."

Ben moved to the bunk and sat down. "So, you know my story. Tell me yours. How did you get involved with Father's Disciples?"

"I don't know how you'll take this," Luther said. "I'm one of the founding fathers." He gave Ben a condensed version of the syndicate's not so humble beginnings. He told him about Father's rule, the arrangement with Duraleigh officials, and how the organization was set up within the prison system.

When he finished, Ben said, "So Father is a real person."

"He is."

They were quiet for a while and then Ben asked, "Why are you in prison?"

"I killed a man," Luther answered in a matter of fact tone. "It was gang related and stupid. If I had it to do all over again, I…"

"Not now," Ben said cutting him off. "Here's an easier question—are Father and Mayo really brothers?"

"Yes," Luther said. "Twins." He told Ben the story of how Matthew Albert Fathers had literally thrown away one of his sons because he'd been born with dark skin.

"Identical twins born with different pigmentation," Ben said. He was trying to get his head around that.

"It's rare. But it happened," Luther said.

They sat in uncomfortable silence for awhile, partly thinking about the cruel weirdness of nature, but mostly about each other. Were they really father and son here together? For Luther, it was a reality of something he'd longed dreamed about. Not that his son would be in prison, but that he would one day share a room and conversation with his first and only born. It was a dream he'd had for so long that now the reality felt dreamlike. For Ben, after having spent his entire life trying to come to grips with the fact that he had no father, his mind was not yet willing to accept the possibility that he was sharing a room with him.

"Luther, your boy here is sprung." The voice came from outside the cell. Ben looked up. Luther turned around. A guard was standing there. "You've made bail. Your attorney is waiting for you."

Ben looked at Luther who indicated that the guard was okay. Ben stood as the cell door slowly rolled open. He looked at Luther for a long moment. But he didn't say anything more. Instead, he reached down and took the photo from Luther's hand. Luther nodded his head, and then watched as the guard led his son down the corridor. When he was no longer in sight, Luther went back to his bunk and laid down. Questions swirled in his head. Mainly, why was Father trying to kill his only son. Thirty-three years ago when Luther had taken sole responsibility for the murder that landed him in prison, Father had promised not only to make sure that Luther's family kept a roof over its head but also not to involve Luther's only son in any type of gang-related business. Although technically, trying to have his son killed was not involving him in gang business, but it surely seemed to violate the spirit of the agreement. What was Father up to?

***

Shortly after 11 o'clock p. m., Officer Lowell Paxton, a sixteen year veteran guard, without forethought or concern as to what he might say to the warden on tomorrow morning, casually hit a switch on the control panel, rolling open the door to cell number fourteen. With lighting speed, two inmates who at that hour should have been comfortably asleep in their own cell calmly strolled into the cell that was supposed to have been occupied by temporary resident, Ben Lovison. Shanks in hand, they attacked the covered mound in the bed with sick malice. It wasn't until after they'd noticed that what should have been splashing blood was actually scattering feathers that they realized that Ben Lovison wasn't there.

Chapter 26

By 10 PM, the news of Officer Mike Molson's suicide had spread amongst his colleagues like a wind-fueled brush fire. Both those with and without knowledge of the conspiracy were equally shocked at the traumatic end to what had been a most imperfect day. Now everyone viewed everyone and everything with suspicion, as no one knew when or if or under what circumstances the next shoe would drop. So was the atmosphere at the station when Jim Crouch approached the desk sergeant about doing yet another story on the police department.

"It's kind of late in the night to be coming around here about a story," Dan Clark said with a raised eyebrow. Clark was a twenty-two year veteran of the force, half of which was spent behind the desk he now occupied. He was a thin man with a full head of dusty-gray hair.

"I know," Crouch said. "But Molson was a friend of mine. If there's anything positive that can be gleaned from this, I want to find it. He has two sons and a widow for Christ's sake."

"What do you think you're going to find by just walking around the station?"

"Hopefully, inspiration," Crouch said evenly.

"You know all media requests go through our PIO who works 8 to 5."

"I'm not asking questions tonight. I'm just walking around. I'm not even sure yet what angle I'm going to use for the story."

Clark hesitated before shaking his head dismissively. "I guess I'll never understand you media types. But suit yourself. And Crouch, remember, no questions."

"Don't worry. No questions."

Mike Molson had given Crouch the letter after their last ride along last September, with the explicit instructions for it not to be opened unless something happened to him. Crouch had asked specifically if that by something he meant death and Mike had replied that death was definitely a something, but it wouldn't be the only something. Therefore, the letter had been opened before Crouch had received the news of his friend's suicide.

The memory card was supposed to have been taped to the underside of a table near the coffeemaker in the break room. Crouch walked around the station for awhile, looking as if in deep contemplation. Few of the officers looked him in the eyes and those that did, flashed either disbelief, suspicion, or a sort of self-pity.

He was in luck. The break room was empty. He walked over to the table near the coffeemaker and casually dropped his pen. When he knelt to pick it up, he shot a glance under the table. It was there. In the letter, Mike had said that even though the police department was the reason he'd had to write the letter in the first place, it was still the safest place for the memory card. The one place the real bad guys probably wouldn't think to look for it. Although as far as he knew, they wouldn't know that it existed.

Crouch looked around the room hurriedly and then snatched the masking taped memory card from the table's underside.

***

After Ben rang the doorbell a second time, Frank said, "You probably should have called. It's almost eleven o'clock."

"Phone calls can roll into voicemail," Ben said. His finger hovered over the doorbell. "I need to see Doc tonight."

He punched the doorbell again and waited. After a few moments, the porch light came on. He shouted at the door. "It's Ben Lovison, Dr. Shepherd."

The door opened. "Ben!" Shepherd exclaimed. "Come in. Come in. I saw the news. Are you okay?"

Frank and Ben entered the house. Shepherd closed the door behind them. "Yes, I'm okay," Ben said. "And I hate to bother you at this hour, but I needed to show you this." He reached into his coat pocket, pulled out the photograph, and handed it to Shepherd.

Shepherd looked curiously at the photograph. "It's your mother and you at probably a few days old." He shrugged and handed the photograph back to Ben.

"A man claiming to be my father had this photograph in his possession."

"Your father?" Shepherd asked.

"Yeah, my father. I know you've delivered a lot of babies, and I know this was over thirty years ago. But do you remember anything at all about my dad?"

Shepherd thought for a moment and then slowly began shaking his head. "I won't be able to think of anything here. Let's go to my office. Just let me get my car keys and coat, and of course tell Ellen where I'm headed."

"Okay, doc," Ben said. He turned to Frank. "Why don't you go on home and get some sleep. I'll get doc to run me home."

"Are you sure?" Frank asked.

"I am."

"Okay. I'll see you tomorrow morning. Remember, your first court appearance is at nine o'clock."

Ben said, "See you then. And Frank... Thanks."

"No worries," Frank said and then he left.

***

Shepherd flipped on the light to his office. "I know this may be rudimentary. But the easiest thing to do first is check my wall. You start at one end and I'll start at the other."

"You think you may have taken a picture of the three of us?"

"I can't say. As you can tell by the pictures on the wall, some parents are included and some are not. But we won't know until we look."

It took about twenty minutes to find the picture of Luther Savannah and his girlfriend, and their days-old newborn son amongst the hundreds of pictures taken by Dr. Shepherd in his over forty years of delivering babies.

"Of course, this is not a DNA test," Shepherd said. "It merely shows he was there at the beginning."

"I know," Ben said almost to himself. He felt numb after the discovery but was keenly aware that besides a request for the DNA test, he would have a thousand questions to ask the man he'd met for the first time tonight, the least of which was why he'd taken a photograph with his girlfriend and newborn son, but hadn't bothered to sign the birth certificate.

***

Back to back phone calls rattled James Etlzer. He sat in the darkness of his living room, trembling. The first phone call had been from his chief prosecutor, Jeff Stone. Stone wanted to know why he Stone hadn't been made aware of any possible wrongdoing by Lovison, and why wasn't he included on any investigatory team. Stone said that he'd researched some of Lovison's cases through the DA's web system and something seemed odd. It looked to him that some of the cases had been altered to appear to be Lovison's files. Stone asked if there were others under investigation. Was Etlzer actually convinced that Lovison alone was corrupt? Had Etlzer considered the possibility that Lovison may have been set up? There appeared to be additional questions, and Stone said he'd be more than happy to assist in the investigation going forward. He'd added, "Lovison was a good guy."

Stone could be a problem, Etlzer realized. An even likelier possibility, he assumed after the message from his second received phone call of the night, advising him that Lovison had made bail. These developments were bad and strong indications that shit was heading toward the fan. Unless...

With his cellphone in hand, he stood and went to his liquor cabinet. He laid his cellphone on the countertop and then poured himself a shot of whiskey. He quickly downed it and poured another. He hated who he'd become. Although he hadn't been the orchestrator of the original deal with Father, he'd been a willing participant in the years since. For most of the city and its inhabitants, Duraleigh was one of the safest places in America. For the most part, innocent people were never killed or even injured. He downed the second shot of whiskey. But if he wished to keep this thing going and keep himself out of trouble and on track for the governor's mansion, two innocents—Stone and Lovison could not be allowed to see the dawn. He poured a third shot of whiskey and then grabbed the disposable cellphone he kept on the top shelf of the bar. A disposable cellphone was the only kind he ever used to contact Father. There would be no known records of this call or any of the others he'd made. He downed the last shot and then picked up his personal cellphone and placed it in his pajama pocket. He went back to the living room, plopped back down in the chair, and with his nostrils flaring, he dialed Father's personal cell number.

***

In the bowels of the federal building in downtown Duraleigh, Caleb Dawson was led down a long corridor by two of his former colleagues. His hands were handcuffed in front of him. His face was solemn. His body felt drained of all energy. He was tired, extremely tired. It wasn't the commonly experienced end-of-a-workday tired. It was the tiredness from years of carrying the burdensome load of betrayal and deceit. It was the kind of tiredness that was felt not only deep in the bones, but in the very fiber of being. The kind not easily rested. The kind that not even continuous sleep could remedy.

The agents stopped in front of an interrogation room and led their former colleague inside. Ram sat in a chair behind a small square table. A single metal chair was in front of it. "You can take those handcuffs off of him. He's not going anywhere," Ram said.

The handcuffs were removed and Caleb was directed toward the metal chair. Caleb sat down. He massaged his wrists and then dropped his chin into the top of his chest.

"Leave us," Ram said to the two agents. They both left. Ram glared at Caleb. "I've read your confession, and I want you to know that it sickens me to be this close to a traitor. You leaked information to a ruthless and vile organization. You betrayed the trust of your country. And I don't know what you're trying to prove with this elaborate 'my bad.' Maybe you found out we were on to you. Maybe this confession of yours is all just part of a Father's Disciples' scheme. But it's not going to work. We're going to prosecute you. On that you can make bank. And fuck a plea deal. We're going to max your ass out."

Caleb lifted his head. "That's what I want. That's what I deserve."

"Cut the crap, Dawson," Ram said.

Caleb said, "I didn't know you guys were on to me. And it really doesn't matter to me if you believe me or not.

Everything you're saying is right. I did betray my country. I betrayed a lot of people. And there's nothing I can do about that. " He dropped his head down and began sobbing.

"Why?" Ram asked. "Why should I believe you? Why should I believe that a syndicate that has spent nearly its entire existence undetected is all of a sudden collapsing in on itself in such spectacular fashion? Why shouldn't I believe that your, er, confession isn't just part of some pissing game?"

"Because they killed him. They killed Tony. They tortured him and then they killed him. I should have done something about it. I should have known," he cried louder. "I should have known!"

"You found out about that, huh?"

Caleb lifted his head, lines of tears streaked down his face. "Yeah."

"We aren't making that information public, yet," Ram said solemnly.

Caleb nodded and dropped his head again.

They were silent for a while as if mutually agreeing that Special Agent Tony Burns deserved at least that much.

Then Ram said, "You've confessed your involvement with Father's Disciples. But you're short on facts about the syndicate. Tell me something we don't know."

Caleb used both his hands to wipe his face and then dried the palms of his hands across the surface of the table. "Father's Disciples is just a front for one man."

"Mayo Fathers?"

"No," Caleb said. "Mayo Fathers is just as much a victim as everyone else. His brother, Father is the leader. Father is Father's Disciples. Everyone else is just a pawn in his world."

Ram leaned back in his chair. "Father, who is Father? None of our information says anything about a Father."

"That's how he wanted it," Caleb said. "He purposely set Mayo up to appear to be the leader. Bledsoe and

McCain too."

"Why?"

Caleb looked at Ram without answering.

"Right," Ram said realizing. "So where does this Father live? What does he look like?"

"He lives underneath the funeral home. And I have no idea what he looks like. I haven't seen him in over ten years. No one has. He only communicates through flat screen monitors."

"This is just great," Ram said sarcastically.

They were silent for several moments. Then Caleb said, "About Lovison."

"What about him?" Ram said.

"Ben was never involved with them. He's innocent. The Disciples have a complicated selection process. They never chose Ben. They chose me. It's not the kind of acceptance you write home about. I used to be angry with Ben about that. I mean, why me? Why my childhood? Why not him? It was the kind of thing that used to eat me up. I hated Ben because of that. I hated him more than I did Father, and Father was the reason my childhood was lost.

"Anyway, the other night, I confessed to Ben about his mother. I told him about how I was told that Father had wanted her dead. And how I'd let my anger at that time lead me to be the one who'd done the deed for him. I shot her in the middle of the street, right in front of her house, in broad daylight." He stopped and sucked in a deep breath and released it. He looked at Ram with tear-filled eyes. "How do you make up for something like that? How can you live with yourself after having done a most unspeakable thing? I went to law school and went into law enforcement, busting everyone in sight, thinking and hoping that if I just put away enough bad guys it would make up for that one terrible act. I thought that maybe enough time and distance would help to erase the memory. But it never did, and even if it had, Father's Disciples wouldn't let me go. Father wouldn't let me forget what I'd done. He had me. As soon as I pulled that trigger, he had me for as long as I drew breath."

"You've done a lot of wrong, Caleb. There's no denying that. But you can do some right. Look at me. You know the layout of the house and the funeral home. We're going in there tonight, and we're going to get this Father character. And you're going to help us."

Caleb shook his head. "That could be dangerous. There are video cameras all over the place. You won't be able to surprise him. He'll see you. He lives beneath those structures. He knows that place inside and out. The basements of both Fathers Funeral Home and Fathers House are connected by a long cement tunnel about eight feet in diameter. Father lives mostly in the area beneath the funeral home. There are rooms within the walls and Father is probably the only one who truly knows how many. He also has the place booby-trapped. So, it's likely you could lose men and come away without a shred of evidence or him."

"Is there a way in or out without going through either the funeral home or the house?"

Caleb shrugged. "If there is, I wouldn't know."

"What does he look like?"

"Ten years ago, he looked very much like Mayo Fathers, just darker."

"Do you think he's changed his appearance since the last time you've seen him?"

"It's hard to say. But there's got to be a reason why he hasn't allowed anyone to see him in a while."

Chapter 27

In most homes, two eleven-year olds missing curfew would create a wave of panic. But at ten o'clock at Fathers house, an hour after both should have been somewhere in the vicinity of their bedroom or one of the second floor bathrooms, the unknown whereabouts of Jamal Morris and Maalik Jackson caused barely a ripple of disturbance.

In over twenty years of working at Fathers House, Miss Helm had abided countless missed curfews by a few of the house's wayward inhabitants. Some had missed curfew simply for the hell of it, just testing what they could get away with. And truthfully, some of the boys had missed because they'd been up to no good. And of course, there were several occasions when the boys had missed curfew because they'd simply lost track of time. But in no instance had she ever had the need or desire to call the police or to bother even one neighbor concerning the whereabouts of any of her boys. The boys knew the rules of the house and they knew where the house was located and they understood there would be consequences for forgetting either. So when Mayo Fathers returned home a little after ten PM, she simply gave him the headcount, all the boys were present and accounted for, save the two youngest.

"Alright, thank you Miss Helm," Mayo said, "You can go ahead to bed. I'll sit up."

He headed for the family room, but then had a strong suspicion of where they might be. Pausing in the hallway, he checked his key ring. The basement key was missing. "Figured," he mumbled. He went to the basement door and turned the knob. It wasn't locked. Jamal had been biting at the bit to see what was in the basement, he thought. He sighed and reluctantly opened the door.

Turning the basement into a virtual den of horrors had been his brother's idea. And now, years after the fact, Mayo liked to pretend that it didn't exist. In fact, it was not part of the house. He liked to believe that Fathers House was only the godsend he'd always intended it to be. That it helped young boys who, through no fault of their own, needed that help. That it was about second chances for boys who needed them. And first chances for ones who never got a break. Ones, he'd assumed had been like his brother, born into circumstances outside their control.

But Fathers House had an underside and undisclosed second purpose that Mayo chose to ignore. The nurturing and encouraging of youthful criminal misbehavior. As his brother had so eloquently put it, "There will always be good and evil in the world. Always. Both exist in varying amounts in each of us. To pretend otherwise would be foolish. To pretend that you can save all boys only with love and kindness would be equally foolish. Some boys are just born to be bad."

Mayo stood at the top of the stairs and stared down at the basement floor, pushing that thought aside. He didn't want to think about good boys and bad boys. He just wanted to go down there and get his boys, both of them, including Maalik who'd already been contaminated with his brother's sick philosophy and Jamal who was as yet untainted. But as he stood there, momentarily unable to move and staring down into the bowels of the family house, he realized what he'd purposely ignored all along. His brother's philosophy hadn't been just a philosophy—it had been a confession.

From the moment he'd learned the truth about his brother, about what their father had done, he'd felt guilty. Such an inauspicious beginning to one's life was surely a precursor to a life of hardship and quite possibly one of crime. Through no fault of his own, his brother had literally been tossed into the garbage by the very people who'd brought him into the world and who should have by natural instinct alone protected him and nurtured him. Because they hadn't, Mayo figured that there was no wonder why his brother was as he was or thought as he thought. It was a logical progression, except for one thing. Not even his brother believed that. By his brother's own admission, he'd been raised by two loving white parents, which he found ironically amusing, given the circumstances as to why they had to raise him in the first place.

Some boys are just born to be bad.

Of course, their father had had no way of knowing, but he'd literally thrown away a naturally bad seed. Circumstances hadn't made his brother who he was. He was as he'd been born to be. Bad. My God! Mayo thought. What had he done? All of those years! What had he subjected those poor boys to? His boys. He descended the stairs rapidly. "Jamal! Maalik!"

When he reached the basement floor, the overhead lights and the flat screen at the end of the hallway blinked on, stopping him where he stood. A digital head appeared on the screen. It was his brother. "I don't have time for tricks, brother!" Mayo shouted at the screen. "Where are the boys?"

"There," Father said. His digital representation nodded to its right. Mayo turned to his left. He saw the boys inside the room, on their knees, facing the wall. Their hands were tied behind their backs. Their eyes were blindfolded.

"What's going on?" Mayo demanded. "We haven't discussed this."

"Didn't you send these boys down to me?"

"No," Mayo said. "One of them took my key. Let me take them back upstairs."

"Too late," Father said. "The new boy has seen something he shouldn't have seen. He's one of us now."

"No, no," Mayo pleaded. "He's not one of you. He's

just a kid. They both are. I want both of them back." At first his own words surprised him as if they hadn't come from his mouth, but from someplace else. But he quickly realized that he had said them, but more than that, he meant them. This ended now. This ended here. These two boys wouldn't make up for Caleb, or Ben, or any of the others. And they wouldn't atone for his acts of betrayal; acts that had been in many ways worse than the original betrayal that had landed some of the boys in his care in the first place. His betrayal had come under the guise of making everything right. But for far too many of the boys, he'd made things as wrong as they could have possibly been made.

Father said, "You can't have them. And we both know that you don't really want them. You never had children of your own for a reason. You're not the fatherly type. You can't raise children out of guilt or some foolish need to assuage the memory of your father's worthless life. "

"I know that's what you think," Mayo said. "And for awhile I believed it myself. But my love and concern for these kids have nothing to do with my father, neither was what I'd tried to do for you. I did so because it's who I am. It's what I'm about. I care."

Mechanical applause erupted from an intercom. Father laughed. "You care. Really. You turned your back on some of these boys, and I didn't have to twist your arm. You're just like me. We're cut from the same cloth. You're just a weaker, pathetic version of me."

"Nevertheless," Mayo said undeterred, "these boys are coming with me." He headed for the glass door.

He suddenly felt the nozzle of a gun poke the back of his head. "I wouldn't do that if I was you."

Mayo stopped. "Who are you?"

"I'm your brother's right hand man," Morant said.

"Well, you'll going to have to shoot me because I'm not leaving without those boys."

"Okay," Morant said. A single gunshot whistled briskly through the air, striking Mayo in the head, splashing blood and skull against the glass wall. The gun had been equipped with a silencer. Mayo's headless body crumpled to the floor.

On the television screen, Father's digital head smiled, "Get that worthless crap out of here and get those two to help clean up the mess. Lovison will be here soon."

***

The first call had been from Father. At least that's who the caller had claimed to be. Until recently, Ben hadn't known Father existed and therefore he had no idea what the man's voice sounded like.

"You're not seriously considering going over there?" April asked incredulously.

They—April and her parents, were sitting around the kitchen table, staring at him. Ben pushed back from the table, stood up, and walked across the kitchen toward the microwave. He leaned over the counter with the palms of both hands pressed against the countertop. The simple answer to her question was yes, he was seriously considering it. Father had said he'd kill the boys if he didn't come. Ben knew in all likelihood it was a trap and that he was the intended target. But if he didn't go to Fathers House tonight as requested, Maalik and Jamal's fates were surely sealed. "He's going to kill those boys if I don't show," he said finally.

April said, "He's going to kill them anyway, and he'll kill you too."

"Maybe, But I've got to try."

"Call the police," Stephen Ellison said. "Let them handle it."

"He said specifically not to call the police," Ben said. "Besides I'm not certain who to trust in the police department."

"You should think of your family," Patricia Ellison said.

Ben didn't turn around. He was thinking of his family. That's all he could think about. But how could he one day look his boys in the eyes if he didn't do all he could to save the other boys?

Stephen Ellison made a barely audible sound, and Ben turned his head and looked in his father-in-law's direction. Stephen Ellison frowned, but didn't say anything. Of course, he didn't have to. His look said it all. I bailed you out of jail at some ridiculous amount and this is how you repay me?

April stood up and walked over to her husband. She hugged him from behind. Ben turned around and pulled his wife into his embrace. He loved this woman, and he loved their two babies. He was getting ready to tell her exactly how much he loved her and how much he loved his boys— his family and that he would not leave the house tonight. That he would figure something else out. But before he could say any of that, his cellphone rang again.

***

Ben understood why April hadn't wanted him to leave the house. He'd just returned home tonight. She needed the reality of his return reinforced by his continued presence in her sight. She needed to see him, hold him, and smell him. He understood that because he needed her in that way as well. The reality of being separated from her had been too much for him to bear. In actuality, their separation had been less than a day. But it felt like so much more, which was why she needed to understand why he needed to go to Fathers House tonight. Not just to save the boys, but in a way to also save himself. Because the unspoken truth was that he could still be locked up, not only in the very real

physical sense, but in a mental sense as well. This Father
character, whoever he might be, held knowledge that could
mentally set him free.

He parked his car on the curb in front of Fathers House
and went up the walkway to the front porch. The house was
dark, but the porch light was on. A note was attached to the
front door. He pulled if off and read it. It read in its
entirety:

Ben, you know where the key is. Come inside, you
know where to go.

It will not be locked.

He looked back at the walkway leading up to the
house. Square bricks traced either side of the walkway from
the sidewalk all the way up to the porch where he stood. He
lifted up the third brick facing away from the house on the
right side of the walkway. They kept it in the same place all
of these years. He unlocked the front door.

The house was quiet. He entered and pushed it almost
closed behind him. He checked his watch. It was just after
midnight. He imagined Miss Helm upstairs asleep. He
hadn't expected to see her. One or more of the older boys
might still be up, watching television. The two younger
ones were down below, in the clutches of a madman.
Ordinarily, Uncle Mayo would either be downstairs in the
study or asleep in the master suite. He considered going to
Miss Helm's room to urge her to get the other boys and get
out of the house. But he knew that he was being watched.
So, he headed straight to the basement door.

The door was unlocked as the note stated it would be.
He pushed it open wide enough for him to enter. He went
inside and let the door close behind him. It slammed shut as
if someone had yanked it closed from the other side. He
wondered if anyone upstairs heard it. Though he'd lived in
Fathers House for over five years and had been in its
afterschool program for at least three years before that, this
was the first time he'd been in the basement. The stairway

leading down to it was completely dark. But a flickering light from somewhere inside the basement pushed against the darkness, offering a glimmer of enlightened hope. Slowly, he descended the stairs.

Halfway down, he called out. "Father!"

There was no answer.

When he reached the basement floor, he tentatively stepped forward. He looked to his left and saw them. He dashed to the glass door, yanked at its metal handle and opened the door.

"Boys," he cried out. They were on their knees in front of a wall, blindfolded. He knelt beside the first one and smelled a hint of disinfectant and some other kind of cleaning fluid. "Are you okay?"

"Yes," The boy answered. It was Prodegee.

"Are you okay?" Ben asked the other boy, Maalik.

Maalik nodded his head affirmatively.

Ben started to remove Prodegee's blindfold.

A voice crackled out from somewhere above his head. "Don't do that." Ben looked up and saw the intercom on the wall between the vents.

"Father, is that you?" Ben asked.

"Yes."

"Let me take the boys out of here."

"The boys will be okay," Father said. "They'll be out of here in due time."

"When?" Ben shouted.

"That, of course, depends on you."

"Me?"

"Step out into the hallway," Father commanded.

"What?"

"You're wasting time. Step out into the hallway."

Ben looked at the boys. "I'll be back." He stood up and walked back into the hallway.

"Good," Father said. "Ah, there stands Luther Savannah's boy. Your father and I go back a long ways. A promise to your father was the reason why you were never overtly involved in our chosen profession. He didn't want his only son to turn out like him. It's funny how things work out sometimes."

"My mother," Ben said angrily. "Why did you want my mother dead?"

"Interesting," Father said. "You've been talking to Caleb."

"He told me you ordered my mother dead."

"Ah, Lizzie," Father said. "Your mother was a very lovely woman, Ben. I'd told your father that I would look out for the two of you. I never intended to fall in love with her. But I did. But she remained loyal to your father, a man who was never again going to see his freedom. I couldn't understand her. I'd merely voiced my frustrations of the situation and my men took it the wrong way. Caleb took it the wrong way. I never ordered a hit on your mother. As I've said, I was in love with her."

"You're lying, you sick son of a bitch!"

"I have no need to lie to you, son," Father said calmly. "But in any event, let's get to the matter at hand."

"Let the boys go," Ben demanded.

"As I've said, that depends on you."

"I'm here," Ben said. "That was the agreement."

Father chuckled. "There was no agreement. I merely said that if you did not come, I would kill them, which I would have. I did not say that if you did come, I would let them go."

"Are you playing word games, Father?"

"No, I'm not playing games. I will let the boys go as soon as you confess to the policemen that you killed Mayo."

"What? You're crazy. What are you talking about?"

"Look in the room to your right."

Ben looked to his right. He hadn't noticed the room before. The door to it was slightly ajar. He walked over to it and gently pushed it open and gasped. A body with part of its head missing was splayed across the floor. Ben backed from the room and kept backing until he hit the glass wall of the room where the boys were located. "You killed him."

"No, son," Father said. "You killed him. And when the officer ordered you to drop your gun, you refused, and he was forced to shoot you."

Ben saw the figure emerge from the shadows where the headless body laid. It was a Duraleigh police officer, brandishing his service revolver.

"Meet Morant," Father said. "Morant and I represent the new Father's Disciples. Of course, the name will change. The feds wanted Father's Disciples and so I gave it to them. Now, the two of us will start a new organization. Of course, your father will continue to do as he's always done for us inside prison walls. And those boys back there, along with the ones upstairs, will resume their roles as foot soldiers James Etlzer will be governor and if fortune holds, one day, president. Of course in order for my vision to be fulfilled, you must be eliminated."

Ben eyed Morant cautiously. Suddenly, the wire that was taped to his chest felt heavy as if an extra appendage had grown there. He prayed that Morant wouldn't pat him down. Hopefully the feds had gotten Fathers delusional wish list on tape. Although he knew even if they had, there was still something that they'd need for sure. "This is madness. You can't expect…"

"But, I do," Father said. "I do expect. Morant will place bullets into each of those boys' heads unless you do exactly as I say."

There was a silence as Ben contemplated his next move. The feds were nearby, ready to pounce, but he had to make a move now. Otherwise, this certifiable nut-job could disappear forever into the night. "Why," Ben said finally. "Why me? Why have you screwed with my life?"

"Ah, the existential question, why."

'Answer me, damn it!" Ben demanded. "Come out here and answer me!"

"I'm afraid I can't honor that request," Father said.

Ben looked grimly at Morant and then turned back to the screen "You coward. You can't even look me in the eyes and answer one simple question."

Father said, "You want to know why?"

"Yes," Ben said.

"There is no why." Father said.

"You're full of shit," Ben said and turned to leave. He heard a click and stopped. "A shot in the back at this distance would be a little difficult to explain wouldn't it, officer?"

"Stand down, Morant" Father said.

Morant smiled impishly, but kept the gun pointed at Ben.

After a few moments, Ben heard a rocky wailing-like sound as if a statue was being dragged across concrete. When he turned back around, Father stood in front of the flat screen.

He looked unreal. He wore a well-fitted white suit. But the hands, neck and head that emerged from its orifices were a pinkish-pale as were the inner corners of his eyes. At first, Ben failed to see any resemblance to Mayo Fathers, but as he stared into the man's haunted-looking eyes, a faint hint of Mayo became visible. The two of them had the same bone structure, the same high cheekbones, pointed chin, flattened nose, and thin ruby-red lips. Though they were both light-complected, Mayo's skin coloring seemed natural, particularly so if he was a white person. But Father's skin was more pinkish as if its outer layer had been peeled away. Ben had never before seen such a severe case of vitiligo. "Finally," he said for lack of having anything more profound to say. Five minutes, he thought. They said they could breach the basement within five minutes.

C. Edward Baldwin

"You ask why," Father said. "Why is such a pointless question. You of all people should know that. There is no why. There is only what is. We are here because we are here. You're here because you're here."

Ben shook his head. "That's mindless dribble."

"Is it?" Father said. "You believe someone is controlling all of this? A god perhaps? Because only if someone is controlling this would there be a need for a why," he paused and smiled. "There is no one controlling this. I'm of the Big Bang school of thought. And the Big Bang and everything since the Big Bang was just a matter of happenings. Things happen with no rhyme or reason. They are simply random occurrences. Why you? It's simple...because you were there and you're here. You're in my realm of being. I've put no more thought in you than I have a thought of putting on a shirt."

For a moment, Ben stood in front of the man, speechless, and not truly comprehending what Father meant. But then, it hit him. Father had essentially said that he hadn't mattered. Father had killed Ben's mother, just because. Ben's father was locked up, just because. Just because they'd had the misfortune of being in that sicko's realm of being. That was unacceptable. Ben reached out, intending to grab Father's neck to squeeze some 'why' into the equation. But as he lurched toward Father, he heard, "FBI! Everyone on the ground!" The voices came from both behind Ben and behind Father.

Morant aimed his gun toward a spot behind Father, but Ben quickly regrouped and dove into him, knocking the gun from his hand. It hit the ground with a metallic clack and slid across the floor. Ben rolled atop Morant, pinning him to the ground. Father was frozen in place like a blinded deer, unsure of what was happening and uncertain about what to do. But it didn't matter as federal agents who'd entered the basement through both the funeral home and Fathers House, quickly swarmed him from behind. They knocked him to the floor and handcuffed his hands behind his back.

Meanwhile, another agent lifted Ben off of Morant and helped him up onto his feet, while two other agents yanked Morant to his feet and then handcuffed his hands behind his back.

Ben went to the room where the two young boys were still on their knees in front of the wall. He took off their blindfolds and untied their hands. "It's over boys. It's over."

Tears streamed down Maalik's face. "I'm sorry, Prodegee," he said. "Father told me to get you down here. I didn't know this was going to happen."

"It's okay," Prodegee said to him before turning to Ben. "There's a book. I need to find the Book."

Chapter 28

At seven o'clock the following Wednesday evening Ben lay across his bed, just about to doze off, when he heard the doorbell. He hadn't the slightest idea who it might be as he wasn't expecting anyone. Moments later, April stood at the bottom of the stairs and called for him.

The drop-in visitors were Emma Tunnel and her caregiver, Maria Rodriquez. "Hello," Maria said as he entered the living room. April had already seated them. "I hope we're not disturbing you and your family. But Ms. Tunnel wanted to see you, and considering her condition, I felt it was probably best to have her do so tonight."

"No, you're not disturbing us at all," Ben said. He remembered that Ms. Tunnel suffered from symptoms similar to the early stages of Alzheimer's. "Did you meet my wife?"

"Yes," Maria said. "She's a very lovely lady."

"I believe my in-laws went to the store. They should be back shortly."

"Well we don't intend to stay long," Maria said. She looked expectantly at Ms. Tunnel.

Ms. Tunnel smiled pleasantly at him for a moment, and then she turned solemn. "This disease that's growing within me, among other things, it robs me of time. Maria tells me that I'm away more than I am here. And I realize that the day will soon come when I'll always be away."

Maria interrupted. "She's been away, as she puts it, since the time you came to the house inquiring about Sarah Leeson's whereabouts. And then Sunday, the day you were, uh, well, arrested, she came back and she's been here ever since. She's watched every news report and read every newspaper account about the corruption scandal and that drug syndicate, Father's Disciples."

"Give him the box, Maria," Ms. Tunnel said.

Ben hadn't noticed the box beside Maria's right foot. Maria stood up and brought the box over to him.

"Those are my husband's files," Ms. Tunnel said. "They're from the case he was working on at the time he died. I believe that all those missing people from his files are related somehow to that outfit that tried to kill you. Since my husband didn't trust his colleagues, neither could I. I didn't know if I'd ever be able to give his files to someone and then you came along. I trust you. You have a good aura about you."

"Thank you, Ms. Tunnel," he said softly.

***

Detective Robert Tunnel had been given the missing person assignments as busywork, something for the old-timer to do on his way out to pasture and whereby no real detective would be bothered having to work cases that didn't really need solving. But for a thirty-year veteran police officer who'd only known honest work for honest pay, and whose sworn oath to protect and serve had been as sacred to him as his marriage vows, there was no such thing as busywork. He'd attacked the assignments with gusto and in so doing, had been the first of the ignorants (the name given by those in the police department with knowledge of the conspiracy to those without knowledge of it) to stumble across the inevitableness of Duraleigh's agreed descent into the abyss.

Tunnel had meticulously laid out his theory concerning the fates of the twenty-two Duraleigh citizens who'd been reported missing in the late eighties by either friends or loved ones. None of the missing had exactly been bluebirds, he noted in an understatement in his case summary. All of them had either a criminal record or a history of pattern drug use. None had been missed by society and most likely all of them, according to Tunnel's theory, had been subjected to some type of street justice. Their remains had most likely been scattered throughout a wooded area somewhere.

Due to his untimely death a few months after the forced start of his retirement, Tunnel had no way of knowing that for the next twenty years, many of the ignorants would give tacit approval to the conspiracy either through knowingly looking the other way or simply by not following through on basic police work. Some ignorants eventually joined in the conspiracy.

Tunnel also had no way of knowing that it would take a combination of his original investigation, Father's Disciples own egotistically self-serving account of its malicious acts, (later deemed the Black Book of Death by the Duraleigh Standard), as well as the late Officer Mike Molson's videotaped confession of his part in the scandal, before the depth and consequences of the conspiracy would fully unfold.

Three months later, the dust still hadn't fully settled in the city of Duraleigh. Despite the more than sixty indictments and counting, including those of the last three mayors, a former and current district attorney, the current chief of police, five judges, five current prosecutors, fifteen police officers— active and retired, and a host of bit players, the citizenry had still expected and rightly so, more. Faith in their government and each other had been severed to the core. People were distrustful of everyone.

Their elected officials had signed a pact with the devil, but it had been their own neighbors who, either through fear or nonchalance had sat idly by while the dregs of their society ultimately ruled. Unconscionably, people had not lifted a finger to help, nor had they voiced even the smallest whispers of concern for their fellow citizens who had either outright disappeared or had slowly, but noticeably been consumed by the perils of inequity. The city's Grand Bargain— the name given to its wholly illegal and highly immoral relationship with the leadership of Father's Disciples, had exposed, the very worst in all involved.

So had been the essence of the Sunday editorial in the Duraleigh Standard. However, Ben did not entirely concur. Sure, the so called Grand Bargain had been an abject failure and had been indeed, reprehensible. But ultimately good had won out, a fact that the editorial's author hadn't fully acknowledged. Instead, he'd broad-stroked everyone with the brush of indifference, callousness, and a woe-is-me attitude. Ben didn't quite see it that way. The people should not be blamed for having had a trust in those they'd elected to serve them. It was the obligation of those who'd accepted the responsibility of public office to have adhered to the highest standards of ethics and duty. And when those individuals had not, the system had ultimately rooted them out. Regrettably, it had taken over twenty years. But still, the system had eventually responded.

And as for Father, he'd thought he could game the system and shirk the rule of law, neither of which he cared about, nor had he cared about the people each had been established to protect. Father had only cared about himself and his desire to potentially control a governor, and perhaps only in his extreme delusion, one day the presidency of the United States and by extension, the world. But the system he'd so callously manipulated had eventually corrected itself and exposed him. And sweet karma and the rule of law were now having their say as well. Father would spend the rest of his life on death row, awaiting the fulfillment of the death sentence he'd bestowed upon so many. And he would do so in a manner in which he'd grown accustomed, alone. He would spend twenty-three hours a day in a small

6 x 9 foot prison cell, just him and his self-aggrandizing thoughts.

In the weeks immediately following the scandal, Ben admitted to himself that he could have been the author of that editorial. He had felt just as the author had felt, vengeful, saddened, and angry. But harboring such emotions, Jeffrey Stone had warned him, was destructive. "Maybe so," he had told Stone, "But that's how I feel. And that's how you'd feel too, if you'd been betrayed, set up, and almost sent to prison for doing what you thought was your job. I felt as if my whole life had been a lie, manipulated for no other reason except that someone could do it."

"But I, too, was betrayed," Stone had said calmly. "Every prosecutor in this office has been, those implicated in the scandal, as well as those who weren't. Most of us had accepted these positions because we believed in law and order, the rule of law. And none of us, not one of us should have been placed in a position where we had to oppose that rule. And none of us should have to face the scrutiny and doubt of the people. People know we've worked in an office where the rule of law has been knowingly and willfully stepped on and pushed to the side. So yes, I, too, have a right to be sad, vengeful, and angry. But as I've said, that's destructive. And it wouldn't change what is."

"Was I gullible?" Ben asked sincerely.

"No," Stone answered sincerely. "You were not gullible. I've reviewed your files. You did nothing wrong. Those were solid plea agreements. We make them all the time. You had no way of knowing that Etlzer had farmed most of the Father's Disciples cases your way. And you certainly couldn't have known that he'd forged your signatures on files you hadn't been involved with. He'd known that he'd made a pact with the devil and that that pact could one day be exposed. So, when that possibility manifested, he'd already pegged you as the fall guy. With your Fathers House background, you were the perfect foil.

"The plan had been for you to be killed before you could defend yourself against the accusations. And when I got close to the truth, he'd planned to have me killed as well," he paused. "Just imagine what would have happened, if it hadn't been for that butt call."

They both smiled at the memory of Etlzer, butt-calling Stone. It had been the night that Ben had gone to Fathers House. Etlzer, who'd always called Father from a separate disposable phone, had done so on that night as well. Etlzer had just taken a call from Stone and had, after ending the call, placed his personal cell phone in his pajamas pocket. When he sat down in the chair to call Father on the disposable phone, he unknowingly butt-dialed the last person he'd spoken with, Stone. Stone then heard Etlzer's declaration that both he and Ben would not live to see the dawn. Stone immediately contacted the FBI who in turn, had immediately contacted Ben. After learning that Ben had just gotten off the phone with Father who'd requested a meeting with him, the Bureau, who had no idea what the supposed mastermind and leader of Father's Disciples had looked like, asked Ben to wear a wire during the meeting, while trying to convince Father to come from behind the walls of the funeral home.

For Stone's part, he practiced what he preached. He showed no signs of vengeance or anger during the prosecution of the first two of his former colleagues. And Ben suspected that Stone would show the same open-minded professionalism during Etlzer's upcoming trial. Stone, who'd accepted the acting DA's position, was a lot further along in that regard than Ben. Although, Ben admitted to himself, Stone hadn't that far to go. He hadn't been the one facing a long stint in prison. In any event, Ben eventually decided that Stone was right. There was no good in those emotions. They were neither healing, nor productive; they were only inhibiting.

Ben understood that now, which was why he'd been able to forgive Caleb. That was also why he was able to stand in the basement of Spring Hope Baptist Church on a fine May afternoon, awaiting the arrival of his father to join him for the christening of the twins. Ben had seen firsthand the level of atrocities that the vilest of mankind could commit; but there he stood, preparing to celebrate the pureness of life and its precious beginnings. Stephen Ellison and Frank Vass waited with him.

Through the window Ben could see the three black government vehicles enter the lot from the side of the church, curb around to the back entrance, and park. Black suited men exited the first two cars and walked back to the third car. Two more suits exited from the front of the third car, and one from its rear driver side. The third car's rear passenger side door was opened and out came Luther Savannah with cuffed hands and chained feet, wearing a new suit which had been bought off the rack at Men's Wearhouse by his only son. One of the government suits said something to him. He nodded. And then the chains and cuffs were removed.

The conversations between Ben and his father had gotten much easier than the first one had been three months earlier. Since then, Ben had visited him at the prison often, even bringing April and the babies a few times, and on one occasion, his in-laws. Ben respected how his father had felt about being in prison. How he hadn't wanted Ben to see him in that capacity. During Ben's brief imprisonment he'd felt the same way. He hadn't wanted April or his boys to see him locked up. But now Ben realized that both he and his father had been wrong. Family was family whether locked up or free. Each member of a family does have something to give. Giving a part of themselves, be it a smile, a thought, or a simple touch, could be just as valuable as gold or silver.

Stephen Ellison asked, "Alright, are we ready to go

up?"

"I think so," Ben said.

"You guys start up," Luther said to Stephen and Frank, "Ben hold back just a sec."

Stephen and Frank went to the basement steps and began the ascent. Ben and Luther stood near the back of the room. "Are you nervous, Dad?" Ben asked.

"A little," Luther said. "But it's not that." He lowered his voice even though they were now alone and already speaking softly. "I just wanted to say that I love you."

"Really," Ben said, astonished. "I never thought I'd hear those words from you. I love you too, Dad."

They hugged. "I always dreamed that this day would be possible," Luther said.

Hugging his father felt good. It was something that Ben had never dreamed he'd be able to do. A lot of things had to fall into place in order for it to happen. Too many things to leave to random chance. To Ben, that was clear evidence that a power much greater than himself had a hand in things. He didn't have all the answers. He didn't know why things happened the way they did. But for now, it was at least good to know and believe that there was a why.

"Are you two ready?" Frank Vass asked. He stood near the top of the basement steps. Vass had graciously agreed to be the twins' godfather. He looked dapper in a custom fitted white Italian suit.

"Yeah," Ben said.

Ben and Luther started up the stairs. Sunlight filtered through the church's multi-colored windows and cascaded down the basement steps. It was as if they were walking up into a rainbow. Luther paused at the top of the stairs and looked back down at his son, who was chuckling. "What's so funny?" Luther asked him.

Ben said, "Nothing really, I just had a funny thought about curveballs."

C. Edward Baldwin

THE END

I really hope you enjoyed reading Fathers House as much as I enjoyed writing it. If you liked the book, please write a review at your place of purchase.

Find C. Edward Baldwin:

FaceBook
Twitter
Pinterest
LinkedIn

Coming Second Quarter 2015

Rememberers (An Urban Fantasy Novel)